Sisters
OF
Sword
AND
Shadow

Sisters OF Sword AND Shadow

LAURA BATES

SIMON & SCHUSTER

First published in Great Britain in 2023 by Simon & Schuster UK Ltd

Text copyright © 2023 Laura Bates

1 3 5 7 9 10 8 6 4 2

Simon & Schuster UK Ltd
1st Floor, 222 Gray's Inn Road
London WC1X 8HB

www.simonandschuster.co.uk
www.simonandschuster.com.au
www.simonandschuster.co.in

Simon & Schuster Australia, Sydney
Simon & Schuster India, New Delhi

A CIP catalogue record for this book is
available from the British Library.

HB ISBN 978-1-3985-2004-2
eBook ISBN 978-1-4711-8760-5
eAudio ISBN 978-1-3985-2005-9

Typeset in the UK by Sorrel Packham

Printed and Bound in the UK using
100% Renewable Electricity at CPI Group (UK) Ltd

MIX
Paper | Supporting
responsible forestry
FSC® C171272

*For my own sister, who inspires
me every day.*

Prologue

Cass was little when it happened. So little that afterwards she could never be quite sure if it had just been a dream. And Mary never spoke of it again, either.

They were gathering firewood in the forest near the farm, Cass collecting the smallest twigs for kindling as she always did, stuffing them into the sackcloth bag slung over her shoulder and grumbling that they'd be late home for dinner if Mary didn't get a move on.

Mary was examining a thorn in the soft heel of her palm, wincing and making a fuss about pulling it out as usual, until Cass sighed and took her hand, worrying at it with her teeth and rolling her eyes at Mary's whining. They were stood like that, Mary's hand pressed to her little sister's mouth, when the woman appeared as suddenly and silently as if she were a spirit conjured out of the air.

Cass dropped Mary's hand and they both stood frozen, remembering the stories about faerie folk that would charm you into their world and never return you above ground, their mother's warnings about bandits and ruffians in the forest, the old stories whispered round the fireside on winter evenings about the wandering druids who followed the old ways and twisted ancient magic to their will.

The woman wore a gold cloak and seemed to shine as if the light came from somewhere within her, brighter than anything else in the gathering dusk. Her face was folded and lined like an old piece of parchment, her mouth sucked in at the corners. Around her neck hung a metal pendant in a distinctive spiral shape, its ends joined so that it continued for ever.

She looked to Mary first, seeing she was the taller and older of the two, asking in a wheedling, lilting voice if she hadn't any charity to spare for a poor woman living wild with nothing to eat tonight. When Mary half turned away, shielding Cass from the woman's sight, she frowned and hissed the air out between her teeth, then swallowed her impatience and returned to the high, whining voice, promising to 'tell a pretty girl her fortune as a fair exchange'. But Mary walked quickly away, pulling Cass behind her, and it was only when Cass glanced back at the woman over her shoulder that she saw the luminous yellow eyes in the haggard face widen and the woman gasp as if all the air had been knocked out of her.

'It cannot be,' the woman whispered, her eyes never leaving Cass's face, searching it as if it were a map to some long-lost treasure. And it was like a golden thread shot out from her and hooked into Cass, holding her fast so that she could not move, could not speak, could not walk away in spite of Mary tugging on her hand. And as if she stood before a queen, the woman fell to her knees, her gaze unwavering, prostrating herself on the ground before Cass until she broke eye contact as her forehead kissed the mossy ground. At once Cass shivered as she felt her body come under her control once again and she tripped as Mary pulled hard, falling and cutting her wrist on a sharp rock. She stumbled to her feet and followed her sister, sucking on the wound as she ran, the metal tang of her own blood in her mouth and her bag of twigs lying abandoned and forgotten in the forest clearing next to the woman's motionless form.

Chapter 1

The leaves smelled of earth and last night's rain. Cass lay on her back, feeling their wet tongues licking at her arms and legs, her precious white dress already damp and soiled. White felt wrong on her, anyhow. She slid off her shoes, releasing her cramped toes from the strange confines of stiff leather, and let her calloused heels dig into the soft soil. Her lungs expanded again. Above her a thousand leaves danced in a symphony of colour: emerald and sea green, acid bright and adder dark. The apples shone like jewels.

You could tell your future husband by the twist of an apple's stalk, Mary always said, counting the letters until it broke and gave his first initial, then stabbing the sharp end at the peel until it pierced the flesh to find his second. She'd pilfered dozens as a child, twisting gently or jabbing fiercely to manipulate the outcome, while Cass watched from the tree above, rough bark clasped between bare thighs.

She needn't have bothered. Mary would marry Thomas today, like she'd known she would since before her back teeth had all come in. Ever since Adam the blacksmith knocked at the door of the farm one night to speak with their father and they'd pressed an eye each to the crack in their bedroom door and seen their mother nod briskly and wipe her hands on her apron and say it was a good match for a farmer's daughter and then break the second-best milk jug into shards and bury one deep into her palm in the washing-up bowl. Then their father had put a gentle hand on her shoulder and squeezed it.

So they knew. And they'd gone silently back to bed, Cass's cheek curled into Mary's ribcage the way it always had, so she could fall asleep listening to the steady drumbeat of her sister's blood.

Yes, they'd always known. But it had always been something for another day. Until this morning, in its strangeness with the Sunday tub full of suds and two new dresses in white, an impractical shade they'd never worn before and wouldn't soon again, and the sweet, ripe smell of blossom boughs piled high on the kitchen floor, ready to be used as decorations for the ceremony. There was a private, distant smile on Mary's face that Cass had never seen before.

So she'd left the baby clinging to the kitchen table leg with a crust and flown out through the back door before she could be seen. She'd whirled down through the field with the long grass slicing at her bare calves and the crisp air thrilling her lungs and the dew bathing her feet until she vaulted over the orchard fence. She felt the tickle of the warm summer air, her toes in the soil – a return to the wilds of childhood, a childhood that still felt a part of her despite her seventeen years. She was still here, rooted to the soil of the farm, but Mary was leaving her behind.

She closed her eyes and let the sunlight stripe her eyelids black and gold. They'd miss her in a minute. She wasn't supposed to be here, nor to feel this way on a day of celebration. It was a bad omen, Ma would say. Selfish, to taint her sister's wedding so. She let her fingers brush the grass blades until the tips sank into something soft. A pulpy mess of split crimson skin, brown edges peeling back from once white flesh now hollowed to a dark yellow cavity. She sucked the sweetness from under her fingernails.

Tucked inside her underclothes, Cass felt the hard lump of her mother's most precious possession. A thick, round silver locket. She took it out and held it up to the sun, turning it over and over between fingertips still grubby in spite of the morning's scrubbing. The little green stone set in the dull grey metal eyed her malevolently, as if mocking her. She knew she should have been proud and grateful when her mother pressed it into her hand this morning. 'It was never really mine, Cass. It is yours,' she had said, uncharacteristic tears in her eyes. But the locket felt heavy and ugly and Cass couldn't help feeling like she was being decorated, ready to be put on display behind her sister.

She dangled the locket from its chain, still holding the softness of the rotten apple in her other hand, probing its pulpy heart with her fingers, waiting for a shout from the kitchen doorway to grab her, jerk her back.

The commotion that came was not the one she expected. Down the stone-pocked road that separated the orchard from the forest a horse came careening, kicking up great clouds of choking dust. She leaped to her feet, necklace still dangling, and everything happened at once. A soot-black horse with its face split by a flash of bright white. A man, face masked, eyes flashing, plump pouch at his belt, straining to look over his shoulder. A moment of sheer terror when time stopped, and the horse reared up in front of her and in the glint of hooves and shriek of its whinny a gloved hand closed round the locket and ripped it from her fingers.

Then time moved again, and she was alone by the side

of the road with her heart pounding and her empty hand outstretched.

Hooves, again, before she could start breathing. Approaching fast. Another man bent low to urge his chestnut stallion onwards, its rich, ruddy mane rippling, nostrils flaring, their bodies flowing together in complete alignment. The rider halted in front of Cass, twisting round to take in the orchard.

'Did he pass this way?' And the voice inside the metal helmet was like honey.

Cass could find no words, staring silently as the rider removed his helmet.

Not a man. A woman, perhaps ten years older than her. A woman with sharp, straight brows tightened together, with hair the colour of the last autumn leaves twisted tight to the nape of her neck. She had a split in her lip that shone bright with cherry-fresh blood. A woman, with her legs encased tight in shining leather, boots gripping tight to the horse's flanks.

'He . . . my necklace.'

Cass was too shocked even to look away. A heavy heat flooded her cheeks as she stared at the strange woman's face, at her collarbone quickly rising and falling above the patterned black leather that corseted her chest. The hollow at the base of her throat was damp.

Cass gestured, wordlessly, in the direction the first rider had gone.

'My mother's necklace,' she said again.

'Well, then.' Her voice was golden honey. 'Are you coming?'

The woman held out a gloved hand and for a split second Cass looked back through the quiet orchard, across the grass turned golden by the morning sun to the door of the farm. Where they'd miss her, any moment. Where another knock might come one night and it would be Cass who would be promised to someone. Given away. So she caught up her sodden, soiled skirts and reached out her hand. And the horse lurched beneath her and jerked her breath out staccato as the apple fell from her fingers into the dust.

Chapter 2

It was like riding into a dream. The horse's flanks heaved between her thighs and the stranger's waist was warm and supple in her hands. Cass gripped tight. She had ridden before, if you could call it that, plodding to market and back on old Ned, the farm cob, but this was something entirely different. She felt like every bone in her body was rattling and jolting, the shock of the horse's pounding hooves vibrating up through her pelvis and into her teeth, her slippery, sweating calves squeezed tight as she tried to keep a grip on the galloping stallion.

As they plunged into the forest in pursuit of the pitch-black horse and its rider, the colours of the late summer leaves swirled and streaked past like dyes running into each other.

A thousand questions clamoured in Cass's head, half meant for the rider whose bent back strained in front of her, and half for herself. Every rushing, panting gallop forward took her further from her home, from her responsibilities, from Mary and her mother and father, and the baby with the crust dangling between its fingers at the kitchen table leg.

Stop.

Wait.

I must go back.

But the words caught in her throat, something preventing them from reaching her lips. And anyway, she didn't have the breath to speak, not while her fingers gripped tight to that supple, leather-clad waist, and it was all she could do to cling on. Yet she knew the thing that stopped her voice was neither the speed of the horse nor the tightness of her chest but her own will.

Because this ride was sheer exhilaration. She had never moved so fast in her whole life. She felt rather than saw the shadows of the tree trunks as they flickered past, the roots and dead leaves underfoot blending into a dizzying whirl.

The heavy scent of honeysuckle bloomed rich in her throat and delicate woodland flowers, red campion and wild geraniums, nodded gaily to them as they rode. As if it were just another Thursday with the washing waiting to be done and the floor to sweep and a posy to be gathered for the table from the fringes of the wood. As if everything hadn't changed in a single moment.

Colour, smell, the fingers of the wind grasping at her scalp: everything was fluid, fleeting, impossible to grasp. Everything except the tiny beads of sweat that stood out on the slender nape of the neck in front of her, and the ruddy hairs that curled damply where they escaped from the thin leather thong that bound them in a tight, glossy knot. She felt *life*, bright, vibrant, breath-taking, coursing through her as if she had never really been alive until this very moment.

The woman was bent forward, urging the stallion onwards, her lips so close to its ears she seemed almost to whisper it encouragement as much as she spurred the horse on with her heels.

They came upon him in a clearing, where his horse had checked momentarily as he considered a fork in the path. He twisted to face them, eyes widening in surprise, and the next moment a dagger whistled past his face so close it left the thinnest streak of blood before it bit deep into the trunk of the tree behind him with a resounding thud.

He froze, his eyes never leaving the rider's face, as she sat astride her stallion, her shoulders rising and falling quickly as the horse panted out great clouds of breath into the space between them. Her gloved hand fingered the empty scabbard where the dagger had been. Cass was frozen, every muscle in her body tensed for his attack, certain they would both be dead within moments. But when the woman spoke her voice was as low and calm as if she had happened upon the stranger on a morning stroll. As if she discussed the weather or the price of milk.

'What you have taken does not belong to you.'

He sneered but did not move, his fingertips searching the wound scratched across his cheekbone. He examined his bloodied fingertips and his lips drew back from his teeth.

'You will regret this, bitch.'

She shook her head, clicked her tongue and reached down beneath the stirrups and suddenly there was a bow strained and poised in her hand, the arrow nocked and drawn back, the quiver pointing directly at the man's heart.

'I have no need or desire to kill you, bandit. So, I will give you one final chance,' she said coolly. Cass could not see the woman's face, but she spoke like one who chastises a child, or checks a dog.

His face clouded as if she had slapped him. And Cass recoiled in horror at the boldness, the stupidity of addressing such a man with crass brutality, and she flinched in anticipation of the blows that would surely come, as his hand moved to the hilt of the sword that swung at his side.

Then two things happened in the same moment. The man drew his sword, the blade flashing in the weak sunlight, and an arrow whistled between the horse's ears, burying itself deep in his left eye. The other was still wide open in an expression of confusion as if, even in death, he could not comprehend what had happened.

Cass sat there, shaking, as the woman dismounted smoothly, strode over to the body as if it were nothing more than the carcass of a fox and stripped it of its belt and sword before yanking the clinking money bag from its side.

She remounted, swinging herself back into the saddle in a single fluid motion, and it was only then that she twisted her body to look at Cass, who felt that she could not move, could not breathe, whose eyes were fixed on the spreadeagled body, the blood gently trickling into the leaves.

'Here.' A cold lump was pressed into her palm. Then the woman clicked her tongue and the horse walked forward, Cass opened her fingers and gazed wordlessly down at the silver locket lying in her palm.

Chapter 3

Hours had passed before they slowed again, the horse coming to a stop before sturdy gates of dark, rough, splintered wood set in a stone wall that seemed to Cass vast and unending. Her thighs ached from the effort of clinging to the horse's back and her head felt numb and heavy, her senses blunted by the shock of what she had seen and the confusing whirl of the miles they had ridden since. The sun was fading fast, and the early September evening was beginning to bare its teeth. Cass shivered in her thin, muddied dress and gooseflesh pricked at her forearms. That blank, unseeing eye was burned into her sight, as if she had looked too long at the sun.

She blinked in surprise as two girls with daisy crowns

in their hair appeared on the ramparts above the gate, giggling and curtseying as they peered down curiously at her. Their dresses were grubby as if they had been playing outside all day.

'Beware,' one of them cried in a singsong voice, as they approached. 'There is sickness here.'

'You should ride onwards, to the next village, for your own sake.' The other girl nodded.

The mysterious rider dismounted with a lithe, catlike jump and removed her helmet. Although she didn't say a word, the giggles faded from the girls' lips and they melted away as if they had received an order. Moments later, there was a clanking and scraping of metal as the gates were unlocked and swung forward.

The rider led the horse into a cobbled courtyard, Cass still clinging wordlessly to its back.

There had been no discussion, no question of releasing her or returning her home. Her stomach lurched as the horse trotted on.

A low stable block ran along the side of the courtyard to the right and an elegant stone manor house rose in front of her like a faerie castle in the gathering dusk. Should she be grateful for the return of her locket or terrified of the murderer who had borne her here without another word? Excited to be a guest in this strange place, further from home than she had ever ventured, or fearful that she might be a prisoner?

As her thoughts whirled, the woman who was both her rescuer and captor looked up at her and held out a leather-gloved hand. Cass hesitated, but there was no other option. And again she felt that strange pull, like something inside her reached out when the woman extended her hand. She was drawn to her, magnetically, this creature who was completely unlike any woman she had ever known.

'Come,' she ordered, as a girl not much older than Cass, wearing a russet woollen tunic, stepped forward to take the stallion's bridle and led it off towards the stables.

'But . . . the sickness . . .' Cass's voice came out as a croak.

The woman just laughed and shook her head. So Cass followed her up smooth stone steps, through an ornately carved stone archway and into a brightly lit hall.

For a moment, the light from dozens of table tapers and the torches in brackets that lined the stone walls dazzled her so much that she almost lifted her fingers to her eyes. And it was not just the light itself, but the colours and brightness of the people within, that gave the impression of stepping into a shimmering jewellery box.

Music spilled gaily from a group with lutes and flutes ensconced in the far corner of the hall, their instruments flashing in the firelight. Along each of the four long walls of the hall was set a wooden table, with benches running the length of it. The tables were laden with platters of venison and rich jugs of redcurrant sauce, trenchers piled high with loaves of crusty bread, earthenware dishes filled with steaming buttered potatoes and greens. There was fruitcake topped with rings of dried apple and drizzled in honey, pitchers of golden ale and the sweet scent of spiced mead.

Women in bright gowns of purple and green, deep blue and blood-red filled the room like butterflies, some clustered along the benches, filling plates, some dancing energetically in the open space between the tables, whirling and laughing beneath a vast chandelier that dripped with flickering candles. Their dresses rippled about them like fluid, gently reflecting the light, clinging to their hips and swirling out light as air when they moved. They were made from a material finer than any Cass had ever seen.

The walls were hung with beautiful tapestries, richly embroidered with hunting scenes and delicate floral motifs. At the centre of the longest table, which ran the length of the back wall, on a chair with a tall, intricately carved wooden back, sat a woman with fiery red hair that hung straight down to below her waist. Her features were small and delicate, her gently pointed nose smattered in freckles. And her piercing eyes were as green and still as a winter pond. She wore an emerald gown, with a delicate golden girdle looping round her waist that caught the light as she rose to greet them. The music petered out and a hush fell over the room.

'We welcome your safe return, Sigrid,' she said with a gracious incline of her head, holding out both her hands to the rider to whose waist Cass had clung for the past several hours without knowing her name.

The woman called Sigrid held out the bandit's purse. The coins inside clinked gently as she handed it over.

'A rich day's work.' The other smiled, taking it and tucking it into her girdle. 'And you bring further spoils?' She eyed Cass curiously.

Cass felt her cheeks flush as those steady green eyes swept over her from her unruly brown curls to her bare feet, the soles of which were now thoroughly blackened. She felt like a child and for a moment, she heard her mother's voice, chastising her for being so careless, and on such a special day. The morning's bath seemed like a distant memory, something that had happened to somebody else, in a different life. For a moment, her heart squeezed with guilt as she wondered if the wedding had gone ahead, or if her disappearance had caused chaos.

'We had a shared quest,' Sigrid said simply, with a shrug of her shoulders, and for a moment Cass felt strangely deflated, as if she had failed some kind of test. Sigrid turned to her, that low, smooth voice as calm as it had been when she had spoken to the man she was about to murder. 'You may rest here tonight and I will return you to your home tomorrow if you wish.'

Stretching her arms above her head and rotating her neck from side to side, Sigrid nodded to the flame-haired woman. 'I am stiff from the long ride.' And she strode from the hall without another word, leaving Cass standing awkwardly alone.

'My name is Angharad,' the woman before her said, and though it was a simple enough greeting, she spoke with such authority that she might as well have said: *I am the King.* 'You are welcome here.'

Cass glanced around her.

'Are there no men here?' she blurted, and a ripple of laughter passed round the hall.

'Not everything here is as it seems,' Angharad replied. 'Lily will see you are made comfortable.' She beckoned to a girl of about Cass's age with cream-coloured skin, crescent dimples set deep in rosy cheeks, and hair hanging in golden ringlets about her shoulders. The girl grinned and darted forward, knocking over a wooden tankard of ale and splashing it down the front of her dress.

'Whoops!' She flashed her dimpled smile at Cass before seizing her hand in a warm, sticky paw. 'Come with me!'

And before she knew it, Cass was sitting on a sturdy wooden bench, filling her belly with tender, juicy meat and fragrant sauce and thirstily swallowing down a cup of mead.

Hunger crowded out the questions that still clamoured at her as she ate until the slow, pleasant warmth of the meal and the mead spread through her body. Then she stopped, looking down at her empty trencher, and her mind was cast back to her own home. She saw the expectant piles of plates and cups lined up on the kitchen table, awaiting the celebrations after the ceremony. Was Mary married? Had she ruined this day for the person she loved most in the world with her stupid, rash, selfishness? Cass felt dizzy, and the room seemed to spin a little.

'Bless you,' Lily exclaimed, 'you're falling asleep at the table!' And she picked up a taper and pulled Cass by the hand, unresisting, out of the hall.

They passed through a maze of corridors and stairways until she found herself in a simple but pleasant tower room, where Lily handed her a clean shift and she fell gratefully into the soft bed, with Lily's gentle snores for company until a deep and dreamless sleep rushed up to swallow her whole.

Chapter 4

When Cass woke the next morning she reached out, eyes still closed, for Mary's warm shape, but found only a hollow in the straw mattress next to her. Of course. Mary was in a new bed now, with a new bedfellow. Her stomach twisted painfully.

She opened her eyes to stone walls and the flickering warmth of a fire in a small hearth at the foot of the bed. There was a slight smell of lavender, which she would later learn Lily had a habit of stuffing inside her straw mattress to make it smell sweeter.

Cass leaped out of bed, the events of the previous day rushing back to her. Her torn and muddied dress was gone, and in its place, draped over a wooden chest in the corner, was a robe of fine, soft rose-pink, its sleeves fluted, its skirts long and full. She pulled it over her head, fingering it gently, a fabric more delicate than any she had ever worn, that slipped about her shoulders and caressed her hips like warm water. 'What is this place?' she murmured.

She remembered her mother's bedtime stories, whispered to her and Mary as the little ones slept in their bed on the other side of the room, their breathing already deep and even. The tales of bold girls who strayed too far into the forest, who let themselves be charmed into following mysterious faerie folk into their enchanted halls under the hills, who returned after what felt like days only to find everyone they knew had grown old and died while they had been away.

She remembered shivering with pleasure, savouring the delicious taste of danger from the safe nest of their shared bed. Because it had only been a story. But now she looked around her at the bare stone walls, the tendrils of woodsmoke curling up from the hearth, and ran her hands again over the strange dress as soft as gossamer. She remembered how the outer walls had loomed up in the dusk as if they had appeared by magic the night before. How heavy and dreamless her sleep had been. And she shivered as she opened the door and slipped through it.

In a tangle of limbs, bouncing curls and flying skirts, Lily skidded down the corridor.

'Oh, good, you're awake', she grinned, her dimples winking into life. 'Angharad wants to see you,' she panted. 'Come with me!'

Angharad's chamber was a beautiful room with carved wooden screens on all sides. The floor was covered in animal skins, the chairs cushioned with fluffy white fleeces. They found her sitting at a writing desk, papers scattered across it covered in fine script. Her pale forehead creased into a frown as she scrutinized them. She rose from her chair when the girls entered, holding out her hands, and Cass noticed delicate rings set with stones brighter and finer than any she had ever seen. There was a low cough, and Sigrid stepped forward from the shadows in the corner of the room. Dressed in a plain, dark maroon gown, with her auburn hair tumbling round her shoulders in gentle waves, she looked different – and wrong somehow. Cass could not marry the image of the gentlewoman before her with the memory of the rider who had shot a man through the eye with so little hesitation or remorse.

'Lady Sigrid intrigues you,' Angharad observed, with a gentle smile. 'Did I not tell you that little here is as it seems?'

She paused, and gently took Cass's hand. 'Few young women would leave their homes to leap on the back of a passing horse with a stranger. There is something in you that has drawn you here, to us. But if you choose to return home, I will arrange it. We will not keep you here against your will.'

Cass hesitated. Something in her chest fluttered wildly at Angharad's words, and not just because she wondered if her face had betrayed her lingering unease about being trapped in this dream. What had they seen inside her? Her fingers sought the thin scar on her wrist – a trophy of that day in the forest. For the first time in years, she recalled the glowing yellow eyes of the old fortune-teller.

She felt torn in two. The voice of reason, her mother's voice, telling her to run home to the safety of her sister's arms and beg her forgiveness. And a smaller, stubborn little voice, the one that kept her up trees until long after dinnertime, and plunged her into the stream in the summer though she'd been told a thousand times that she was no longer a child and that a proper lady would not continue to behave in such a way. That voice reminded her that Mary wouldn't be there any more, even if she did go home, and that her father might bring home a match for Cass any day. That this was the first chance she had ever had in her whole life to seek something different for herself. And the little voice seemed to be getting louder.

'What is this place?' she asked simply. 'Where are we?'

'Those are two very different questions,' Angharad replied. 'And the second is far simpler to answer. We are in Northumbria. You have travelled a long way from your home in Mercia. We are not far from the border.'

'And the answer to the first question?'

Angharad hesitated.

'It would be easier to show her, would it not?' The words burst out of Lily who seemed to be almost vibrating with excitement beside Cass. 'Forgive me,' she apologized, stepping back contritely after speaking out of turn. But a ripple of amusement passed across Angharad's face.

'Perhaps you are right,' she said.

Together they walked out of the chamber and down a set of stairs to a small door at the bottom that led out into the main courtyard where Cass and Sigrid had arrived the night before. Girls in short tunics and hose were hard at work in the yard, heaving great forkfuls of soiled straw out of the horses' stalls and sweeping manure. Cass stared at them. They were shouldering their loads like stable boys, wiping sweaty brows with dirty hands that left brown streaks, meeting her gaze frankly as if there was nothing remarkable about what they were doing.

Instead of continuing through the main entrance gate Sigrid had led her through, they turned and walked round to the back of the courtyard instead, taking a narrow pathway between the walls that led behind the main manor house and coming out through a small postern gate into a lush meadow bordered by thick trees on three sides and the walls of the manor on the fourth.

The meadow was bright with wildflowers: cuckoo flowers the pink of a morning sunrise, bright blue cornflowers and tall daisies bloomed amid the long grass. But it was not the flowers that made Cass stop and stare.

The meadow teemed with activity. The clash of swords rang out as small groups of young women met in noisy combat. Cass gasped as one of them rolled backwards almost across her toes, before leaping back to her feet with a triumphant shout, catching up her shield and re-entering the fray.

A group of younger girls practiced drills with wooden batons, stepping forward, striking and defending as an older woman with a curtain of straight silver hair barked commands at them. Along the east side of the meadow stood a dozen wooden targets. An arrow slammed into the centre of one with a great hollow *thunk* as a plumpish girl with light brown skin and her hair pulled into tight, narrow braids, released her bowstring. At the far end of the meadow, horses galloped back and forth, their riders carrying long, narrow wooden poles with balls at the tip.

'Are they . . . jousting?' Cass whispered.

'They are training,' Angharad answered.

'Who *are* you?' Cass gasped, mesmerized by the girls, her

eyes never leaving their forms as they darted and lunged, rolled and struck, stabbed and retreated.

'We are a fellowship,' Angharad answered.

'A sisterhood,' Lily chimed in, beaming.

'We are knights,' Angharad finished simply. You are inside the stronghold of the Sisters of Sword and Shadow.'

Chapter 5

'**K**nights?' Cass blinked. 'But . . .'

'Tell me the qualities of a knight,' Angharad said coolly, pre-empting the obvious objection Cass was about to raise.

Cass stopped to consider the question. Knights had never been a part of her world. Of course, she had heard of them, was aware of the adventures of King Arthur and his shining fellowship of the Round Table in Camelot, but they had always seemed more like bedtime stories than real people. In the rural depths of Mercia, where lesser kings held sway and lesser knights occasionally rode out hunting, the tales were of land disputes and petty scuffles, not grand exploits and daring rescues.

So she closed her eyes and remembered the bedtime stories. Remembered the thrill of the maidens saved and treasure sought, of noble quests and brave deeds.

'A knight shows valour,' she began, uncertainly. 'A knight is brave and courageous and puts the needs of others before his own.' She frowned. 'A knight saves damsels – or at least he is sworn to fight to protect women, and to uphold the values of chivalry and courtesy.'

'You are almost completely right.' Angharad smiled. 'We are brave and courageous. We fight for the needs of the many, not the few. We are sworn to protect those less powerful than ourselves, and to uphold values of kindness and decency. We are a group of women who, for many reasons, have not found lives for ourselves that we can accept outside these walls. So we gather here. And we make our own rules. We defy anybody who believes that only men can fight; that valour is inherently a masculine virtue. We believe there is a life for us with a higher meaning than marriage and servitude, which so often come interlinked. We believe we have as much right to knighthood as men do, and we do not timidly seek permission to call ourselves knights. We simply prove it.'

And she whirled round, catching up her emerald skirts in one hand and seizing a nearby girl's sword with the other, before throwing herself headlong into the fray with a spine-tingling shriek. Cass watched, open-mouthed, as Angharad's sword slashed through the air like lightning. She parried the first blow that came her way, caught up a shield and used it to send the next opponent tumbling headlong into the grass. A deft sidestep and the next girl stumbled; a flick of her wrist and another saw her sword leap out of her hand. That left just one final adversary, a tall young woman with dark, flashing eyes and sharp cheekbones, with smooth, dark brown skin and black hair cropped close to her head. She bowed to Angharad, grasped her sword and stepped determinedly forward. Angharad feinted, light on her feet, sending the young woman lurching in the wrong direction, then darted round behind her. But the girl recovered, spinning on her heel, her sword flicking back and forth so fast Cass could barely keep her eyes on it, though Angharad swerved and ducked, avoiding the blows as fast as they came.

It was like no fight Cass had ever witnessed: they seemed to dance with the delicacy and grace of two butterflies, circling and swirling around each other in a dizzying, joyful spiral in the morning sunshine, even as their blows rained down fast and sharp round each other's bodies. Cass did not realize she was holding her breath, that her fists were balled and her brow tightly furrowed. She was completely transfixed, her muscles tensing and clenching in sympathy with the whirling young women, as if she, too, might take off from the ground and spin through the air like a sycamore seed.

And then, as suddenly as it had begun, Angharad's sword swished down, catching the girl's wrist a glancing blow, and her sword fell from her hand. Angharad leaped forward, her foot upon the hilt of her opponent's blade, and pressed the point to the younger woman's throat.

'Well done, Rowan, you show great promise.' She nodded approvingly, dropping the sword, and the young woman's eyes shone with pleasure as she gasped to regain her breath.

Angharad calmly wiped her hands on her dress and smiled at Cass. 'You see,' she said lightly. 'Not all is as it seems.'

'So you . . .' Cass turned to Lily.

'I am Angharad's squire,' she said, swelling with pride. 'A squire sees to her mistress's needs, helps her to arm and disarm, cares for her armour and weapons, and learns from her, as she is training to be a knight herself one day.'

'Aye, although I sometimes think twice about it when she worries at my ankles like an overeager spaniel,' Angharad replied, giving Lily an affectionate cuff on the shoulder.

'I will take you as my squire,' Sigrid announced abruptly, her dark eyes appraising Cass. 'If you stay.'

Cass noticed that Angharad's eyes widened slightly in surprise, and that some of the young women who were watching them gave each other curious glances.

'I am glad, Sigrid,' Angharad murmured. 'Your pursuits are so often solitary. It is clear the girl has shown courage already in accompanying you here. I am sure she will serve you well.'

'But . . .' Cass's mind was in turmoil, her questions spilling over one another, and underneath it all something inside her swelled and pulsed at Angharad's words. 'Under whose authority . . .' She trailed off.

'Under whose authority was Arthur made High King?' Angharad asked scathingly. 'An archbishop and a supposed sorcerer and a sword we are told was drawn from a stone before a great tournament gathering?' She raised a sceptical eyebrow. 'Men, all of them. In the church and at the tournament and at Arthur's side. What greater authority has he than we do to declare himself what he is? And to gather others to follow him? And what about all the lesser kings with their fellowships and their knights who pillage and plunder as often as they uphold the knightly code?' Her face darkened. 'What difference is there between our fellowships, if you forget what you have been told about who in our world has the power to make decisions and announce decrees?'

Cass felt dizzy. None of it made any sense. There were rules, and traditions and things had been this way for centuries. And yet . . .

And yet hadn't she herself dreaded the knock at the door

of the farm? Only yesterday she had lain under the apple trees, feeling rebellion in her heart at the thought of Mary being taken from her, fear at the idea of being taken from herself too by a man who would choose for her, a life decided without her saying anything at all. Hadn't she reached out for Sigrid's hand on that dusty road for a reason? Because something inside her yearned for escape, something more? Angharad was offering her that.

'How is it possible that I have never heard,' she began slowly, 'of a fellowship of women knights? If this were real, wouldn't people know about it? Wouldn't it be forbidden?'

'You have answered your own question,' purred Sigrid, a twisted smile on her face. 'When we ride out, we conceal our identities for our own protection.'

'And we have—' Lily began eagerly.

'We have ways of keeping our lives here private and have done for many years,' Angharad interrupted, her eyes flashing a warning in Lily's direction. 'Ways you will learn should you choose to stay.'

Cass remembered the girls who had warned them away from the gates.

'And if I don't?'

'Is it likely anyone would believe you, should you choose to tell the tale?'

Cass knew Angharad was right. She tried to imagine

herself describing the events of the past day to her mother or father. She would be chastised for inventing wild stories, or chided for letting her imagination run away with her. Told that she should have left such things behind in childhood.

'But the bandit,' Cass wondered aloud. 'The man you confronted. Had he lived . . .' She stopped abruptly. 'Do you kill every man who sees your faces?' she asked, aghast.

Sigrid laughed, a spill of honey notes. 'No, country girl. We do not slaughter indiscriminately. I killed that ruffian only when he posed a direct threat to my own life. We were fairly matched, and he reached for his weapon first.'

'And if he hadn't?' Cass asked. 'Or if he had lived to tell the tale? What then?'

Sigrid's lips curled back from her teeth in a smile that was almost a snarl. 'An interesting thing happens, when a man is defeated in combat by a woman.'

Angharad nodded. 'He tells nobody.'

Chapter 6

Cass lay on her back in the long grass at the edge of the meadow, sucking the remaining scraps of flesh from one of the last of the season's plums.

'So will you stay?' asked Lily, who lay beside her, her yellow curls spread wildly round her head like a halo, an angelic effect she immediately ruined by spitting the pit of her plum high into the air.

Cass sighed and closed her eyes. A succession of shadowy figures chased each other across her eyelids. Her mother, wringing her hands and crying out her name. Her sister, face twisted in confusion and hurt. Sigrid, leather-clad and mysterious. And suddenly those yellow eyes from all those years ago, burning into hers with an intensity that startled her and made her sit bolt upright, blinking in the sun.

The meadow had almost emptied, the women and girls gone to attend to their tasks in the kitchens and stables, feeding the animals and preparing the evening meal. ('Arthur boasts of his Round Table with all its fairness,' Angharad had explained, 'but who do you think roasts the meat in his court? Not the knights themselves, that is for certain. Here we share everything, glory and labour alike.')

'How is this possible?' Cass asked curiously, watching Lily braid daisies together into a long chain. 'How do you afford to live?'

'The Lady Angharad's husband was a wealthy merchant,' Lily answered, running the fine edges of Cass's gown through her fingertips. 'He imported silks and other rich cloth to sell throughout Northumbria and beyond. When he died on a trading expedition seven years ago, he left behind stuffed coffers, and a glut of his wares as well.' She smiled. 'So every girl who finds her way here, no matter where she has come from, is clothed in silk and given a safe, warm place to stay.' She turned the daisy chain over in her fingers, examining it closely. 'And we repay that kindness in loyalty, and love of this place,' she said quietly. 'The sisterhood becomes our family and we have no need of any other.'

'What happened to the other men?' Cass asked curiously.

'When the lord died, the women working here were offered sanctuary, but Angharad hid it from the menfolk and dismissed them on the lord's order. She had to pay substantial sums to some of them to persuade them to move on, but once it was done, she was free.'

'Free?'

'Her husband was not known for his kindness. Nor were some of his men. And letting his death become known would have opened the floodgates to suitors greedy to absorb the wealth he left behind, and Angharad with it. Keeping it a secret was the only way for her to live with true autonomy.'

'How long have you been here?' Cass asked, squinting at her.

'Since I was fourteen,' Lily replied. 'I wish I could tell you I left home the first day my father laid hands on me, but it can't have been the fiftieth, or even the hundredth.' She sighed, looking straight up at the sky. 'I don't know what was different about that day. It was just the two of us, always had been. My mother died giving birth to me and I had no brothers or sisters. And I think some part of me always felt guilt, that I had somehow made him the way he was, by taking my mother from him with the murder that was my birth. It was my fault he couldn't cope, my fault he drank, my fault his grief exploded out of him in great bursts. So I stayed, like I was doing penance. But that day, he knocked out a tooth. And I don't know why, but I couldn't stop looking at that tooth. Just sitting in my hand, a little white thing smudged with blood. And I put it down on the table, like I was paying the last of what I owed him, and walked away.'

'I'm sorry,' breathed Cass, taking her hand.

'I walked for so long my feet went numb, with no sense of where I was going and no idea in my head about what to do except that I couldn't stay. And, when I was near to collapsing, I saw a knight riding towards me, in fine armour and a helmet, and he lifted me onto his horse and brought me here. Except that it wasn't a man, it was Angharad. Her last squire had been knighted just a few days before. And I've been apprenticed to her ever since.'

Lily gave a little shake of her head, as if to scatter the memories, and her dimples appeared again. 'You won't regret it if you stay,' she said. 'I promise you won't.'

They subsided into silence, and Cass shielded her eyes from the sun, feeling uneasy. She had no monster to flee, no reason to drive her here the way Lily had been driven. Her parents were traditional, her mother busy with caring for their home and the little ones, her father brusque and seldom emotional but hard-working. They were not cruel. Her parents' worst crime was to hope for a stable future and a family life for her, and this was how she repaid them: by running from the very idea of such a future, running so far from it that she had abandoned them for ever.

A shadow fell over them and they looked up to see Sigrid standing there, her body encased in the intricately patterned black leather armour once again. 'Ride out with me today,' she said. 'And perhaps you will find the answers you seek.'

So it was that Cass found herself astride another horse, wearing a borrowed linen shirt and hose that faintly retained Lily's lavender scent.

'Here,' Sigrid said, tying a piece of cloth round Cass's face to conceal all but her eyes, and gathering her hair in a knot at the back of her neck. Cass noticed with a jolt that as well as the bow slung from the side of the saddle, Sigrid also wore a belt with a long, thin sheath and protruding from its top was a finely wrought silver sword grip, the pommel engraved with the single letter 'J'. As Cass watched, she caught up a great white shield in one arm and finally pulled on a plain, domed silver helmet that entirely covered her face with only narrow slits through which she could see.

And so, with some trepidation, Cass found herself plunging into the forest with her arms round that straight, strong back once again.

'Where . . . are we . . . going?' Cass gasped, her breath jerking with the rhythm of the horse.

'We will know when we get there,' Sigrid replied, her voice echoing and strange from within the helmet. 'We follow adventure, reward, destiny . . . a quest will find us, not the other way round.'

They rode along country lanes where the hedgerows hung thick with yellow-green hops and dripped with ripe, glossy blackberries. The sky was calm; feathery wisps of cloud floated lazily across the blue, and the road was deserted.

The borrowed clothes felt strange against Cass's skin, between her legs. She itched to adjust her position, tug at the material, but she dared not take her hands from Sigrid's waist as the horse galloped on.

'What . . . led you . . . to the sisterhood?' she panted. Sigrid stiffened, but before she could reply, or rebuke Cass for her forwardness, the serene countryside air was torn by a piercing scream.

'Yah!' Sigrid wrenched the reins round immediately, galloping without hesitation away from the track and into a nearby copse of trees in the direction from which the scream had issued.

In a small clearing, a young woman lay on the ground, a bright red welt standing out angrily on her cheek. Her dress was torn down the front, her hair in disarray.

Sigrid slid down from her horse. 'Lady, are you hurt?' she

asked, and Cass noticed that the melodic voice had dropped several tones.

'A little,' the woman sniffed, struggling to sit up. Her clothing was coarse and home-stitched, her nails caked in dirt. 'But he has taken my brother.' She broke into a sob, her shoulders shaking, and ran a trembling hand across her face.

'Who has taken your brother?' Sigrid asked, more gently than Cass had yet heard her speak.

'A knight,' the woman cried, 'a most ungentle knight who lay in wait and attacked us from his vantage point in a tree as we returned from market with what little our crops would sell for. The money should last us for a month, though the harvest has been so poor, but he has taken it. And without my brother to work the farm . . .' She dissolved into shuddering sobs.

'He shall not keep the money, nor your brother,' Sigrid growled, leaping back into the saddle in front of Cass, who had to grab on suddenly as the horse took off through the trees, sending her jerking painfully backwards.

Sigrid rode furiously, following a trail of broken branches and flattened undergrowth.

A few minutes later they came upon a gently babbling stream, and beside it a pavilion of scarlet and black. A pennant bearing the head of a boar fluttered proudly atop it and a mighty warhorse was hobbled nearby, where it could graze and drink from the stream. A little way off a great oak tree grew, and a man of about twenty was bound to the base, his head slumped onto his chest. One side of his face was caked in dried blood and his features were grotesquely swollen. Beside him from the branches of the tree hung a huge shield, divided into four quarters of black and red, with the gold outline of the boar painted in the centre, its tusks glinting cruelly.

Sigrid dismounted, and drawing her sword, struck the shield with its metal pommel until it rang like a great gong. Hearing the signal, a knight strode from the pavilion to meet her. He was a giant of a man, his armour gleaming black, a gigantic sword in his hand.

'Come out and defend your actions, coward,' Sigrid shouted, her voice ringing out across the woods.

The knight bore down on her, sneering. 'And who are you to challenge me?'

'One brave enough to take on an equal opponent, rather than prey on the poor and defenceless,' Sigrid spat.

'Equal opponent?' The knight let out a great guffaw, and leaned on his sword. 'Let us see you try your might against mine, sprat, and you will soon beg my forgiveness for that insult.'

Cass watched, her heart in her throat, as Sigrid stepped forward without hesitation, her sword raised in front of her. But the knight laughed again.

'Nay, lad, it will be too simple to slaughter you where you stand. I will tie my right hand behind my back, to give you a fighting chance.' And he returned to his pavilion and emerged with a length of rope, which he used to tie one hand behind his back, while Sigrid watched silently.

Sneering, he stepped towards her, but Sigrid was quicker. She seemed to take leave of the earth as she flew forward and upwards, her sheer speed and the height of her ascent taking the knight by surprise so that she caught him a great, glancing blow with the top of her shield under his chin, and darted backwards again out of reach as he swiped out in retaliation with his sword.

'No runt, perhaps, after all,' she mocked quietly, as he rubbed his chin with the back of his free hand, sword dangling.

'You shall pay for that, and in blood,' he retorted, no longer laughing, and lunged towards her, armour clanking. But she was too fast, darting behind him with lightning speed, the tip of her sword finding a gap between his breastplate and his helmet, so that the knight cried out in pain and blood trickled from a wound below his shoulder blade.

Cass gazed at Sigrid in open awe. She was so unlike any woman Cass had ever met that she might as well have been a sprite or a will-o'-the-wisp. She imagined, for a moment, what Mary would say if she could see this. But she knew that Mary would have buried her face in her skirt by now. No, Mary would never have let her get this far, would have seized her by the elbow and dragged her back home before they ever left the safety of the edge of the forest. And that uncomfortable sensation of her heart being stretched until it might snap in two throbbed in her chest again.

There came a faint moan, and Cass saw that the young man had come to his senses and was watching, his eyes moving between his captor and his potential rescuer, and that his sister had crept through the trees to stand beside him, her face alight with hope.

'Damn you, gadfly,' the knight cried, whirling round with the flat of his sword as if to buffet Sigrid full across the chest. But she ducked nimbly, her sword seeming far lighter and less cumbersome than his, and as she stooped she slashed it across the back of his legs, just at the bottom of the armour where his ankles were unprotected, and he screamed in pain and fell forward onto his knees, blood spurting onto the ground.

'Would you like me to untie your other arm, perhaps?' Sigrid asked politely, her voice a low purr, and as she spoke the knight roared in fury and stumbled forward, throwing the full weight of his body behind his sword as he stabbed towards her heart. But she stepped neatly aside, and he toppled at her feet. In a blink, she stood astride his body and stooped to wrench off his helmet, then straightened, the point of her sword hovering above his neck, both hands poised to drive it down and into the earth beneath.

And the knight cried mercy, begged to yield and be allowed to live. Cass saw the disgust in Sigrid's eyes and knew in that moment that Sigrid would sooner die at the point of a blade than grovel as the knight did, but she spat in the dust next to his face and stepped aside.

'See that you remember this the next time you are tempted to line your own pockets with the money of the poor,' she said, as she strode past the cowering knight to enter his pavilion and emerged with a leather money bag. 'Now get out of my sight, before I change my mind.' And the knight stumbled to his feet, groaning and limping, mounted his horse and disappeared into the trees.

Sigrid cut the ropes that bound the young man with her sword and dropped the money bag into the lap of the girl who had emerged from the trees where she had been hiding and now sat beside him, crying tears of relief and gratitude into his shoulder.

'Thank you, sir, and may God reward you. We can never express our gratitude,' she sobbed.

'Thank you,' her brother repeated, dazedly.

Sigrid simply nodded, and turned to find Cass gaping at her.

'You are a hero,' she said simply. 'Why do you not let people know?'

Sigrid bent over for a few moments, hands on her knees, to regain her breath.

'Watch,' she said quietly.

And she strode over to the youth who was blinking his swollen eye and rubbing at his chafed wrists.

'Their word will be of little consequence.' She shrugged in answer to Cass's enquiring glance, as she lifted the helmet off her head and shook out her hair like a skein of ruddy wool tumbling from its binding.

For a moment, sister and brother simply stared at her, their mouths slack, their eyes swivelling from Sigrid's face to her armour to her sword and back again as if they strained to make sense of what they were seeing. Then the girl recoiled in horror and the boy's face flushed a painfully dark red.

'What are you, witch?' he asked, grasping the bark of the tree behind him to draw himself to his feet. 'What kind of unnatural display is this?' He made no effort to conceal his naked disgust, even as Cass could see the flush of shame beneath it.

'Stay back, doxy,' the sister cried, her voice shrill and cruel. 'We want nothing to do with you or your kind.' And she grasped her brother's arm and supported him to hurry away into the forest.

Sigrid grinned at Cass and replaced her helmet. 'Anonymity has its benefits,' she said as she swung herself back onto her horse. This time Cass did not hesitate to grasp the gloved hand and leap into the saddle behind her.

Lily was not in the hall when they returned and went to eat supper, but she found Cass later, in the small bedroom, where they huddled close under the wool blanket and Cass recounted the adventure. Lily provided a most appreciative audience, gasping and covering her mouth at all the most exciting moments, and clasping her hands together with excitement at the climax of the evil knight's defeat.

'Will you stay, then?' she asked eagerly, when the story was done, but Cass stared into the darkness and did not answer.

'I used to sleep always arm in arm with my sister,' Cass said quietly. The ache when she thought of Mary had not lessened with the day, but if anything, seemed to have sharpened, like a blade waiting beneath the skin to pierce her when she least expected it. She sighed and turned onto her side, and her eyes pricked with tears when Lily's soft hand crept into hers in the dark.

Chapter 7

Impact. Sky. Pain.

A dull ringing that seemed to shake her skull and the iron grip of a great gauntlet squeezing her lungs.

The first day of training was the hardest of Cass's life so far. She had known she was going to stay, really, from the moment the evil knight fell to his knees, or perhaps from the moment Lily had spoken of this place as home, lying on her back in the meadow. Or was it from the moment she had first seen Sigrid, bearing down on her along the dusty track? All she knew was that it wasn't a choice, not really, but a feeling of complete certainty that this was where she was meant to be.

She had buried the silver locket deep inside her mattress,

as if submerging it there would somehow make her decision final. Like it could muffle the guilt she felt at leaving her family.

She had hoped that training would provide a sense of thrilling clarity; that she would sit upon a horse and feel a sudden sense of purpose and strength; that she might weave and dance as fluidly as the women she had watched the day before.

But within ten seconds of picking up the blunt wooden baton she lay on her back in the mud, gasping for air that would not enter her bruised lungs.

'Up. Again.' Vivian swished her curtain of silver hair back from her face, frowning at Cass.

'She's not as fierce as she sounds,' Lily whispered sympathetically, as she took Cass's arm and pulled her to her feet. 'She is one of the bravest knights here, and Angharad's closest adviser. Learning from her is a great hon—'

'If you've breath to talk, you're doing it wrong,' Vivian snapped, appearing from behind them and whisking her baton across the back of Lily's calves, sending her sprawling into the indent Cass had made in the mud just moments before.

'A great honour, you were saying?' Cass grinned, as she helped Lily up. Thick mud dripped from Lily's earlobes.

Vivian's face was round and soft, her skin smooth and pale. The silver hair was premature, Cass thought, making her look older than her years. Her eyes were a piercing blue, bright as the periwinkles that dotted the edges of the meadow.

'You will improve,' she told Cass, briskly but not unkindly. 'But only with practice, and hard work. What seems difficult here in the meadow will be a thousand times more challenging on a roadside verge with three knights surrounding you or in the murk of the forest at night.'

Cass gulped. The idea of finding herself in such a situation still seemed absurd. All this still felt like a dream, the exercises like children's games, not part of real life. That she could one day herself become a knight seemed ridiculous, impossible. And yet here was Vivian, her own black leather breastplate studded with metal rivets, confidently discussing Cass's future skirmishes as if they were a matter of simple fact, not figments of wild imagination.

'Now concentrate,' Vivian urged, holding out the wooden baton. Cass grasped the end with one hand. 'Grip.' A small notch was carved into the wood where the cross guard of the sword would be, and she indicated the next few inches of wood, the bottom of the 'blade'. 'Forte. The strongest part of the sword. Use it to defend and to parry your opponent's blows.' She slid her hand along the smooth wood, until it reached the section nearest the tip. 'Foible. The weakest part. Use the point to thrust, to stab, but not to slash and hack, or you will find yourself standing with a broken stump in your hands and nothing left to fight with.'

All this sounded quite reasonable in theory, except that every time Cass picked up the wooden stick it twisted and jumped disobediently in her hands, refusing to do her bidding. She lashed out wildly at Lily, but her opponent was more experienced and easily batted the blows away with her own baton. Cass felt lucky if she made contact at all, let alone trying to determine which part of the 'blade' she was using.

Step. Parry. Thrust. Sidestep. Plunge. Retreat. Slash. Duck.

Never had it occurred to her how closely aligned a knight's feet had to be with their hands. It was more like learning to dance than learning to fight, memorizing complex steps and routines and treading them over and over again until she felt dizzy and her thighs ached for rest.

Just as she felt certain that she would have to give up, that she could not bear one more bout, they moved on to the archery targets. Rowan, the tall, slender young woman a couple of years older than Cass who had sparred with Angharad the day before placed a simply carved bow of supple ash in her hand and a quiver of arrows at her side. The bow was far heavier than it looked, the wood polished to a rich sheen. Each arrow was fletched with brightly dyed feathers, and for a moment, if she let her eyes slide out of focus, they looked like the posies of flowers she and Mary would pick and bring in from the garden, bright petals clamouring together in a burst of colour. But then her vision focused and she saw their straight shafts and the carefully sharpened metal arrowheads. She tested a point with her thumb, leaving a red dent. She felt clumsy as she tried to raise the heavy bow, her left arm held straight out in front of her like Rowan's, her right hand drawing back the string with the arrow nocked. She trembled with the effort, the shaft of the arrow clacking and clattering against the bow as her arm shook.

'Turn your body side-on,' Rowan called, 'open your stance, or you will . . .' But it was too late. Cass let the arrow fly, soaring far above the target and into the woods beyond the edge of the field, as the bowstring snapped angrily forward, delivering a sharp smack to the tender flesh on the inside of her upper left arm, she rubbed it, smarting.

'Too valuable to waste,' said Rowan, returning from the trees with the errant arrow and dropping it back into the quiver. She lowered her voice, so that only Cass could hear her. 'I did that about the first thousand times I fired an arrow too. You'll soon get the hang of it.' She moved on to coach Lily.

Cass's muscles were aching by the end of the session. But she had at least managed to hit her target when she realized Sigrid had been observing her – for how long, she did not know.

'So, how does it feel to train?' Sigrid asked.

'Like freedom,' said Cass simply, 'but it is more work than you make it look.' She pulled the sleeve of her dress down to reveal a bruise from the bowstring.

Sigrid ran her fingers across it gently. 'You'll need a poultice: ask Lily to take you to see Alys this evening, if she can find her.'

She clapped Cass on the shoulder and returned to the manor, leaving Cass to prod the sore place on her arm, wincing as it throbbed at her touch, and wondering who Alys might be and why she might be difficult to find.

That afternoon, her muscles still aching, Cass was summoned to the stables, where a very quiet, gangly youth named Blyth shyly whispered from behind a sweeping dark fringe that Sigrid had ordered her to be matched with a horse, so she might begin riding lessons in earnest.

'You'll find Blyth a little . . . different,' Lily had whispered when she'd told Cass where to go. 'Blyth arrived one day with no story or explanation of the path that led here . . . went straight to the stables as if the horses were a sanctuary . . . slept there the first night and has never left since. I've never seen anybody else who can handle them in the same way. Even the most spirited colt or the fieriest stallion. It's like they share a language, somehow.'

Stepping into the stables was like stepping outside time. All the hustle and bustle of the courtyard and the manor faded away, as the clashing of swords and the hubbub of the students practising their melees could not penetrate the thick, stone walls, and the air felt cool and smelled rich with straw and dung.

Bright, inquisitive eyes peered at Cass over the wooden latched doors to each stall, the horses harrumphing gently as she approached. Blyth walked next to her, scratching the horses between the ears, suddenly more animated than shy, as if the animals' presence brought confidence and ease. 'This is Star,' Blyth said, reaching out a lightly sun-browned hand to a glossy roan mare that nudged affectionately closer, pushing her nose over the stall. 'She's Angharad's mount. Doesn't scare easily – she has nerves of steel in a fight, much like her mistress.' Cass smiled.

'I can't imagine it,' she admitted, letting the horse snuffle her soft, velvety nose into the palm of her hand. 'Even riding as hard and fast as Sigrid did, let alone . . .' She swallowed. 'Let alone fighting myself.'

'You'll find you are capable of things you never dreamed of, if you give yourself a chance to stretch beyond the idea of yourself that you've always known,' Blyth said quietly, then flushed a little and retreated to the next stall, as if saying so much had overstepped some private limit.

Then, with a little cough, 'This is Bessie, who belongs to Vivian.' Bessie was a fine piebald horse, white with liver spots and a dark brown mane. 'And that's Sigrid's charger, Brimstone, who you've already met.' Blythe gestured towards the tallest of the horses, his nostrils flared and his neck arched regally, looking ready to fly off on another adventure at a moment's notice.

'But these striplings,' Blyth chuckled affectionately as they reached the smaller stalls at the far end of the stables, 'these are still learning, aren't you, little ones?' The horses snickered and jostled in their stalls, still growing into the full length of their limbs. Their ears pricked excitedly at the sound of Blyth's voice. There was a rich mahogany-brown colt that pawed impatiently at the dirt-packed floor as if to demand adventure, and a quieter bay mare that butted her nose curiously towards Blyth, but Cass could not take her eyes from a scruffy little black cob that seemed to linger shyly behind the others, its mane askew and its eyes skittering nervously from the other horses to Blyth and Cass and back again.

'Hello, little one,' Cass whispered, reaching her fingers out towards it and feeling an instant kinship as it nudged towards her, acorn-brown eyes fixing on hers from beneath absurdly long lashes.

Blyth laughed. 'That's Pebble, the runt of the pack. But

she's got spirit, more than enough to match her size, and I think she might surprise us yet.'

Like me, Cass thought shyly. But there was something inside her, a little flame of hope and determination, that she could feel burning steadily. She nodded firmly, held out an apple and said, 'Pebble. She's the one.'

It was the same little flame that led her back to the meadow that night, as the crickets chirped and the lowing cows heralded the quiet end of the late summer day. The warm dusk held the scent of the sweet meadow grass and she felt something like exhilaration as she breathed it in deeply, closing her palm round the wooden practice sword that already began to feel as if it belonged in her grip.

That was where Lily found her, baton in hand, practising her steps for the hundredth time, her bruised arm tender and stiff but her limbs suffused with that pleasant glowing ache that comes from good exercise and fresh air. It was a feeling Cass had always loved, riding proudly home lying atop the mountain of straw in the cart after working from dawn to bring in the harvest, or limping home with bedraggled hair and bruised thighs after a day running wild in the forest with Mary. But Mary had accompanied her less and less as the wedding approached, staying indoors with her mother, sewing the quilts and sheets she would take to her new home, learning to make hot-water pastry and how to use the last of the carcass of a slaughtered a pig to make brawn.

'You can't carry on like this much longer, sweet,' her mother would chide her gently, picking the leaves out of her wild curls when she slipped in after dusk, her clothes muddied from a day spent lying on the riverbank trying to tickle fish. 'It'll be your turn before too long, Cassandra.' And Cass had felt her stomach ache without really knowing why. She had never really questioned that she would follow Mary out of their father's home and into another man's. But she had always known, in some deep, quiet part of her, that she wasn't ready to be still and quiet and clean. That her lungs would never stop needing the rush of that fresh-cut grass nor her thighs the satisfying afterburn of clamping on rough bark. That when her mother used her full name it felt as uncomfortable and strange as the stiff leather shoes she had forced her feet into on the morning of Mary's wedding. She had known it then without really knowing that she knew it, and she knew it now with more certainty than ever. She wasn't going home.

'Hurry,' Lily urged, breaking her reverie. 'Alys may be asleep if we arrive much after dusk and believe me, she doesn't take well to being woken.'

They made their way out of the manor gates in the gathering gloom. Somewhere deep in the woods a warbler was singing, its trilling notes spinning faster and faster before stopping abruptly.

'Where are we going?' Cass asked nervously, as Lily picked her way confidently through the trees, moving deeper into the forest.

'It's not far,' Lily reassured her. 'Alys prefers to live outside the walls. She's a little brusque, but she can do things with a radish-and-vinegar poultice that'll turn your skin to silk.'

As they approached the hut, Cass couldn't help but remember the stories the villagers had shared about strange women who lived in the woods. The warnings about those whose knowledge of herbs and spells gave them unnatural powers, who might use their dark skills to charm a man from his wife or cast a sickness on the child of an enemy. The whispered snatches of scandalous rumours: women who cavorted with the devil and danced in the moonlight . . .

The little wattle hut loomed suddenly out of the shadows, its lumpen walls crouching like a toad among three tall birch trees. In front of it somebody had cleared the ground to create a bed of earth, bursting with sage and comfrey, parsley and chamomile, hyssop and sweet woodruff, lemon balm and yarrow and others Cass didn't know the names of. Their scent mingled and clashed intoxicatingly, a confusing mixture that made her head spin a little so that when the door opened at Lily's quiet knock it seemed for a moment that the figure silhouetted against the candlelight inside leaped and distorted into grotesque shapes as the flames flickered in the draught.

Then the flames stretched tall on their tapers again and the door opened a little wider.

'Come in, then, if you're coming,' Alys snapped impatiently, and they stepped inside.

The packed-earth floor was smartly swept and the walls and ceiling loaded with dried herbs and grasses, onions that swung in long plaited rows, chamomile flowers clustered upside down, and lavender in neatly tied bunches.

An iron pot sat amid the embers of the fire, a thick stew simmering gently inside it, filling the hut with a delicious savoury smell that made Cass's mouth water.

'Well? It is late, and I was on my way to bed.' Alys turned to face them, a plump, plain woman in a shabby brown tunic, her frizzy, dark brown hair streaked with grey. She was short and her face pinkish, her slightly stooped gait putting Cass in mind of a hedgehog as she bustled towards them.

'I see it.' She tutted, but the fingers that probed Cass's arm were gentle, her voice not unsympathetic as she grunted, 'Bowstring?' and Cass nodded.

'I am not what you expected,' she observed bluntly, a twinkle in her eye, as she pressed Cass onto a wooden stool by the fire and brought a pot of sweet-smelling salve. 'No snaggle-tooth or bristling chin, perhaps? Mutton in the pot where you might have looked for a love potion?' Cass flushed at the thoughts she'd been having moments earlier. 'You will not be the first to benefit from my wisdom while you disparage my character,' Alys said curtly, rolling up her sleeves and pounding radish peel into a paste with a heavy pestle. She mixed it with honey and then uncorked a bottle of sour-smelling vinegar.

'I didn't know . . .' Cass faltered. 'I am sorry.'

'You were taught to fear me.' Alys shrugged. 'It is not your fault.' And as she delicately smoothed the paste over the bruise that was already beginning to bloom, Cass thought she understood why Alys chose to live here, alone and apart.

They stood to leave, but Alys caught Cass's hand a moment after Lily had bent her head to pass through the low doorway, her rough fingertips pausing on the scar at the base of her wrist. Her eyes met Cass's searchingly, curiously, but she said nothing, only nodded her on her way and closed the door firmly behind her.

Lily led her back to the manor, to the kitchen, where they scavenged some slightly stale rolls and cold venison.

'Enjoy it while it's here,' Lily mumbled, her mouth full of the smoky meat in its sticky sauce. 'We only have meat when someone's had a successful day's hunting. Sometimes it's bread and soup for weeks.'

Cass bit into the crusty roll. 'Can't you buy meat?'

'Yes, but our funds are limited. We have to make them last, and we can only supplement what's left in the coffers when a knight brings home money from a tournament or wins it on some quest. So someone has risked their life for each bite we take.'

Cass swallowed hard, the lump of bread suddenly leaden in her throat.

'Are you not scared?' Cass whispered into the inky dark that night, as she lay next to Lily's warm body on the straw tick mattress.

'Scared of what?'

Cass hesitated. In the darkness, she saw the sharp blade of a sword slide silently between her ribs like a knife slicing through butter. She saw herself fall from a horse as it cantered through the forest, her skull smashing on a rock and spilling out its contents. She saw blood trickle from her unseeing eye as an arrow pierced it and found her brain.

Her throat ached. 'Scared of getting hurt. Or worse.'

Lily was quiet for a long time, so long that Cass thought she might have fallen asleep, but then she spoke softly.

'I've known what it is to be truly scared. Now I have a sword at my side, and the strength to use it. I know how to defend myself with my shield. And if I die, I know it will be doing something I believe in. Not cowering from my father's fists.' She sighed. 'Of course I'm scared. But isn't it better to burn through life with joy and excitement and adventure than to sit at home and wait for a life of servitude to ebb slowly away without ever really knowing what it is to live?'

Cass thought of Mary, of her secret little smile on the morning of her wedding. She thought of her father, coming in from the fields at the end of a long day, how he would touch her mother's arm gently as he passed her on his way to the kitchen table. 'It needn't always be that way,' she said, a little defensively. 'There's happiness to be found in a quiet life, in family, for the lucky ones.' And yet a little twist of betrayal, that same pain she had felt in the orchard on the morning she had left home, plucked at her.

'Perhaps.' Lily didn't sound convinced. 'Yet you're in as much danger giving birth to a babe as you are facing the point of a bandit's sword. We don't call mothers knights yet they're jousting with death, every one of them, and enough of them lose the fight too.'

That was true. And Lily knew it better than most. But it didn't banish the spectre of blades that danced before Cass's eyes in the darkness. It was a long time before sleep came. And when it did, the locket burned white-hot beneath her

71

in her strange dreams, that she would only remember snatches of in the morning – the woods, a lake and the strange feeling of being watched.

Chapter 8

Next morning as they breakfasted on porridge and barley bread and butter made with freshly churned milk from their cows, a clattering of hooves echoed in from the courtyard, followed by a commotion in the hall as a group of young riders spilled inside, their short tunics caked in mud and ringed with sweat at the necks. Cass watched curiously as they clustered before Lady Angharad's chair, their voices clamouring together as they delivered seemingly urgent news. She watched Angharad's eyebrows tighten, her long, slender fingers drumming on the armrest of her chair as she fired quick, low questions at the riders and listened intently to their answers. Then it was over and the young women left the hall, while Angharad leaned towards Vivian, who always sat at her right hand, and began to converse with her in hushed tones.

Vivian spoke, calmly, quietly, and Angharad nodded and gestured to a nearby squire, who rushed forward. She listened to Angharad's bidding, then nodded and raced out into the courtyard, gathering several others as she went. All around them, young women in bright silk dresses continued to eat and to chatter as if nothing were amiss. Cass frowned. 'What was that all about?' she asked Lily curiously.

'Scouts,' Lily mumbled, her mouth full of bread and honey. She swallowed. 'They are positioned throughout the surrounding woods and in every major town from here to the Scottish border and as far south as Wessex. Arthur may have driven out the Picts and the Irish sea wolves for now, but there are always more raiders, and upheaval closer to home could cost us dearly.'

'We are always prepared,' said Rowan, listening in from further down the bench. 'And being forewarned is the best type of preparation.'

'Not that it's necessarily bad news.' Lily shrugged, reaching out to ladle porridge into her wooden bowl. 'Perhaps they've picked up the trail of the black stag.'

Rowan's head jerked towards Angharad and Vivian with interest. 'I'd give anything to be the one to fell it,' she breathed.

Cass raised her eyebrows at them quizzically.

Lily leaned forward conspiratorially, her eyes dancing. 'There is a rare stag in the forest hereabouts, its coat as black as charcoal, its antlers so powerful that they are said to shine almost like silver. But it is rarely seen and nobody has ever successfully hunted it. Local legend has it the animal is enchanted, that only a pure, chosen hunter will ever successfully subdue it . . .'

Joan, the plump girl with the braids, chimed in eagerly, 'Some people believe it is not an animal at all, but an omen, or a messenger . . .'

At that moment, Angharad rose from her seat and the hubbub in the hall hushed as all heads turned expectantly towards her.

'A tournament has been declared in Eboracum. We ride in two weeks.'

A great rumbling seemed to vibrate from the very bones of the hall, as knights, squires and even the pages who Lily had told her were too young yet to practise combat began to roar their full-throated approval. They hammered the wooden tables with their fists, their elbows, the bases of their tankards, until the hall rang with the noise.

Rowan jumped up and grinned, running a hand through her short-cropped hair and letting out a wild whoop.

Cass turned to Lily. 'Tournament? I . . .'

'Don't worry,' Lily jumped in, 'nobody's expecting us to compete.' She grinned with excitement, completely unaware of the honey dripping from the single errant ringlet that had escaped from her hastily pulled back hair. 'But it's a rush to watch. And Sigrid will need you.'

Sigrid did need her, in ways Cass couldn't have imagined. The next two weeks were physically and mentally exhausting. She moved from Lily's chamber into a small anteroom off Sigrid's apartment, where she could be summoned at any hour when her mistress needed her. When Lily had spoken of becoming a squire, she had imagined herself riding behind a gleaming knight on a fine horse, but the reality felt a lot closer to the endless cycle of washing, cleaning and chores she thought she had left behind at the farm. And that was on top of the intense training she was now undergoing.

Each day began at sunrise, when she would light the fire in Sigrid's rooms and lay out her armour. Some days the door to the bedchamber would be closed, the low, rhythmic sound of her mistress's breathing audible. Others, the door would stand ajar, the bed neatly made and empty. Sigrid came and went like a spirit, noiseless and aloof, asking nobody's leave. When Cass tried to ask what adventure she had been on, Sigrid was evasive. Sometimes she would be gone for days, then return with a saddlebag full of coins or gold, presenting them to Angharad for the coffers with neither boast nor explanation. Then there were long days when the door never opened at all, when near total silence descended on the rooms like a velvet cloth, but Cass just occasionally caught snatches of what sounded like low, desperate sobbing.

Once she had prepared Sigrid's fire, Cass would tiptoe out of the sleeping manor to meet Blyth for a riding lesson. The moment she entered the stables each morning to find Pebble's shining eyes and eagerly butting nose awaiting her was one of fierce joy. Together they learned from the beginning, her own awkwardness in mounting and sitting astride the pony matched by Pebble's uncertainty about carrying her. Together they lurched round the meadow, Cass trying and failing to find the rising and falling rhythm that seemed to be so natural, so fluid, when she watched Sigrid ride, Pebble sometimes responding to the squeeze of her heels, sometimes stopping abruptly with an indignant snort and sending her sliding to the ground.

She had never formed a relationship like this with another creature, each of them bonded to the other, learning and falling and getting back up again together, exhausted and frustrated and still loving each other with a stubborn kind of affection. With Pebble, she could be exactly who she was, caught between the confidence of the girl who climbed every tree and laughed at her big sister's horror, and the young woman who felt nervous and untested in this strange new world of warriors and thrilling, terrifying possibility.

And slowly, day by day, they made progress. By the fifth day, they could walk round the edge of the meadow – more or less – without Blyth leading Pebble, and with only one sudden stop, which, Cass reasoned, was actually quite understandable considering that Pebble had stepped in a very cold puddle, and wouldn't she herself have halted abruptly and more than likely shrieked in the same circumstances? She scratched Pebble behind the ears and with a little shake of the horse's shaggy black head they moved off again.

By the eighth day, they could trot, and Cass felt more like she was riding and less like she was hanging on for dear life. By day twelve, they were approaching a canter, and Cass could mount and dismount at speed. Not quite with the same elegance and catlike grace as Sigrid, but still smoothly enough for Cass to prickle with pride and bury her face in Pebble's soft mane as she helped Blyth rub her down before breakfast. 'We're getting there, girl. We're getting there.'

After breakfast, which was usually punctuated by Lily's giggles and gossip about what was going on around the manor, Cass rushed back to Sigrid's chamber to help her to arm. It was an intricate process involving fiddly buckles and straps, fitting the leather breast and backplates together and fastening them securely, then strapping on the pauldrons that protected the shoulders, the pieces she learned were the rebrace for the upper arms and the vambrace for the forearms, then the thick, boiled-leather gauntlets that had to be held still as Sigrid worked her fingers in, tight and close-fitting to enable a dexterous grip on her sword. Cass learned how to carefully lace up the leather boots that encased the muscular calves, feeling somehow powerful and exhilarated as her fingers worked to create the gleaming knight in front of her eyes.

Then there were drills in the meadow – some days she had sword fighting and fencing, others archery, although her own lessons had to fit into snatched hours and free moments around the training to fulfil Sigrid's needs on the tournament field. There were weapons to carry, the sword and lance surprisingly light but unwieldy nonetheless, the shield to pass up to her mistress once mounted, the careful exchange of lance for sword, the preparation of the quiver of arrows ready for Sigrid's fingers to fit and fire one at a moment's notice.

Again and again they practised the handover of the lance, a long, smooth wooden pole striped gaily with blue and white paint. Cass gripped it below the conical vamplate and passed it up to Sigrid as their horses walked past one another in opposite directions. Cass nudged Pebble with her knees to keep her walking steadily when she seemed tempted to stop and rub her neck against the older horse.

Once a week, there were fascinating, challenging lessons at Alys's hut, where she and a group of the other squires would learn about plants and herbs: which leaves you should use to staunch the flow of blood from a wound, which draughts you could add to a boiling kettle to bring a deep and dreamless sleep, and which berries and bitter roots should be avoided at any cost, because even the slightest taste could kill you in moments. She would return to the manor exhausted, her head spinning with the long, strange names of plants she had never heard of before, and always at the back of her mind the sense that Alys seemed to have been watching her, warily, curiously, throughout the whole session.

And in between there were peaceful, comforting moments with Lily, who always had a sweet roll in her pocket and a quick laugh ready. She shared stories of her days in Angharad's rooms, the buckle she had slipped off and lost through a crack in the floorboards, the oil she had accidentally left unguarded while cleaning the armour and the hours it had taken her to clean up the vomit after Angharad's favourite hound, Mason, had lapped it up before she could stop him. She recreated the scene, exaggerating the poor dog's retching until Cass let out peals of laughter.

At night her aching fingers would fumble to unbuckle Sigrid's armour, her nails rimmed with dirt that would have earned her a scolding at home. On the fifth night, and every fifth night after that, she drew Sigrid a bath, heating the water over the fire and adding it, bucket by bucket, to the wooden tub she had carried into the antechamber. She spread animal-skin rugs beside it and added the sweet-smelling lavender oil and rose petals Alys had provided her, along with a powdered salt to soothe aching muscles. And as the steam rose high, she helped Sigrid to disrobe. Cass stopped, frozen, as Sigrid's tunic slipped over her head to reveal a jagged scar, the skin puckered and distorted around it, beside her right shoulder blade. Sigrid heard her sharp intake of breath, felt her fingers falter, and turned, without shame.

'The arrow entered here,' she said, pointing to a smaller, more faded scar above the sloping curve of her breast. But she offered no more, and Cass didn't ask, aware of the vulnerability and intimacy of the moment, as Sigrid stepped into the water and sank down with a sigh, her rich reddish-brown hair floating out in all directions as if it, too, could finally unclench itself from the tight winding of the day.

Sigrid's eyelids fluttered closed and Cass stood quietly, holding the drying cloth, her eyes tracing the sinew and muscle of Sigrid's stomach, the soft hair beneath, the supple strength of her thighs, the solid bulk of her calves and the violet bloom of a bruise round her right ankle, where Cass had fumbled as she'd tried to pass her the lance the previous day. It was strange and fascinating to see a body like this, so different from the soft, undulating folds of her mother's and Mary's waists. Strange to take in the taut, battle-ready strength of Sigrid's muscles juxtaposed with the soft, pale mounds of her breasts above, her hair rich against the sun-browned skin of her neck and chest. Cass stood there, contemplating her, aware of the little new muscles very slowly starting to thicken round her own upper arms, her own calves, feeling herself adrift between two different images of womanhood.

Sigrid was fair and patient on the training field, but she had never spoken of anything personal, never allowed Cass to see behind the armour and the shield. When Angharad and Vivian and the other knights gathered round the fire in the hall to listen to music and share battle stories in the evening, Sigrid sat apart, or retired early to her chamber, when she was at the manor at all.

'Were you always destined for this life?' Cass wasn't sure whether Sigrid would answer.

Sigrid's chest rose and fell among the petals. 'The path that brought me here was not straight, but I know it is where I am meant to be. For now.'

There was no noise in the room except the gentle crackling of the fire and the occasional swish of the water.

'I believe I am meant to be here too,' Cass started uncertainly, 'but I think of my sister . . .' She trailed off, half expecting a rebuke from Sigrid, an insistence that she should be more focused on her skills.

'I would have followed my twin to the ends of the earth,' Sigrid said in that low, honeyed voice, and Cass looked up at her in surprise.

'Perhaps if I could just send my family a message,' she ventured eagerly, 'let them know that I'm safe, without telling them anything of where I am . . .'

Sigrid rose out of the bath with a splash that sent water cascading onto the waiting animal skins. 'It is too dangerous. We don't allow any correspondence with the outside world: the risk of it being traced back here is too great. Imagine if the families of every runaway and abused woman who ends up in the safety of these walls came clamouring at the gates.'

Cass felt the hot tears pricking at the corners of her eyes and nodded, passing Sigrid her robe.

'What I have learned,' Sigrid continued in her low voice, her back to Cass, 'is that the only way to avoid the distraction of love is focusing your mind on your current goal so completely, so obsessively, that there is no room for anything else. I advise you to do that with your training.' And Cass would have asked her more about what she meant, about why love was so dangerous, but Sigrid padded into her chamber and shut the door, leaving only a trail of wet footprints behind her.

And so the time slipped away until the night before the tournament found Cass sitting on a sheepskin-cushioned chair before the fire in the hall, carefully sharpening Sigrid's sword on the whetstone that had been brought in and placed next to the hearth. The blade sang against the stone, and she tested the edge with her thumb, watching the light from the flames play across the deep 'J' engraved into the pommel. The atmosphere crackled with tension and excitement as the other squires jostled for position, waiting to sharpen their mistress's weapons. Lily burst out of the pack to kneel beside her, Angharad's sword with its delicate, twisted silver crossguard under her arm.

'There's nothing like a tournament, Cass,' she enthused, as she started to draw the sword across the whetstone with slow, careful strokes. 'It's a rush of excitement like nothing you've ever felt before. The colours, the smells, the noise . . . And watching the knights, seeing our mistresses joust and hold their own against men who would sneer and rage at them if they had any idea who they really were . . . It's . . .'

She clenched her fists, her eyes sparkling. 'It's like a fire lights inside you. And all you want is to serve them, and one day to follow in their footsteps.' She leaped to her feet, the sword waving in her excitement.

'Whoa, fledgling!' Rowan stepped out of the crowd and seized Angharad's sword, replacing it in its leather scabbard. 'Angharad will need you at the tournament, and her sword too: neither will be much use to her if it's stuck in your gut!' And Cass laughed, feeling a fluttering excitement that had nothing to do with the cup of watered wine on the hearthstone beside her.

Chapter 9

They rose at dawn and were on the road while the wrens and the blackbirds still sent their morning song spilling out through the trees. It was a festive procession, fifteen or so knights resplendent in their newly oiled armour and gleaming helmets, their squires riding behind them wearing brightly coloured tabards, fastened about the waist with leather belts. The horses stepped smartly forward, unburdened by the weight of weapons: Blyth rode behind them on a great carthorse, pulling a wagon that contained the lances and equipment as well as the cloth and fixings that would form their tents at the tournament.

Cass wore the flat wool cap of a squire for the first time, its square sides covering her cheeks, her hair firmly bundled up inside it, and when they rode past a still pond beside the path, she felt a shiver of pride and excitement pass through her as she looked down at the water and saw a cheerful, confident squire trotting there, as if following his master to tournaments was the most natural thing in the world.

'It's two days' ride to Eboracum.' Lily rode up beside Cass, her eyes sparkling. 'Which means we will have to camp out tonight, Cass!' And Cass laughed aloud at the thrill etched across her dimpled face, but she couldn't help but feel Lily's infectious excitement bubble up in her too.

They kept away from major thoroughfares, riding down dirt tracks and narrow lanes, between hedges studded with bright hawthorn berries and dark purple sloes.

Once or twice, they passed other riders. When a group of smartly dressed men clattered importantly past them, Cass stiffened, her face suddenly feeling exposed and feminine beneath the warmth of the wool cap, but they barely spared a glance in her direction as they shouted brief greetings to the women ahead in their armour and helmets before riding on without a backwards look.

'Nobody looks twice at a squire.' Lily smiled, seeing her face, and she reached out and squeezed Cass's hand briefly as their horses' noses touched in delight.

Later in the day, they passed a small procession of villagers, their carts laden with produce and their feet wrapped in rags, who pressed themselves into the trees and hedges to allow the knights and their entourage to pass.

'They fear us,' Rowan said grimly, as Lily waved playfully at a little girl with a grubby face who stared up at them in fascination. 'Because experience teaches them it is wise to be afraid.'

'Experience of Angharad and her knights?' Cass asked, surprised.

Rowan shook her head. 'Of other knights and nobles in these parts,' she replied darkly, and she took a coin from her purse and flipped it in the direction of the delighted child as they rode onwards.

Before nightfall they left the path and rode deeper into the woods, stopping at last in a secluded glade where a stream bubbled through the trees. They tethered the horses where they could easily reach the water to drink, Cass giving Pebble's neck an extra pat to reward her for managing their longest ride yet. Then they made a fire and spread thick cloaks on the ground round it.

Sigrid drew a little apart as always, standing among the trees at the edge of the clearing, keeping a self-appointed watch, her back straight, fingers ready at her quiver.

After they had dined on hard sheep's cheese wrapped in leaves and flat bannock loaves, Lily and Cass sat, backs pressed together, amongst the other squires, allowing the pleasant warmth of the fire to soothe their tired limbs. Joan was idly playing dice with Susan and Elizabeth, two of the other squires, as the older women's talk turned to tournaments in years past.

'How many lances did you break at Alnwick?' Angharad laughed, jabbing Vivian in the ribs with her elbow.

'At least four, and I should remember: I'm the poor squire who had to keep finding fresh ones to bring to her!' Rowan protested loudly.

'I have no recollection of that,' Vivian said quietly and smiled, finishing her cheese and licking her fingers. 'And if I did break four lances, it was only because the turd who rode against me was so slow that there was no momentum to topple him from his horse!' The others roared with laughter.

'Need I remind you,' Vivian continued, 'that the winnings from that tournament kept us in wine for a whole winter?'

This was met with a resounding cheer. 'The tournament prizes are that great?' Cass whispered to Lily.

'Of course! Why else do you think we ride to them?'

'For glory and honour? To practise swordsmanship?'

'I think you mean swords*womanship*,' Rowan laughed, overhearing.

'Well, yes.' Lily nodded. 'But though Angharad's lord left

rich goods behind, it is not wealth enough to sustain us all indefinitely. We fight to live . . .'

'. . . And some of us live to fight,' Rowan roared, to another rowdy cheer.

'I'll remind you of that on the next cold morning when you'd rather lie abed than get up and spar,' Vivian remarked drily.

'Our conduct at tournaments is governed by three rules.' Angharad addressed Cass and the other squires. 'Fight bravely. Win fairly. Conceal your true nature at all costs.'

'What would happen,' Cass murmured to Lily, 'if they were unmasked?'

'It is too awful to contemplate,' Lily whispered back. 'We could be imprisoned, forced into marriage or worse.' And with a jolt, Cass realized that it was not 'they': that she, too, was now part of that 'we'. 'We would lose the manor,' Lily continued. 'If they realized the true nature of what was happening there. We would no longer be able to provide sanctuary for any of the women and girls who have made it their home.'

'Then why do you . . . do *we* take the risk?' Cass asked, horrified.

'Does anybody ask that of other knights?' Angharad spoke from the other side of the fire, her red hair catching the light like a flaming crown. 'Wonder why they take the risks they do, or what drives them to such boldness? Is it not our right to risk everything for honour and glory, and the life we want to live, as it is theirs?'

'And have we not the skill to match a troll who soiled his breeches when the fourth lance finally toppled him?' Sigrid's barking laugh came out of the darkness and broke the tension.

'The honour isn't quite the same, though, is it?' Cass mused quietly to Lily. 'If nobody knows who the victor is.'

'No,' said Rowan shortly, padding over to hand out sheepskins to cover them from the chill night air. 'Sleep now. And perhaps after tomorrow you will no longer need to ask about the value of glory.'

Cass slept fitfully, her dreams uneasy and filled with rearing horses and thundering hooves. They woke at dawn, scattering the ashes of the fire and remounting. Cass winced involuntarily as she swung into the saddle and Rowan grinned. 'You're not the first to have a sore arse after your first full day's ride. It will ease as you become accustomed to it.' Cass wasn't sure whether to be offended or reassured by this, so she settled for grinning at Lily's stifled giggle as she urged Pebble back towards the path that led south-west, towards Eboracum.

They arrived just before sunset, and already the wide, level field where the tournament would take place was ablaze with activity. Gaily striped pavilions emblazoned with the colours and symbols of dozens of knights dotted the edge of the field.

In the distance, Cass could see the huddled mass of buildings that made up Eboracum, rising within its sturdy stone walls.

Sweating workmen filled the field, hammering the last supports onto the wooden stands where spectators would gather the following day. The banging of the carpentry, the clash of swords as knights skirmished with their squires, the shouts of peasants hawking meat pies and ale, all blended into a bewildering cacophony that left Cass's head ringing. At the centre of the field the lists stood ready: long, straight wooden fences that looked somehow completely inadequate for the task of separating the multitude of hurtling beasts and fighters that would face each other within it tomorrow.

She was glad when Sigrid instructed her to help the other squires with assembling their tents: grateful for the solidity of the wooden mallet in her hand and a physical job to focus on as she forced the tent pegs into the soft earth. The wood biting slowly deeper into the dirt was real, tangible. The whirl of colour and sound behind her was not, could not be. This was a reality Cass was not sure she was ready for. She had imagined the fighting, the tournaments, yes, but to be here, in plain view, dressed in her boy's clothes, the cap feeling like an ever-flimsier barrier to her exposure . . . She was not ready for it to be real. So she hammered at the stakes until the sweat ran into her eyes and her palms blistered round the wooden mallet.

Chapter 10

When they awoke the next morning, the field was twice as dazzling as it had been the day before. The emerald velvet of the turf was studded with jewelled colours: scarlet and cobalt-blue pennants fluttered above the pavilions, squires clad in a dazzling rainbow of bright tabards attended knights in armour of leather or mail or shining metal, their shields proudly displaying their coats of arms. Spectators were already streaming into the stands, children waving homemade flags and clutching painted wooden swords and shields, women wearing their best clothes with flowers woven into their hair. Traders jostled among the crowds, selling everything from roasted pork to lucky trinkets and bunches of herbs.

A stall on the edge of the field displayed yellow pots and bowls, brightly painted with crimson patterns.

The scent of freshly mown grass mingled with the savoury smell of the meat and the smoke from braziers burning round the edge of the field.

But there was little time to stand and gawp. Cass was responsible for grooming and watering Brimstone, then saddling him and putting on the boiled-leather chanfron that would protect his head and ears from the tip of Sigrid's opponent's lance. Brimstone snorted and stamped his hooves, shaking his head, unused to the feel of the armour. Cass spoke gently to him, patting his neck until he settled and allowed her to slip it past his ears, though he still shuffled his feet grumpily as she fastened it.

'You're good with him,' a soft voice observed, and Blyth stepped out from behind the charger, carrying a bucket of water. 'He's a highly strung fellow . . . aren't you?' Blyth's singsong voice and gentle hand calmed Brimstone immediately. The horse lowered his nose, breathing out softly as he butted Blyth's chest.

'You treat them as if they were human,' Cass said admiringly.

'They treat me as if I were human, too,' Blyth replied quietly, putting Brimstone on a long tether so he could graze until Sigrid needed him.

Then began the laborious process of strapping on and buckling Sigrid's armour, her helmet slipped on last, visor closed so that she could only see through a thin horizontal slit in the metal. Like Angharad, Vivian and the others, she carried the plain white shield that indicated they chose to remain anonymous.

'It's why we ride as far as Eboracum,' Lily had explained to Cass the night before. 'Where any chance of exposure is much reduced. We would never attend a tournament closer to home, for fear of being recognized or sparking suspicion amongst our neighbours.'

At last, Sigrid was ready, and Cass, clad in a simple belted white tunic and the square-sided cap, mounted Pebble, taking Sigrid's lance from Blyth and carefully balancing it upright, its bottom steadied on top of her right foot as she had been taught. The lances were topped with wooden balls for the tournament, so that no real injury should befall the participants, save a blow to their pride in defeat. But Lily had breathlessly regaled her with stories of gruesome accidents at tournaments past: grotesquely twisted arms and brutal lacerations and knights dragged unconscious from the field, some never to ride again.

Cass's heart hammered in her chest as they rode out for the first bout, the crowd cheering and waving excitedly at the spectacle. She half expected a shocked gasp: a shout from the onlookers as she passed. Her cheeks burned as her eyes wildly searched the waving, raucous faces, waiting for a set of eyes to narrow or an accusing finger to point at her. But the people continued to clap and shout exuberantly, conferring animatedly and pointing at the different knights as they passed. Cass pulled her cap down more firmly and sat up a little straighter, letting herself begin to believe that she was really here, really doing this.

As a trumpet blared to signal the approach of the first contenders, Cass carefully passed Sigrid the lance, feeling a little burst of pride and exhilaration when the handover was completed successfully. Then she turned Pebble's head towards the stands, riding well clear of the lists where the two knights faced each other from opposite ends, and reined her in to watch.

Sigrid sat imperious and calm, lance perfectly level, Brimstone pawing excitedly at the grass. Her opponent's squire carried a flag of green and gold, the knight's shield emblazoned with an eagle on a background of moss green, his horse pure white.

They began their first pass, the white and chestnut horses thundering towards each other, clods of earth flying beneath their hooves, the ground seeming to shake with the weight and speed of their charge. As they sped towards the inevitable collision, Cass found that she was holding her breath, her fingernails digging into her palms as she braced her whole body as if she too would feel the impact.

In a crashing, splintering moment it was over. Sigrid's lance had found its target with ruthless precision, so that the green knight sprawled wildly over the back of his horse, his own lance soaring harmlessly skywards over Sigrid's head. He crashed to the ground and lay there winded and motionless as his horse galloped on without a rider, its eyes rolling white. Sigrid trotted nonchalantly to the end of the lists, and Cass gasped and shook herself into action, racing to take the jagged, ruined butt of the lance and help her to dismount. Silently, Sigrid acknowledged the cheers and clamour of the crowd with a curt nod, before striding back towards their pavilion, Cass trotting at her heels.

Angharad was next, in a nut-brown breastplate Lily had polished until it shone, her helmet engraved with leaves and vines. From inside the beige canvas walls of the pavilion, Cass listened to the swell of excitement from the crowd, heard the roars and cheers rise to a crescendo and then quiet suddenly. She pictured the combatants facing each other, Lily eagerly preparing Angharad's lance. And then the roaring began again, not fading away this time but exploding into a triumphant din before Lily bustled back in, her face shining. Angharad came next, pulling her helmet off, her face sweaty and flushed but triumphant.

Next came Leah, a middle-aged knight with straight, jet-black hair, sharp cheekbones and a beauty spot next to her eye that gave her a permanent slightly disdainful expression, as if she were always raising one eyebrow. She rode well, but fell at the second pass, overcome by a lanky knight some twenty hands tall who towered above her and used his superior height to force her from her horse.

Then Vivian stepped out, sweeping her long silver hair into a tight knot underneath her helmet before she strode from the tent, Rowan at her side. The cheers built steadily, just as before, and Cass imagined Rowan confidently handing Vivian the lance, and pictured the older knight turning smoothly to face her opponent.

But this time the roars broke off suddenly and sickeningly, replaced by gasps and screams, then a low, uneasy murmuring. And every head inside the tent turned urgently to the flap, waiting.

Rowan's face was grim as she supported her mistress back into the tent, Vivian's gloved hand clutched tightly to her side. Angharad leaped to her feet and took Vivian's weight, lowering her to the floor as she shouted at Lily to make the pavilion secure. While Lily and Rowan raced to stand guard, Cass watched as Angharad ripped Vivian's armour from her body with trembling fingers, her breath coming in short gasps as if it were she herself who had been wounded.

'It's all right, Angharad, it's just a scratch,' Vivian gasped, wincing as Angharad tore back her undershirt, not noticing or caring whether the surrounding squires were watching, and pressed her lips to the bleeding wound beneath.

'It's shallow,' she cried, letting the tears come, and she lifted her bloodied mouth to Vivian's, kissing her fiercely, holding her close, shoulders shaking.

Cass stared openly, too shocked to look away, the moment stretching out as her brain reeled.

Vivian lifted a hand to Angharad, stroking the damp red hair away from her face and gently shushing her. 'I knew it was of little consequence. A stupid mistake. I checked at the last moment and the broken end of the lance scratched me as I fell. I will be well enough to continue after a moment's rest . . .'

'You will do no such thing,' Angharad snapped, her sharp green eyes flashing.

Then Rowan burst back into the tent, gasping, 'The steward is coming,' and Angharad scrambled to cover Vivian's chest, pressing a handful of rags to the wound and fumbling to replace both their helmets as the door flap was swept aside and a tall, thin man in a black tunic strode in, brushing aside Lily's panicked objections.

'Forgive my intrusion, sir, but my lord has sent me to enquire as to the health of the knight and ask if he requires assistance? As tournament host, he wishes to provide any necessary comfort.'

'Thank you, seneschal,' Angharad replied, and her voice was calm and low, with no trace of tears. 'But by good fortune the wound is not deep. My brother will retire from the tournament but he faces no great danger. I will not return to the field to joust, for I wish to stay with him until his strength returns.'

'I am glad to hear it,' the seneschal replied, inclining his head courteously. 'But you will need another to add to your number for the melee if your brother is unable to fight.' He bowed and withdrew, and Angharad drooped, removing her helmet once more and resting her forehead on Vivian's chest.

'I am well, my love,' Vivian murmured, stroking her hair. 'All is well.'

'It is time,' Sigrid said, and Cass tore her eyes away from the couple to follow her mistress to the field once again.

The second bout was more competitive than the first, each knight having already unseated another to progress to this stage. This time the man at the opposite end of the lists carried a shield of dark blue with a double chevron blazoned across it in white.

At the first blow, both knights caught each other square in the centre of their shields, their lances splintering with a great crash, but each kept their seat as the horses cantered past. Cass hurried to replace Sigrid's lance, and they wheeled about and raced together again. This time Cass saw how Sigrid adjusted her technique, swinging her lance to the side at the very last moment so that it took her opponent in the upper corner of his shield, surprising him and catching him off balance. He swore loudly as he crashed to the ground and the crowd's roars surged for Sigrid once again.

This time the break between bouts was brief, and they stayed on the field to witness a tall knight stride out of his pavilion clad in pure black armour, everything from his shield to his helmet glinting darkly. But his shield flashed with a silver emblem: a proud pair of antlers, their points cruelly sharp. His visor already lowered, the knight jumped astride his horse and cantered to the starting position, pulling sharply on the beast's bridle to come to a sudden stop as he passed the stands.

'Now witness a knight of real skill,' he boomed, addressing the crowd, 'unlike these whelps and wretches.' And he gestured towards Sigrid and the others, as the crowd responded to his show of bravado with whoops and jeers.

His opponent, a short man who waddled nervously to his horse, whispering anxiously to his squire, seemed to struggle with his helmet and had only just seated himself when the knight of the silver antlers began to bear down furiously upon him. Panicking, the other fumbled with his lance, shifting awkwardly in the saddle, and as the black knight advanced upon him his horse sensed his fear and reared up, neighing shrilly, sending the knight tumbling straight into the mud.

Cass gasped to see that the charging knight did not check his horse but continued, lance still levelled, taking the poor beast square in the neck and sending it writhing and screaming beside its rider, its flanks heaving as its hooves flailed wildly. The crowd exploded, some jeering at the knight's unkindness but others whipped up into a frenzied chant, and as he rode past them the knight swept off his helmet and inclined a shaggy head of thick black hair to acknowledge them. His face was sallow and his yellow teeth were bared in a triumphant grin as he passed Cass and Sigrid, who seemed visibly to recoil.

'Sir Mordaunt.' Sigrid's voice echoed inside her helmet and she looked quickly back to the pavilion as if she were searching for the others, or half considering retreat. But the tent flap remained closed, the trumpets were blaring and before Cass could ask her about the man, he had replaced his helmet and Sigrid squared her shoulders and spurred her horse forward to meet him.

The trumpets rang out three times, the signal that this was the last bout. Cass saw Sigrid's foot tapping slightly in her stirrup, the only outward sign that her composure had been disrupted. The two knights hurtled forward, their horses' necks straining, hunched over their lances and travelling faster than any other in the competition so far. The audience collectively gasped as they came together like a thunderclap, the impact so great that both were knocked backwards, their lances broken, but neither unseated. Sigrid rode over to Cass and she could hear the woman's breathing, fast and ragged in her helmet, as she handed her a fresh lance, before Sigrid whirled immediately to face Sir Mordaunt again.

The second blow seemed harder still, with both lances shattering again and the crowd shrieking for more.

But the third time they came together, both were unseated in a fierce explosion of splintering wood, and both rolled clear of their horses' hooves and drew their swords, turning on each other. For a moment it seemed Sir Mordaunt would stop, this part of the competition being focused on jousting alone, but before he could speak, Sigrid was upon him, her sword ripped from its scabbard, the metal slicing through the air to buffet the side of his helmet. With a roar, the knight drew his own sword and dealt her a mighty blow in return. She took the full force of it at the base of her sword, staggering backwards as the great clang of metal rang out. They leaped towards each other again like dogs in a fight, as the crowd bayed with delight, but before they could strike again the seneschal was standing between them, and the conflict was over as suddenly as it had begun.

'Noble knights,' he shouted, his hands held high to quiet the raucous spectators, 'the joust is at a close and we will see no single combat today. Only the blunted swords provided for the melee will be permitted in the contest, as well you both know.'

They parted, Sigrid leaning on her sword, breathing heavily, Sir Mordaunt throwing his helmet to the ground and doubling over, hands upon his knees.

'You should let me have satisfaction, and finish this,' he growled, eyeing Sigrid angrily. 'At least do me the honour of revealing your identity, sir knight,' he sneered in mock courtesy. But Sigrid simply turned and reached for Brimstone's bridle, patting him on the neck and leading him away from the field.

'Then I will meet you in the melee,' Sir Mordaunt shouted after her, 'So be ready!'

Chapter 11

When they returned to the tent, Vivian was sitting up, a bandage bunched beneath her breastplate, the colour restored to her cheeks.

'We must speak,' Sigrid said in a low, urgent voice, and she, Angharad and Vivian clustered together, their backs to the squires.

'What's happening?' Lily whispered curiously, and Cass told her.

'Sir Mordaunt?' Lily's eyes widened. 'Are you certain?'

Cass nodded, watching Angharad's shoulders tense as she gesticulated furiously. 'Who is he?'

'He is the noble who controls the land surrounding our manor, as far south as the Mercian border and eastwards to the coast,' Lily whispered with a frown. 'It is terrible luck to meet him here. He must have some reason to have travelled north.'

'Is it not the same risk, whether we are exposed by strangers or by a neighbour?' Cass asked, puzzled.

'You don't understand,' Lily shook her head. 'Sir Mordaunt is . . .' A rare shadow passed over her face. 'He is the reason the folk we passed on the road feared us. He and his household knights.'

'Like the knight I met with Sigrid, the first day we rode out together?'

'Like that, and worse. They collect their portion of produce and income whether or not their villagers starve, and extract higher patronage than almost any of the surrounding landowners. They preside over so much suffering and misery, all in service of stuffing their own coffers.'

She looked over at the older knights, still deep in conversation. 'We do what we can to help the people they mistreat, but it isn't always easy, so close to home, not without attracting suspicion.'

'Then it would be a great satisfaction to Sigrid to fight him, would it not?'

'But also a great risk,' Lily hissed. 'For he knows of Angharad and her court; he is an occasional and unwelcome visitor to the manor and demands she pay homage and duties to him too, as our overlord. And should he recognize any one of us, should he unmask us . . .' She lapsed into uneasy silence. 'Even if he were to learn of the death of Angharad's husband, it would put us in great danger,' she said eventually. 'A wealthy widow is a rich prize and Sir Mordaunt has a greed that never seems to be sated. Her lands and property would all be in danger, and she would have little power to rebuff him.'

'Is he not suspicious, that the lord is never at home?'

Lily shook her head, eyeing the older knights worriedly. 'We put about the word that he is increasingly occupied with trade missions,' she explained, 'and make excuses for his absence when visitors come to the manor. It is vital for Angharad's safety – for all of our safety – that nobody discovers the truth.'

Cass paused, her mind reeling. 'What is a melee?' she asked, remembering Mordaunt's challenge to Sigrid.

'It is the culmination of the tournament,' Lily explained, before chewing on her lip distractedly. 'A great spectacle, where two sides meet each other in hand-to-hand combat and battle until only the victors are left standing, and their opponents have either fled, surrendered, or are too badly wounded to continue.'

Barely had Cass had the chance to digest all this before there was a commotion at the door of the tent and a messenger could be heard remonstrating with Rowan outside. 'Then pass on the message, stubborn lad,' came an annoyed voice, and Rowan entered, casting a wary look over her shoulder to ensure the messenger had retreated.

'I would not allow him in,' she said unnecessarily, 'but he said that the melee will commence shortly and as the joust did not result in a clear winner the outcome will determine the tournament's victors.'

'We should go home, Angharad,' urged Vivian, concern etched across her forehead. 'It is not worth the risk, no matter how rich the spoils.'

'We must continue,' Angharad insisted hotly, her mouth set in a grim line as she got to her feet, releasing Vivian's hand. 'We deserve to claim our prize. He shall not take this from us.'

'Besides,' Sigrid added curtly, 'our funds need replenishing, Vivian, as well you know, and a prize this rich will not be easy to come by again.'

'It would seem stranger and attract more curiosity to leave now,' Angharad reasoned, putting a hand on Vivian's arm. And Vivian seemed to relent, though the worry did not leave her face.

'We will need another knight,' Sigrid pointed out, as she pulled her helmet back on. 'To take Vivian's place.'

'Rowan,' Vivian said immediately, her voice resigned.

'She has earned this chance.'

Rowan's face lit up and she stepped forward. 'I won't disappoint you,' she said, bowing her head to her mistress.

Cass and Lily followed as they left the tent and made for the field once again. Vivian shook her head as Angharad swept out, fists clenched, but she sighed and watched them go.

The lists had been cleared, and the open field thronged with knights clustered at each end. Angharad, Sigrid, Rowan and the others of their fellowship joined the nearest pack, each selecting a specially blunted sword from a pile nearby, and Cass and Lily halted a short distance from the throng.

The sun was beginning its descent, so that the shadows from the wooden stands began to creep across the grass towards them. In the quiet before the melee, a rabbit broke cover and bounded out from the edge of the field, then froze in horror and fled at the sight of the crowd. Shielding her eyes against the sun, Cass watched Sir Mordaunt arming himself amongst the opposing knights, cuffing his squire roundly on the ear when he took too long to fasten the buckle on his gleaming breastplate.

'That armour's worth a small fortune,' Lily breathed, following Cass's gaze. 'Chainmail and solid metal plates are beyond the means of most.' She was right. Almost all the other knights on the field were clad in leather like Sigrid and Angharad, some with patches of metalwork sewn in or chainmail beneath.

The two groups turned to face each other and began to advance slowly, shields held firm and swords at the ready. Cass saw Rowan's face, set and determined, and wondered how it must feel to be striding out towards the bristling swords of the other side, unexpectedly thrown into the heat of the battle.

The rose glow of the fading sunlight glinted on the metal helmets so that for a moment as the two sides warily moved towards each other the scene looked like an ethereal dance, lit by a strange pink glow. And then they met, and the moment was shattered.

The noise of their coming together was so great, so unlike anything Cass had ever heard before, a screaming of strained voices and crashing of metal and thundering of swords on shields, that she started in alarm and gripped Lily's arm.

The field was pure confusion. Swords arced in great, hacking blows, legs crumpled and shields jerked wildly. The two neat lines disintegrated almost immediately into a great, thrumming throng of limbs and heat and noise, knights pounding at one another with such force that it made Cass's eyes water just to see it. It had not rained in days and the dust began to rise from beneath the trampling, armour-clad feet until the pink haze that surrounded the melee made her feel as if it were her own eyes, not just those of the fighters, that were obscured with trickling blood.

For brief moments, figures she recognized emerged from the mass of heaving bodies: here Angharad, her back straight and proud as her sword arm descended with clinical and deadly precision. Then Sigrid, whirling around as she engaged two opponents at once and bested them both before charging back into the fray with a satisfied grunt. And Rowan, grimly gripping her sword with both hands as a heavyset knight forced her gradually backwards, the sheer weight of his blows shaking her like an aspen leaf.

Cass and Lily clung together, watching in helpless horror as Rowan staggered back a few steps, then sank to her knees, her shield now held above her head with both hands, sword forgotten, as the blows rained down from above. She was brave, her face set in stony determination, but she was slight, only a little older than Cass, and the knight towered over her, dwarfing her slim stature. And then, suddenly, Sigrid was there, pounding the knight with such a blow to the back of his meaty neck that he fell to his knees, dazed, and did not rise again.

Even beneath her helmet, Cass could see Rowan droop, but she gathered herself, nodded to Sigrid and flung herself back into the fray.

All the late afternoon, as the sunlight stretched and

deepened to wine red, the knights traded their blows. And the ground began to redden like the sky as even the blunted swords found purchase on unshielded forearms and thighs, and the weapons that had whirled and swept began to slow their movements into sluggish, desperate thrusts. The crowd had thinned now, with the wounded and exhausted slumped at the edges of the field, being tended to by their squires, or limping, supported, to their pavilions to nurse their damaged pride.

Fewer than half a dozen knights remained on the field, and Cass saw how time and again the knight with the silver antlers on his shield lunged in Sigrid's direction, his frustration growing as others seemed always to stumble into his path. Then with a great crashing blow he felled Rowan and left her dazed, in the same moment that Angharad brought the pommel of her sword under the ribs of the green-clad knight and winded him so badly that he withdrew, gasping, from the field. Sir Mordaunt turned to them and lifted his visor, asking with a smirk that they do him the courtesy of revealing their identities likewise. And, when they silently declined, he bared his teeth at Sigrid and asked, 'Will you at least do me the honour of meeting me in single combat then, Sir Knight of the White Shield?'

'Gladly,' she replied in that low, unctuous voice, and as Angharad helped Rowan to her feet and off towards their pavilion, Sigrid was already upon him. With a burst of strength that belied the exhaustion she must have felt, she pounced like a wild thing, forcing him to step backwards and bring up his shield to ward off her blows. Then he advanced in return, batting her sword to the side with a blow from his shield and striking her breastplate with the flat of his sword so hard that she doubled over, wheezing to regain her breath.

As he paused, surveying her crumpled figure with satisfaction, she surged suddenly forward, with a blow to the calves that found the unprotected soft flesh at the side of his knees and left him swearing on the ground. Then she raised her sword to his neck, to claim her symbolic victory, but as she stayed its blade and looked to the seneschal to declare the victory hers, the black knight reached out to jerk her by the ankle, felling her heavily, and rolled his full armoured weight on top of her, as she struggled for breath.

'Cheat,' she spat, gasping, as he knocked her sword further from her grasping hand. 'The victory was mine.'

His pointed yellow teeth showed as his lips spread in a cruel grin. 'And yet I seem to be on top, don't I?' And he thrust suddenly and forcefully downwards with his armoured elbow, so that Sigrid groaned with the pain of it.

There came a soft snort and Cass and Lily wheeled round in unison to see Sir Mordaunt's squire, a whey-faced boy of about fifteen with a straggling attempt at hair growth clinging to his upper lip.

'Over-trusting idiot,' he scoffed, sneering at Sigrid, who strained still beneath the weight of Sir Mordaunt, refusing to yield. 'He should have kept his eyes on his opponent.'

'He should not have needed to,' Cass protested hotly. 'The fight was over. Or it would have been if your master had any honour at all.'

'It's almost as if honour does not win tournaments.' The boy smirked, as Sir Mordaunt propped himself on one elbow, clearly enjoying the humiliation he was causing Sigrid as she struggled and spat.

'A victory gained through cowardice and cheating is no victory at all,' Lily angrily retorted. 'Nor is it any wonder your master fails to find himself a bride, if he behaves so disgustingly,' she continued.

Before the words were even out of her mouth she realized their rashness, her face reddening as the boy scowled suspiciously at her.

'And how would you know about my master's personal affairs?' he demanded.

Lily gripped Cass's hand so tightly that her fingers turned white, horror at her mistake written all over her face.

'It has been the talk of the tournament,' Cass blurted out. 'Do you think there are not those within his own household who mock him for it?'

The squire blinked stupidly, his bushy eyebrows narrowed as he looked uncertainly towards his master as if he might shout to him.

'And who can blame them?' Cass continued, desperate to distract him. 'Is there any man who would not be ashamed to serve such a snivelling, cowardly . . .'

'Say that again,' the boy screeched furiously, grabbing a sword and shield from the blunted pile that lay beside the field, discarded by the knights who had quit the melee. 'And I will force you to take it back.'

'Not if you find yourself arse down in the mud you won't,' Lily gleefully retorted, with palpable relief at having turned his thoughts away from alerting his master to her indiscretion. Eagerly, she thrust a sword and shield into Cass's reluctant hands. 'You don't know who you have challenged, idiot, but you have brought chaos down on your own head,' she taunted loudly, before ducking behind the shield in pretence of helping Cass to buckle it to her arm.

'Lily!' Cass hissed frantically. 'What are you doing?'

'You can take him, Cass!' Lily's fingers fumbled clumsily with the buckles. 'Wipe that smug smirk off his face for all of us. And if you happen to distract him so completely that it doesn't occur to him to mention to his master that someone here knows a bit too much about his personal affairs, well . . .' she finished the buckle, clapped Cass on the shoulder and grinned. 'So much the better.'

'But Lily, I've only been practising a few weeks. With a *wooden stick.*' Lily wasn't listening. She was rubbing her hands together in glee, practically vibrating on the balls of her feet.

'I pity your stupidity in making this challenge,' Lily shouted loudly, in the direction of the squire, as Cass cringed.

'Lily!' Cass gave a last, strangled whisper.

But the snarling squire was already advancing, and Cass had no choice but to turn to meet him, the strange sword heavy and clumsy in her hand, the shield unwieldy on her unpractised arm.

'Swing . . . to the left . . . *the other left!*' Lily shrieked, entirely ineffectively attempting to help Cass as she lumbered clumsily to avoid the squire's first sword stroke. This was nothing like the careful, methodical exercises she had barely begun to master at the meadow. There was no choreography here, no time to rehearse her steps or think twice about which part of her sword to make contact with. The attack was relentless, the boy making up in enthusiasm what he lacked in skill, prodding and flailing with his blunted sword so that Cass had to dodge and turn repeatedly, only narrowly avoiding the worst of the blows.

And yet, even as her head spun with the absurdity of it, even as she reeled with the strangeness of finding herself here, her feet sinking slightly into the soft grass, a metallic tang in her mouth from a glancing blow that had drawn blood from her lower lip, she felt the strangest sense of calm creep over her.

It was an almost trance-like state, a feeling Cass would experience many times after that first day, but never truly be able to explain to anyone else. It was as if she felt herself slipping into her own body, her own skin, with a certainty and control that she had never experienced before in her life. A feeling like coming home, like the sun on her skin on a warm summer's day, like fitting her hand into the hollow at the base of her sister's ribs as they slept. A feeling of total belonging, that flowed through her and into the sword and the shield like a golden light. And the sword somehow flew with the intent of her thoughts rather than the pressure of her palm, so that it struck always just at the place that the boy least seemed to expect. Catching him hard beneath the chin, so that his teeth clashed with a painful crunch. Knocking his hip just below the jutting edge of his leather breastplate. Bashing his ear so that it glowed red and he released a string of profanities so impressive that even Lily stopped cheering to give a low, appreciative whistle.

Then the shield, almost of its own accord, seemed to twist

in the air at the perfect moment, so that it connected with the boy's wrist and with a sharp intake of breath he dropped his sword, right at Cass's feet. And she leaped on it, gasping, still almost dazed, as Lily's triumphant whooping filled her ears and the boy spat out a gobbet of blood-flecked spittle and turned sullenly away.

And for a moment there was a golden ringing that was almost as much a colour as a sound in Cass's ears, until it was abruptly broken by the cold fury of Angharad's voice behind her. The feeling vanished as she turned and saw pure anger on Angharad's face. Sigrid staggering to her feet behind her, the smirking knight collecting a fat pouch of coins from the seneschal.

'COME!' Angharad ordered.

The sword was suddenly heavy in Cass's hand again, and she dropped it with a clatter among the others as she trailed behind Sigrid and Rowan alongside a white-faced Lily as they returned to their own tent.

Chapter 12

'To be uncertain. To withdraw. These are not qualities of weakness, but of strength.' Angharad was shouting so loudly that Cass almost took a step backwards. 'You could have cost us our freedom. Stupid girl.'

Angharad was striding backwards and forwards now, turning sharply within the confines of the small tent, her temper burning as bright as her hair.

'To leap into an ill-advised fight with no experience, no armour, with every chance you might have been exposed . . .' She threw up her hands as if in despair at Cass's recklessness.

'It was my fault,' Lily piped up bravely. 'I accidentally blurted something out and Cass was trying to cover for me . . .'

'Of that I've no doubt.' Angharad turned her blade-sharp glare on Lily. 'You are as foolhardy and as rash as each other.' She continued to pace, muttering under her breath about barely broken colts and youths who behaved like infants, while Cass stood, flinching from her anger but sensing that she was required to stand and wait until it had run its course.

'No harm has been done,' came a quiet, calm voice, and Vivian appeared, her hand steady on Angharad's shoulder. 'They will learn from this, I have no doubt. But we should leave, and quickly. There is nothing left here to gain, but much to risk the longer we linger.'

Angharad sighed, and Cass sensed that Vivian's was the only voice in the world that could have reached her and calmed such a rage. Angharad covered the hand on her shoulder briefly with her own.

'Yes, I am strong enough,' Vivian said firmly, answering Angharad's unspoken question. 'Let us go home, where we can lick our wounds in peace.'

And at Angharad's nod, Sigrid strode forward from the shadows, her helmet still on and her visor down, and marched out of the tent without a word.

As Cass hurried to help her mount, she bowed her head, expecting a tirade similar to Angharad's, Sigrid's tongue perhaps sharpened by the humiliation of her own defeat.

But the question that came was not one she expected. Not 'What were you thinking?' or 'How could you have been so stupid?' but 'Has it happened before?'

'No,' Cass murmured, feeling her cheeks flush. Already the sudden certainty and confidence of the fight felt like a strange memory, as if she had heard about it happening to somebody else. She had been quite certain it had been a mirage, her own distorted mind playing tricks on her. But Sigrid had seen it. And she lifted her visor and gazed at Cass for a moment with a new, calculating look in her eyes, as if she were trying to solve a puzzle that Cass herself could not see. Then she nodded and swung herself into the saddle.

'Then we will work to find it again. Now we know what is inside you.'

In spite of everything, as they set off in a dejected, straggling procession, heading homeward under strict reprimand and with no winnings to show for their exertions, Cass felt a warmth in her chest and a smile creeping onto her lips. She squeezed her heels together and urged Pebble into a faster trot.

It was a weary journey, made drearier by the drab autumn weather. The last lingering summer warmth seemed to have been left behind them on the tournament field and their limping procession homeward was dampened by drizzle that seemed to leak continuously from the flat grey sky.

Though they had left immediately to avoid any further contact with Sir Mordaunt and his household, Blyth had stayed behind to dismantle the tents and caught up with them at the same campsite they had used on the outward journey, Vivian riding with the equipment in the wagon. There was a poor fire this time compared to the bright blaze of their previous journey, with only a few sticks dry enough to burn. And the conversation that had sparked and crackled on their way to the tournament was stilted and weary now, with long silences and yawns, as they shivered in the damp air and tried to get warm by pressing in close to the meagre flames. The feeling of failure hung heavy above the camp.

But there was one moment that brightened the evening, as Rowan pulled a simple, battered wooden vielle from her pack and started plucking the strings unexpectedly to play a mournful tune. The notes seemed to slide round the sparse camp, uniting them in their weariness and discouragement. As Cass sat next to Lily, both brooding on Angharad's disappointment in them, the music was like a salve both to her bruised spirit and her aching, chilled limbs.

'Rowan has had the hardest life of any of us,' Lily told Cass under her breath, as the music rose and fell. 'She was orphaned as a child and spent years begging crusts and shelter as a travelling musician before she happened upon the manor one afternoon.'

Cass watched Rowan cradling her scratched instrument, her eyes bright with firelight. She remembered the nights Rowan had remained on the training field long after the others had gone to bed, her fierce anger in the hall one night when a clumsy younger squire had overturned a plate of meat onto the floor and wasted it. She wondered what it must feel like to know that if they were exposed there was no safety net, no family home to go back to.

And then the melody stopped, on a single, lingering, sweet note. Vivian climbed down from the wagon, her sword in her hand, and touched Rowan's shoulder gently.

'You fought well today, my girl,' she said simply, and there was pride in her voice that set Rowan's face aglow. 'It was not easy and there was no simple victory, but there rarely is, and there is more to knighthood than spoils.'

Then she drew her sword from its leather scabbard and touched Rowan, lightly, once on each shoulder, the simple gesture that conferred knighthood on the young woman. And Lily squeezed Cass's hand tight, so tight, and whispered, 'Imagine, Cass, just imagine!'

As they huddled together under their cloaks that night, their breath puffing out soft clouds into the darkness, Cass whispered, 'Mordaunt's shield . . . the antlers.'

Lily snorted and pulled her cloak more closely round her. 'Of course he chose the symbol of the most powerful local legend for his coat of arms. It doesn't mean the stag has anything to do with him. Just that he'd like people to think it does.'

There was a long pause, then, quietly, 'Why did you lie to me, Cass?'

'Lie to you about what?'

'You said you hadn't fought before.' And there was a hint of reproach in her voice.

'I hadn't, Lily. I can't explain it. It was like . . .' She sighed, and turned over, looking up at the silhouettes of the branches over their heads in the dim light of the dying fire. Here and there, bright stars flickered in and out of view as the leaves moved gently in the breeze. 'It was like somebody else came into my body . . . or like I remembered somebody I had never known I could be.'

'That makes no sense whatsoever.'

Cass grinned, knowing that Lily's left eyebrow would be quirked sceptically without being able to see it in the dark.

'I know.'

Lily sighed and snuggled closer.

'Well, you'd better share some of these new tactics with me, wherever they came from. We're going to need some miraculous performances in practice if we're ever going to win back Angharad's favour.' She gave Cass a squeeze, and Cass sighed and closed her eyes, squeezing back.

*

It was Cass who was sent to run and fetch Alys when they arrived back at the manor, to tend to Vivian's wound. She found the woman on her knees outside her hut, hair more frizzy and unkempt than ever, surrounded by the ruins of what had once been neatly planted rows of herbs. Alys looked up quickly as Cass's footsteps approached, her hand tightening round a thick stick, before she saw who it was and sighed heavily. She passed her hand through her hair and wiped her eyes, leaving a smudge of earth across her forehead.

'What happened?' Cass sank to her knees beside Alys, fingering the crushed stems of a thyme plant that had been ripped up by the roots.

'I am a woman who lives alone and doesn't seek to hide her knowledge of plants and their uses,' Alys replied, her voice dull and heavy. 'It is not the first time and it won't be the last.' She gestured wordlessly towards her front door and Cass gasped.

BURN WITCH. The words were daubed in thick, dripping white letters and horse excrement was smeared round them as if to frame the message.

'Who has done this?' Cass asked angrily, taking Alys's weathered hand in her own. 'We should not let it pass unchallenged.'

Alys smiled and patted her hand. 'Bless you. But the men who ride through these forests are far more dangerous and wicked than the faeries and people of the old ways they claim to despise. Except they are protected by chainmail and coats of arms. And challenging them comes at too great a cost.'

'Mordaunt's men?'

She nodded.

Cass tried to tuck the roots of the pitiful thyme back under the soil, scooping up a handful of mud and pressing the plant back into the earth.

'Living things are not so easy to kill,' Alys said, watching her. 'There is wisdom in nature, for those who know how to listen for it. And those who remember the old ways know that change always comes eventually, with patience.' Her eyes roved again to Cass's wrist, where her linen shirt cuff was rolled up slightly, her old scar seeming to shine almost silver in the fading light. 'Listen to the voices of the forest, Cass.' Alys smiled, tucking another plant back into the soil. 'They will lead you even when you are lost.'

Chapter 13

Cass was still turning Alys's words over in her mind later that evening, as she returned from accompanying her to Vivian's bedchamber and prepared to sit down to dinner with the others.

They had hardly begun to eat when a scream split the air in the hall and knights and squires alike jumped to their feet. Angharad drew a concealed sword that must have been strapped beneath the table in front of her seat, Sigrid pulled on a breastplate that leaned against the hearth and together they ran from the room, out into the courtyard, others streaming after them. Cass and Lily gave each other a wide-eyed look and sprang after them, Cass grabbing a knife from the table as she went.

A young woman lay on the cobbles, an arrow embedded deep in her shoulder. Another was bent over her, calling frantically for help.

'Five of them, maybe six,' she gasped, as Angharad reached her and bent down. 'Saxon raiders. In the trees. They haven't breached the gates, but we challenged them from the top of the wall and this was their response.'

At that moment, there came a great hammering at the gates, a beating so loud that it rang round the courtyard and the cobblestones seemed to sing with it. Angharad grasped her sword and leaped to her feet, drawing a rigid finger urgently across her lips, her eyes burning into the small crowd of women that had gathered on the manor steps.

Her eyes darting from side to side, Angharad pointed silently to Leah and Rowan, who had not emerged from the hall immediately, but run to their chambers to arm themselves and now appeared with helmets and swords. She gestured to the gates, and they each moved silently to stand ready before them.

Blyth came running from the stables with a bow and a quiver of arrows; Sigrid grabbed them and leaped up the steps that led to the ramparts, bent double so that she would not be seen above the outer wall.

The doors creaked under a third battering, and this time, Angharad cried out, one hand still raised behind her to warn the others to remain silent.

'Please wait, my lords, I am opening up now. I am a woman alone without kin here and nervous to leave my gates open at night. But I assure you I will provide you whatever hospitality you desire.'

'We'll take more than "hospitality" if you do not open these gates quickly,' came a leering, threatening voice, with a strange, flat accent Cass did not recognize. She felt Lily's hand creep into hers. Behind them, some of the other squires were huddled together, their faces slack with fear. She gripped the knife more tightly, her hand damp with sweat.

'NOW!' Angharad bellowed, heaving the great crossbar down from the gates and allowing them to swing open.

Sigrid rose to her feet and immediately loosed three swift arrows in quick succession from the ramparts, angling her bow directly down so that they rained on the unsuspecting invaders from above. Cass heard one of the men bellow in pain and the others swore and lurched forward through the gates.

Before they had even crossed the threshold, Angharad and Leah had felled two of them, stepping out from the shadows beside the doorway and running them through with their swords before they could so much as cry out. The cobbles were slippery with blood as the last two men staggered to a halt, their heads turning wildly between their felled comrades and the group of women before them. They began to stride forward, and for a moment there was silence. Then each woman and girl raised the weapon she had grabbed in the moment of the disturbance: some had knives and broken pieces of crockery, others candlesticks or flaming torches ripped from the wall brackets. And in a single, terrible cry, they gave voice to their fury at this violation of their sanctuary.

The men stumbled backwards, their faces covered in confusion and fear, and began to run towards the cover of the trees. But before they had taken more than a dozen steps there was the delicate whistle of two more arrows and they fell to the ground and lay still.

All eyes turned to Sigrid as she descended the steps from the ramparts.

She shrugged. 'Couldn't let them live to tell the tale. Imagine the result if the Saxons learned there was a conveniently secluded manor in the woods of Northumbria, defended only by a small group of women.'

Angharad sighed and nodded. She beckoned to Blyth, who helped the uninjured gate guard to raise her wounded partner from the cobbles, each of them wrapping an arm round her waist. 'Take her to Vivian's chamber. Alys is already there.'

She turned and rattled off a stream of orders. 'That was

too close. Double the guard. And send extra riders to search the woods. Hopefully it was an isolated band of scouts without others behind. But we cannot take any chances.'

As they filed back into the hall for dinner, there was rumbling and muttering among some of the women. Cass watched as Angharad heavily took her seat and picked at her food, her face clouded with worry. Suddenly she rose, pushing her chair back with a loud grating across the flagstone floor.

'If you have things to say, let us say them in the open. A witan.'

The women and girls began to leave their seats along the table benches, gathering in a semicircle round the fireplace.

'What does she mean?' Cass whispered to Lily. 'The witan in my village was held once a month, and never in public.'

Lily nodded. 'In most places, they consist of the village elders, the most powerful men, but here everyone is included. And we call them whenever we need one.'

Joan stepped forward, nervously, but raised her chin and spoke defiantly. 'We could have imprisoned those men. They did not need to die.' There was a murmur of agreement from around the circle as she stepped back to her place.

'And risk everything we've built here? For the sake of a band of bloodthirsty Saxons who would have murdered us all in our beds if they'd caught us unawares?' Rowan's voice was harsh, scornful. She spat into the fire.

'We could have voted on it, at least,' suggested a spotty girl with slightly protruding front teeth standing next to Joan, who Cass recognized as Susan. 'We should be consulted about such choices.'

'And ask the Saxons to just wait patiently at the gate while we decide what to do with them?' Lily laughed incredulously.

'You've only been here a year, Joan,' Leah told her squire, her voice gentle but firm. 'You don't yet know the sacrifices we've had to make to protect our way of life.'

'Well, who says it's worth those sacrifices?' Joan asked, looking as if she might cry. 'What does our freedom mean if it comes at the price of others' lives?'

'Listen, idiot,' Rowan began, but Angharad raised a warning hand.

'She has the right to speak, Rowan, and each voice here carries the same weight, knight, squire, page or stable hand. We are all in this together.'

There was a little snort from the back of the circle. 'But you will not be the one scrubbing their blood from the cobblestones, will you, *my lady*,' someone said quietly.

Angharad stiffened, but before she could respond, Vivian walked slowly into the room, one hand clutching her bandaged chest.

'She has made sacrifices so much greater than you know,'

she snarled, uncharacteristically angry, panting a little.

'We all do our part,' Leah said, her voice conciliatory, putting an arm round Joan. 'Your hard work as squires is not to shame or burden you, but to prepare you for the demanding challenges of knighthood. It is part of your training, a rite of passage.'

'And if you don't like it,' Vivian added, 'you can go and try your luck elsewhere, and see how much more magical life here seems compared to the domestic servitude you find.'

She wheezed, and Angharad moved to her side. 'Come, you should not be out of bed.' With Vivian's arm round her shoulder, she supported her from the room.

The witan was over. And Vivian had made it clear whose decisions would stand.

Chapter 14

As autumn set in, the sisterhood found themselves in the meadow each morning as the sun rose, feet slipping on the ruddy piles of dew-drenched leaves that sloughed from the forest trees and blew towards the manor. Every spare moment when they weren't tending to Sigrid and Angharad or practising their riding skills with Blyth, Cass and Lily were out in the long grass, hacking away at each other with the wooden batons until the sweat ran into their eyes and their palms chafed with splinters that they picked at by the side of the fire in the great hall each night.

Sigrid would stalk the edges of the meadow, a hand shading her narrowed eyes from the sun as she surveyed

Cass's progress, giving a curt nod and sweeping away when Cass caught sight of her.

It was a hard autumn, but a satisfying one, in ways Cass had never known. The work was wearing, but she felt alive, purposeful, driven, as she never had before. There were tasks to attend to: pummelling bread dough in the kitchen one day, rustling through the undergrowth of the surrounding forest to check the traps for small game the next. She blocked out the thoughts of home that inevitably crept in when she carried out her domestic duties. The pangs of guilt when she wondered how her mother was coping without either of her two eldest daughters to help with the household chores. The daydreams about Mary, mistress of her own house now, and whether she was kneading bread dough, just like Cass, at this exact moment, and thinking of her little sister too.

In the evenings she would sit in the candlelit hall in a soft, silk dress, playing dice with Lily and the rest of the squires or listening to one of the other girls playing a song of valour and daring on the harp as they gazed quietly into the great fireplace.

The Saxons did not return and the grumbling from the younger squires seemed to subside, at least for the time being. It helped that Angharad, Vivian and the other older knights were always busy too, either riding out to hunt, training their squires or locked away in Angharad's rooms, poring over complicated letters and financial affairs.

They never went hungry, but supplies were as unpredictable as Lily had warned, especially as the weather turned, and game grew less plentiful.

Angharad swept into the hall one night with flushed cheeks, a bright wound that streaked across her forearm like a blaze and a fat leather money bag, and they cheered when she declared they would dine like queens that month. But later, as Cass passed the bottom of Angharad's staircase on her way to the kitchens, she heard Angharad and Vivian's voices, raised and sharp.

'Too great a risk to go looking for bandits to rob—' Vivian was shouting, before Angharad fired back, 'And how will we survive? We cannot eat our pride, Vivian! We cannot eat safety! I have been confined and restricted so much of my life, I will not accept it from you too.'

Then the voices subsided back into murmurs again and Cass moved guiltily away.

Sitting in the cooling suds of Sigrid's leftover bathwater late one evening, she caught sight of herself in the glass leaning against the wall of the antechamber and startled for a moment to see a stranger looking back at her. Her rich brown curls were just as wild, but now they were streaked with gold from the sun, and tumbled down from a bronzed forehead. Her nose and cheekbones were dotted with freckles and her cheeks flushed with health and fresh air. The shoulders that rose above the sides of the tub were powerful and tanned, the muscles of her upper arms defined and taut. And there was a watchfulness, a certainty and determination about her straight dark eyebrows and blue-green eyes, that had not been present in the girl who sat playing with her locket in the orchard that morning just a few short weeks ago. She wasn't sure that girl would even recognize her now, and the thought made this new Cass's lips curl in an irrepressible smile.

Sigrid took a new interest in her too, arranging private sessions in the evenings when she would sometimes sit, talking her through swordcraft and tactics for hours, other times waiting for her in a firelit chamber with weapons to study or freshly spliced arrows to fletch. But most frequently of all she would insist, over and over again, that they spar together.

A few days after they returned from the tournament, Sigrid had sent Cass to find Iona in the courtyard after breakfast. She had found her in a small, stone-walled building next to the stables, a slight girl with a serious, slender face, delicate, bird-like limbs and dark blonde hair in a tight, neat plait that reached almost to the floor. She looked up from the heat of the fire, and grinned at Cass, sweat trickling down the side of her face. She wiped blackened hands on a leather apron before offering one to shake, and Cass was taken aback by the strength of her grip.

'So you are here for your sword?'

'My . . . ?' Cass swallowed, looking beyond the girl to the fire, and saw a stout black anvil, with a dull blade laid atop it, not yet finished, the sharp point still glowing red from the fire. It was a fine, slender sword, crossed with a slim silver hilt and ending in a simple, black leather-wrapped handle with a round silver pommel. The hissing flames seemed to whisper and murmur behind it.

'Sigrid believes it is time,' Iona grinned. 'She has had me working on it day and night since you returned from Eboracum.'

The small, hot room suddenly felt smaller and hotter. Cass felt her breath leave her body as if it were being pulled, irresistibly, towards that red-gold blade, shimmering hot and glowing like a living thing.

Iona watched her and grinned.

'Sometimes, you choose the sword. Sometimes it chooses you.'

Iona held out another sword, laying it flat across her two uplifted palms so that the metal glinted in the light. 'This,' she said, 'is a typical knight's sword. Sigrid relieved a particularly objectionable gentleman of it in the woods outside

Cambodunum a few months ago, if I remember correctly.'

Cass reached out eagerly, grasping the golden handle. As she pulled it out of Iona's hands, she was unprepared for the great weight, and immediately dropped it across her toes.

'Ow!'

Iona laughed as Cass hopped on one leg, her foot throbbing.

'Then how do they use it so deftly?' she asked incredulously, remembering Sigrid's light-footed, darting blows, and Vivian's quick sword strokes.

Iona's eyes gleamed. 'That's where I come in.'

She took the slim sword from the anvil and plunged the tip into a pail of cold water so that it hissed and frothed and sent a great plume of steam up towards the roof. As the steam cleared, she turned the blade round and held the handle out towards Cass.

'It needs sharpening and shining yet, but you can feel it.'

Cass reached out slowly, her fingers caressing the soft black leather, feeling the hard certainty of the metal handle beneath. She braced herself to lift it, but it flew easily to her side, lighter even than the wooden batons they used to practise. She laughed in delighted surprise and tested it, moving it gently through the air and transferring it from one hand to the other.

'How?' she breathed.

'Tin.' Iona smiled. 'Most swordsmiths use bronze, mixing

copper and tin, or steel. The swords are sharp and durable, but heavy. It puts us at a disadvantage to fight men with weapons they can lift more easily than us.'

She handed Cass a length of bright silver metal.

'This is tin. Feel it.'

Cass put down the other sword and took it – it was light as silk, but it bent easily in her hands.

Iona shook her head. 'No good for swords.'

She picked up two other pieces of metal, both dark grey, one a great, thick lump, the other much more slender.

'This,' she held out the larger piece, 'is the raw steel you would usually start with to make a sword. And you would heat and hammer it to the right shape.'

'But if you start with this,' she took the strip of tin back from Cass, 'and add this . . .' She placed the tin on top of the thinner piece of steel. 'Then you can fold the tin into the steel and make a sword that is much lighter, but still just as hard on the outside, where it matters.'

She grinned, and caught up Cass's half-finished sword, suddenly spinning it in her hand and slashing the air with a series of perfectly executed strokes. 'And your opponent will never know.' She handed the sword back to Cass, who weighed it wonderingly in her hand.

'How did you learn this?'

'My father taught me,' Iona answered proudly. 'And sent

me here as soon as I came of age.' She smiled at Cass's look of astonishment. 'His mother raised him alone,' she explained, 'and he has very different ideas about women and their place in the world than most. He is Angharad's brother, and one of only a handful of people trusted to know the truth of what goes on behind these walls.'

'Was he not concerned about Angharad's husband?' Cass asked curiously.

Iona's face clouded. 'It was not until after her husband's death that Angharad wrote to him a little of what her life had been like, and why she had chosen to stay on here and turn the manor into what it has become. Her pride would not let her tell him the truth of her husband's cruelty before. But he always felt guilty that he had not been able to help her through those years of suffering, and he supported her from the first moment she made the choice to live on her own terms.'

Iona sighed. 'My home is very far away, and he has my mother and brothers to provide for, but I know he thinks of me, and of my aunt.' Her eyes shone with pride. 'Sending me here was the greatest display of confidence and trust he could have shown in her.'

She took the sword carefully back from Cass and returned it to the anvil. 'I will send for you the moment it is ready,' she laughed, seeing the longing in Cass's face. 'I promise. And in the meantime, you will need your own armour too. Come.'

She led Cass to the back of the room, where a pile of brown pieces of leather sat beside a steaming vat.

'Boiling wax,' Iona said, 'to harden the leather so it will protect you from arrows and blades.' And Cass felt the familiar shudder again, as spectral points seemed in her imagination to float slowly, menacingly towards her, but this time she saw in her mind's eye a bright sword, warding them off, and the shiver faded as quickly as it had come.

Iona held up a piece of tan-coloured leather, measuring it against Cass's shoulders and stomach and deftly carving off an edge here or there with a sharp tool. When she was satisfied with the size, she gripped the edge of the leather with a pair of metal callipers and plunged it into the wax, where it fizzed and bubbled. For a moment, Cass saw her mother, with Mary at her side, plunging the little Easter cakes into hot oil and watching them puff up and bob to the surface. Then the leather burst from the wax, and Iona quickly transferred it to a workbench, where she shaped and hammered the now dark brown leather, her hands protected by thick gloves. Her plait whipped back and forth as her eyes darted from Cass's body to the leather, working it into the soft curves that would fit and protect her, curling the sides to fit snug round her ribs. Then she used a hammer and a finely pointed metal chisel to beat out the holes where the armour would be connected to the other plates, either by metal rivets or leather thongs.

Cass watched, amazed at the deftness of Iona's fingers and the skill of her hands, as the leather came to life in front of her eyes, transforming from a flat sheet to a quickly hardening breastplate.

'Have to work it quickly,' Iona grunted, 'before it sets.'

She paused, and held the breastplate up against Cass's body again with a nod of satisfaction. 'It'll gleam like a horse chestnut when it's properly oiled and polished. But first it needs time to harden and set.'

And so it was that just a few short days later, Cass raced to the smithy at Iona's summons and collected her first set of armour and her own shining sword.

Chapter 15

Cass still used the wooden batons at the daily practice in the meadow, but when Sigrid sent word that they should meet for a sparring session, her whole body shivered with delight at the opportunity to use her new sword.

Standing in her small chamber with the borrowed glass leaning against her low wooden bed, Cass watched, delighted as the armour seemed to meld perfectly with her body. The breastplate, simple and unadorned except for the bronze rivets at its edges, shone like copper just as Iona had promised. The pauldron encased her shoulders, making them look broad and masculine, and the fauld, with its horizontal rings, hung beneath her breastplate, protecting her pelvis and thighs. Lower down, her calves were shielded by simple, curved greaves. And although she wouldn't need it for these sessions, she eagerly pulled on the borrowed steel helmet Iona had given her from the weapons store, desperate to see the full effect for the first time.

'Could you stop posing and help me with these fastenings?' Lily grumbled, her fingers straining with the stiffness of the shiny new buckles. Cass grinned and discarded the helmet, but the image of the knight looking back at her from the glass remained in her mind long afterwards.

Her heart fluttered as she knocked on the door of the practice room, waiting a few moments before she pushed it open and went inside. Torches flared in brackets lining the walls, but her eyes were still adjusting to the low light when a sword sliced the air a hair's width from her nose, stopping her in her tracks. Her stomach leaped and she dropped her own sword with a crash that echoed off the walls of the sparsely furnished room.

'Always be ready,' Sigrid's low voice came from the shadows. 'And never carry your sword without a shield on your arm.' She handed Cass a light, blood-red shield, which she hooked over the smooth vambrace that sheathed her forearm.

'Now, let's see if we can reawaken the spirit that showed itself at the tournament, shall we?' Sigrid began to circle her slowly, cat-light on the balls of her feet, sword held up and ready.

Cass bent her knees and tightened her grip on her sword. She tried to remember everything she had learned from Vivian and the others: watching Sigrid's feet to predict where the next blow would land, defending with her shield while she prepared her next attack, trying to surprise her opponent by varying the direction and strength of her attacks.

But sparring with Sigrid was like trying to attack a stone wall. When she faced Lily in the meadow, Cass could often surprise her with a swift, low strike to the knees or a sudden jab in the ribs, but Sigrid seemed to predict her every move, the taut sinews of her neck straining as she flew out of reach of Cass's sword, time and time again.

'Good,' she smiled, her voice softer than Cass was used to hearing it, as they stopped to take a drink. Cass wiped the sweat from her brow, while Sigrid barely seemed to be out of breath.

'Good?' she asked a little bitterly, aware of her already-aching muscles. 'My blade has not yet touched your armour.'

'But neither has mine felled you.' Sigrid sounded amused at her impatience. 'As it would have done almost any other squire in her first year of training.' Cass felt some of the soreness lift with her mood at Sigrid's praise, wiped her mouth and took up her sword again.

It was not always possible to find the light inside herself:

the warmth that had flooded out so unexpectedly that day on the edge of the tournament field at Eboracum. Some days she was bone-tired and weary before sunset and dropped into bed full of frustration at the impossibility of it all. Certain that this was all a mistake, hearing the voices of the village gossips at home, imagining what they would say if they could see her now.

But there were days, moments, when it burst out of her again, sometimes when she least expected it.

One night, she entered the practice room prepared, shield already raised and ready to meet the blow that descended the moment the door closed. Sigrid nodded approvingly then shifted her weight onto the other foot and slashed back in the opposite direction, smiling when Cass jumped nimbly backwards, denying her contact. Sigrid laughed, and punched her approvingly on the shoulder, as Mary might have done when she ate one too many of the peas they were podding for dinner, crouched together in the patch of afternoon sunlight that played across the kitchen floor. And the feeling of knowing who she was flowed into Cass again, as if the memory of that child who had climbed the highest trees, sure-footed and unafraid, laughing at her sister's hesitation, was reaching towards some other confidence, some other certainty yet to come. Her sword leaped in her hand, sweeping in an arc of its own making, finding the elbow of Sigrid's sword arm more swiftly than she could dodge, hitting the most vulnerable point of the joint with such accuracy that her mistress gasped and almost dropped her sword, hastening to regain her grip.

She saw Sigrid's eyes take her in as if reappraising her, her mouth tightening in determination. Then she struck again, her sword slicing downwards this time, aimed squarely for the centre of Cass's forehead. But Cass was ready for her, bringing her own blade up to resist the blow, using both hands to force Sigrid's sword aside. Sigrid was swept backwards, one hand flung out to steady her as she fell towards the floor, and before she could recover, Cass lunged forward, the very tip of her sword finding the soft hollow of Sigrid's throat. Sigrid froze, her body horizontal, knees bent, one hand on the floor, arm crooked at the elbow, the other still holding her sword in mid-air. A brief pause, every muscle in Cass's body trembling as she held her sword-point to the delicate, exposed skin, and then Sigrid opened her hand and her sword clattered to the floor.

Cass's breath caught in her throat, her heart hammering. Then Sigrid gave her wolfish grin, and clapped her on the back with a satisfied nod. Cass felt pride burst warm and intense in her chest.

*

Cass lay in bed for hours that night trying to remember the feeling. Not just the glow of almost disbelieving pride that she, Cassandra Ellory, had disarmed a *knight*, and one of the fiercest fighters in the fellowship at that, but also trying to solidify the sensation of it in her memory. To imprint it on her body. The warmth flooding into her cheeks and fingers, the sudden, joyful rush of her limbs as if some long-distant muscle memory were returning to them, the confidence that suffused her like a drug when it overtook her. She wanted to be able to do it again, to replicate that state at will, not for it only to take her by surprise at odd moments, unbidden. And always at the back of her mind that little voice she tried to push away: 'If only Mary could see you now.'

Lying there in the dark, willing that warmth and certainty to return to her body, feeling only the prickle of the straw tick through the linen sheets, she heard the distinctive creak of the floorboard at the entrance to Sigrid's chamber and started semi-upright in the darkness, all her senses suddenly alerted. Her hand flew to the hilt of the sword that leaned against the head of her bed, in reach of her pillow. But before she could speak or move again she saw a shadowy figure that slipped, not into Sigrid's doorway, as Cass had feared, but out of it. The tall, proud bearing, the purposeful stride were unmistakable: it was Sigrid herself, swathed in a long, heavy travelling cloak and moving swiftly towards the stairs.

Cass hesitated, torn between her curiosity and her respect for her mistress's privacy. But the tingle of energy she had awoken in herself earlier that evening still remained, restless energy with nowhere to go, and in an impulsive instant she leaped out of bed, pulled on her overshoes, threw a bundle of clothes beneath her blanket to give the appearance that her bed was still occupied, and followed.

Sigrid moved like a shadow through the manor, down the stone spiral staircase, through the silent kitchens where baskets of apples waited by the fire to be baked for breakfast, and out of the postern door. Cass followed, frowning as Sigrid strode confidently into the woods. Goosebumps rose on Cass's bare arms as the cool October night air slipped beneath her simple cotton nightshirt. She hurried closer, for fear she would lose Sigrid in the darkness of the clustered trees, then stopped in horror as a twig snapped loudly under her foot. She shrank into the black shadow of a hazel tree, frozen, as Sigrid wheeled round, scanning the area slowly and methodically, her hand on her hip, where a dagger or sword must hang. But before Cass could be discovered, there came a low hoot, like that of a tawny owl, and Sigrid turned towards the sound and lifted her hands to her lips, sending a long, quavering note back in return.

Out from the shadows came a figure, swathed in a cloak, a bow and quiver of arrows slung across his back. He lowered his hood as he neared, and Sigrid stepped forward, sweeping him into a tight embrace. They bent their heads together, whispering urgently, and though Cass strained her ears she could not make out their words, nor did she dare to venture any closer for fear of discovery. The conversation was brief and intense, each of them at different times gesturing passionately, and as it ended the man turned away, his face for a moment in Cass's full view. A cloud drifted away from the moon and the clearing brightened a little, so that Cass could see he was young, perhaps only a few years older than herself, with a weak, pointed chin and softly curling hair that framed an unlined face. But one cheek, from the corner of his mouth to the hairline above his ear, was split in two by a vivid, straight scar.

She held herself quite still, body pressed fast into the rough bark of the tree, as Sigrid embraced the youth again, watched him melt back into the trees, and then swept past Cass on her way back to the manor.

Cass waited, shivering slightly, until she could be sure that enough time had passed for Sigrid to return to her own chamber, before she slipped through the postern gate, across the flagstones of the kitchen, up the stairs and back into the warmth of her own bed.

Lying in the dark, listening to the pounding of her own heart, she thought back to the look of shrewd reappraisal Sigrid had given her earlier in the evening and wondered not for the first time why Sigrid had chosen her as squire. Was it because she thought Cass had showed real promise? Or had she thought that a simple, inexperienced country girl would pay little heed to her movements? Was she a protégée? Or simply a convenient shield for whatever secrets Sigrid was keeping from the other knights?

Chapter 16

'Well, what did he look like?' Lily whispered, as she and Cass discussed the odd events the next morning, while they swept stale straw out of their horses' stalls.

'I told you,' Cass panted, leaning on her broom. 'Young. Intense. Scar.'

'Lover?' Lily's eyes twinkled mischievously with the possibility.

But Cass shook her head slowly. 'It didn't seem that way,' she said in a low voice, as she pitched fresh hay into Pebble's manger.

'Son?'

'I doubt it. Sigrid doesn't exactly seem the maternal type.

And besides, he can't have been more than seven or eight years younger than her.'

'You don't think . . .' Lily's eyes darted round the stable, checking they were alone. 'You don't think she means any harm?'

Cass grimaced. She had been asking herself the same thing since the night before. Sigrid had been meeting alone with a man, with no hint that she had tried to hide her appearance or gender. Was she betraying the sisterhood? Should it be reported to Angharad?

'There's no reason to believe so,' she said, trying to sound more confident than she felt. 'If she wanted to bring trouble, she would only have had to remove her helmet at Eboracum, or nearer home for that matter. She could have exposed us in a matter of moments if she wanted to.'

'Sigrid is one of the newest members of the sisterhood. She arrived at the beginning of the summer, not long before you,' Lily said thoughtfully, as she sloshed water from a bucket into the horses' drinking trough. 'She revealed very little about her past or where she had come from. Nor how she was already so skilled in the sword. But she made her allegiance clear and has proved it ten times over.'

Lily picked up a short, bristled brush and started to rub it in gentle strokes over her pony Elise's flanks. 'There was one incident, only a few weeks after she arrived, when she and Angharad were hunting and were set upon by bandits who took them by surprise. One of them dropped from a tree, and Angharad's horse panicked, threw her and bolted. She was at his mercy, he had a knife to her throat, but Sigrid felled him with a single arrow and then fought off the other three single-handed. She saved Angharad's life. And brought home all their stolen goods too. Why stay so long and fight so loyally over these past months if she wanted to betray us? It wouldn't make any sense.'

'Angharad and Vivian clearly trust her,' Cass added. 'They take her into their confidence more than any of the other knights. Perhaps she was meeting him on their instructions, or with their knowledge.'

'And if you report her, it might show disloyalty,' Lily mused.

'That's what I thought,' Cass agreed. 'I couldn't very well continue as her squire if I repaid her confidence in me by following her about her private business and then reporting her to her own fellowship, could I?'

And, Cass added silently to herself, Sigrid seemed set on helping her to harness the burgeoning power that Cass hardly understood, let alone knew how to wield. Without Sigrid, who would help her learn how to control what was inside her?

'You say nothing,' Lily decided. 'But keep your eyes and

ears open and see what happens next.'

What happened next, as it turned out, would immediately dominate the imagination and the gossip of the whole manor.

Late the following evening, when the meal had been cleared away, members of the fellowship sat round the fire in the great hall, sipping from cups of hot spiced cider, listening to the whine of the wind as a storm raged outside. Cass was using a rag to rub oil into the detailed embellishment on Sigrid's armour. The flickering firelight made the whorls and patterns look as if they were dancing, and along with the warmth of the flames and the heady scent of the cider the effect was almost hypnotic. Beside her, Lily was staring pensively into the fire, Angharad's smooth, chestnut-brown breastplate forgotten between her knees as she daydreamed. A rag dangled from her fingers, dripping oil down to sizzle on the edge of the hearth. On the other side of the fire, Joan was bent over a whetstone, sharpening Leah's sword with grinding, repetitive strokes. The firelight played across the jewelled tones of their dresses, Lily's ringlets spilling untamed round her shoulders and falling onto the mint-green silk. Blyth, who rarely joined them, seeming to prefer the company of the horses, was sitting quietly in a cross-legged chair, hands wrapped round a steaming cup.

Suddenly there came a clamour at the edge of the hall and

two young women approached Angharad, speaking low and urgently. With a start, Cass recognized them as the carefree girls who had seemed to play aimlessly as she and Sigrid approached the outer walls on the day she had arrived. She saw now that she had been right to suspect they were scouts, in the invisible disguise of unthreatening girlhood, and that they had come to warn Angharad about some danger at the gates.

Angharad rose, her lips thin. Almost immediately, there came a loud knock at the main double doors that led into the hall from the courtyard outside.

'Quickly,' Vivian said, jumping to her feet and lifting the lid of a large carved wooden chest that sat beside the fireplace. Together, Cass, Lily and the other squires tumbled the armour and weapons inside in a tangle and heaved the lid closed.

Blyth, the only one of the company still clad in the day's tunic and hose, melted quietly into the shadows.

The doors swung open, letting in a sharp gust of storm-driven wind that sent the torchlight leaping wildly up the walls.

It was a messenger, and even as the light flickered and flashed, Cass could clearly see the silver antlers embellishing his black velvet tunic. She looked at Lily in alarm. A messenger from the household of Sir Mordaunt.

The man bowed to Angharad, who rose to her feet to receive him, the urgent frown she had worn mere moments before replaced with a smile of complete serenity.

'You are welcome, sir.' She smiled, her voice softer and higher than Cass had ever heard it. 'Won't you sit by the fire and warm yourself?'

'I thank you, madam,' he replied stiffly, 'but I have many more missives to deliver tonight.' He indicated his velvet bag, loosely secured with a drawstring, in which dozens of folded parchment letters could be glimpsed, the top one adorned with a maroon wax seal bearing Sir Mordaunt's arms. He pulled one out and hesitated.

'I am tasked with delivering a message to your husband,' he said, looking expectantly round the hall.

'Alas, he has been called away on business,' Angharad replied smoothly, 'and has left me here with my ladies until his return, as you can see.'

Beside her, Cass heard Lily give a tiny, stifled snort. She jabbed her elbow into Lily's ribs.

'But I assure you my husband entrusts me to run all matters of the household in his absence,' Angharad continued, a very slight warning tone creeping into her voice. 'In consultation with him by letter, of course, where necessary,' she added with an imperious smile, as the messenger continued to hesitate.

Reluctantly, he nodded and passed the letter to Angharad, who took it with a gracious inclination of her head, then left the hall as suddenly as he had arrived.

Angharad took a knife from the table and slit the parchment open, and Vivian leaned close to her, her forehead creasing in concern as they scanned its contents together. Angharad sighed heavily and raised her head.

'It is not unexpected,' she murmured, putting her hand on Vivian's. 'And not avoidable, either.' And Vivian nodded once, curtly, though the worry did not leave her face.

'Sir Mordaunt has invited us to a midwinter feast,' she announced.

'Summoned, more like,' Vivian muttered bitterly, as murmuring broke out amongst the assembled knights and squires.

Sigrid rose from a seat in the shadows at the far corner of the hall, pushing back her chair so suddenly that it clattered to the floor. Her face was white, her nostrils flared. 'We will not attend, surely.'

'It would be foolish to decline,' Angharad said firmly. 'And risk attracting unnecessary attention. No doubt he wishes to extend his hospitality to his neighbours –' she grimaced a little – 'or reinforce his superiority over us. We will attend as expected.'

'But we all know how he and his knights treat the

villagers,' Rowan protested hotly. 'We should be attacking them, not dining with them!'

'We bide our time,' Angharad snapped. 'And do nothing to arouse their suspicion. It would be madness to attack them now; everything we have worked for would be put at risk.'

Rowan looked rebellious, but subsided, her sharp, dark eyebrows angrily drawn together.

Sigrid stood taut, her eyes boring into Angharad's, and her voice suddenly dripped with a venom Cass had never heard in it before. 'I will not dance with men who deserve to feel the sharp end of my sword, not the caress of my hand.'

'The rest of you will all be expected to dance,' Vivian sighed, as Sigrid swept from the room without another word. Lily clutched Cass's hand, her eyes sparkling with excitement. 'Lessons will begin shortly, in the evenings. They will *not* come at the expense of your training,' she snapped. And though Angharad placed a consoling hand on her arm, she turned and followed Sigrid out of the hall.

Chapter 17

One blustery day, when they had been given a rare afternoon's rest, their chores completed for once and their training finished for the day, Cass saddled Pebble and rode into the woods with Rowan and Lily at her side, all of them itching for adventure. They had barely left the manor since the disastrous trip to the tournament, and while the knights frequently rode off for days at a time on various expeditions and quests, the squires were rarely afforded a break from the cycle of work and training that filled their days.

There was a sharp nip in the air, and Cass was glad of the face covering that allowed her hot breath to warm the tip of her nose. Somewhere somebody was burning leaves, and she enjoyed the rich tang of the woodsmoke and the newly powerful feeling of the sword resting at her hip. Every now and then she reached down and fingered the pommel, running her fingers over the smooth, cool metal again and again.

They rode with little incident for an hour or two, the rustling of their horses' hooves through the golden autumn leaves accompanied only by the occasional trill of a goldcrest hidden in the trees. Then suddenly they found themselves in a grove of elders, their slender leaves flaming crimson. It was as if the light changed, as if they had moved into a realm of amber and gold. And on the other side of the clearing, between the trees, there was, just for a moment, a dark shadow that seemed to quiver and blaze in the metallic light.

'The black stag,' Rowan and Lily gasped, in unison. The shining creature turned its majestic head, crowned with great gleaming antlers as powerful as blades, and seemed, Cass thought, to look directly at her. Then it was gone, and they were left in the amber silence.

'I thought it was just a legend,' Lily whispered, sounding awestruck.

'It is a quest,' Rowan declared, her voice filled with excitement as she reached for her bow. 'It found us for a reason.'

'It was so beautiful,' Lily faltered, gazing doubtfully at the gap between the trees where the stag had been.

Rowan snorted. 'It would feed everyone at the manor for a week,' she reasoned. 'And the pelt would fetch a handsome price, let alone the antlers. But imagine the glory, Lily: the tale of the black stag ending with our names! We would become the Knights of the Black Stag Quest; our names would *mean* something . . . '

Lily still hesitated, the thrill of a hunt battling with her sympathy for the creature. 'It *would* be a knight's quest, to capture the stag,' she burst out at last. 'Even if not to harm it . . .'

'And the quest is yours as much as mine,' Rowan urged, her eyes sparkling at them both, though Cass strongly suspected she was only playing along with Lily to get her to join in. She didn't rate the stag's chances highly if Rowan cornered it first.

As they continued to speak excitedly, Cass sat thoughtfully, only half aware of their chatter. She was trying to hold on to a feeling she couldn't quite place; an uncomfortable feeling that the stag was there for her, that it had a message for her. Alys's voice echoed unsettlingly in her mind: 'Listen to the voices of the forest, Cass. They will guide you.'

'Cass?' Lily's eager voice interrupted her thoughts. 'Are you with us?'

Cass shook herself a little and looked up at the arched

canopy where the elder branches reached towards each other from each side of the glade. It was a cathedral of burnished orange and bronze, vermilion and yellow. Perhaps it was just the setting that had made her feel such intensity. Rare or not, the creature was just a stag, after all. She was letting the strange light run away with her.

She grabbed the bow that hung from her saddle. 'I'll go this way.' She indicated, trotting off to the right, and Lily and Rowan split up, Lily taking the path to the left and Rowan riding off in the direction the stag had disappeared.

Cass hadn't gone far when Pebble began to whine and toss her head, the whites of her eyes showing as she flattened her ears nervously.

'What is it, girl?' Cass whispered, scratching the shaggy mane. But Pebble snorted and stopped, taking a few steps back. Ahead of them was a tree with a blaze cut into it, the bark scraped away and something carved into the soft wood beneath. Cass patted Pebble gently and dismounted, looping her reins round a low hawthorn branch.

She crept forward, peering at the tree's scar. Carved deep into it with the point of a knife was a symbol that dragged a memory from deep in Cass's stomach, the memory of a feeling of fear, of shock and then of something else: excitement, maybe, or possibility. It was rough and splintered, but unmistakable. An infinite spiral.

Something rustled somewhere nearby and Cass's head snapped up as she peered through the trees. Behind her, Pebble was still snickering nervously. But Cass didn't feel scared. She felt exhilarated, as if something were calling to her. As if she were meant to be here at this exact moment. Her bow clutched reassuringly in her hand, the quiver of arrows slung across her back, she crept forward. She felt the powerful sense that something was waiting for her, just beyond the trees.

There was a slight movement ahead and she froze, finding herself gazing directly at the majestic stag, half silhouetted in the amber light. Beneath the glossy coat, its muscles were tensed as it sniffed the air. Then, as if it picked up her scent, it slowly turned its head until she was gazing straight into its deep brown eyes. It blinked once, then leaped away again, and Cass threw herself after it without hesitation, crashing through the undergrowth, neither noticing nor caring as sharp branches caught at her boys' clothes and grazed her bare forearms with deep scratches.

She was deeper in the forest now, the trees above her head evergreen, their leaves blocking out the light so that it felt suddenly later and more dangerous. She stopped, panting, and listened, rubbing absently at the bright beads of crimson blood that streaked her scratched arms. Silence.

She moved forward again, fists clenched, holding her

breath, as if her heart were waiting to beat. And she emerged into another clearing, this one ringed with tall, ancient oaks. The autumn light filtered through the leaves in bright rays, dust motes floating and sparkling within. At the very centre of the glade was a pool, edges fringed with tall reeds, water as still as a sheet of black glass. The stag had led her here. She knew it had.

And as she stood, her feet transfixed to the spot, the light danced and dazzled on the surface of the water and for a long moment she was certain she saw a translucent hand, the arm below clad in a sleeve of the finest white samite, rise up out of the surface of the pool and beckon to her.

Cass moved towards it slowly, as if in a dream, hardly knowing that she pulled off her face covering as if in greeting. As she peered into the pool, she saw what at first appeared to be her own reflection, pale and wide-eyed. And then suddenly the silver antlers of the stag seemed to flower out of her skull, beautiful and awful, transforming her into something grotesque, unrecognizable. As quickly as they had appeared, they faded, and her own startled blue-green eyes looked back at her. The water seemed to begin to roil and churn, and her reflected eyes swirled and faded, becoming Mary's eyes, wide and terrified. And then they changed again, becoming golden and terrible, fixed on her in adoration and fear. Fixed on her with an intensity so great it seemed excruciating, as if it might burn Cass alive.

The lined face of the woman in the forest so long ago rose, etched and sharp, towards the surface of the water, her wrinkled hands reaching out towards Cass's shoulders. She wanted to scream, wanted to run, but she could not move, and the woman's hands were at her shoulders now, fingernails scratching and digging into her skin, pulling her towards the surface of the pond. She was powerless to fight, powerless to resist, as her head broke the surface and the cold hit her like a dagger as her shoulders and chest followed and her body plunged forward into the icy cold.

Cass felt her skin catch aflame, felt herself falling further and further downwards, the pool seeming to have no limit. And then a great shout came from behind her and Rowan was dragging her backwards out of the water onto the muddy bank of the pond and she was coughing and wheezing, hacking out great barking cries as she spat out rancid water and her skin burned with the cold.

'What happened?' Rowan's eyes were wild with concern and confusion above the cloth that obscured the lower half of her face. Her forehead was scratched, her hair dishevelled. 'What happened, Cass?'

Cass shook her head, unable to speak.

Rowan cast her eyes round the clearing, looking for an assailant.

'Slipped,' Cass managed to wheeze, her lungs still burning from the cold and the water she had inhaled. 'Stupid of me. Concentrating on tracking the stag.'

Rowan looked at her doubtfully, but nodded. 'Did it come this way?' Cass raised her hand and pointed in the direction where she had last seen the stag. Rowan gave her one last concerned glance, then raced after it, Lily close behind. Cass was left alone in silence once more.

She found herself crouching on her haunches at the edge of the pond, her hands clasped in front of her as if in prayer, the empty water in front of her dull and unremarkable.

Cass stayed there for a long time, kneeling by the water, struggling to come to terms with what she had seen. She told herself it was her imagination, sparked by the strangeness of the stag's appearance and the beauty of the elder trees, nothing more. And yet she knew that was untrue. She rubbed her shoulders where they still seemed to ache with the pressure of those long, sharp fingernails, and the crescent-shaped scar at the base of her wrist seemed to throb a little, as it had not done for many years.

Rowan and Lily returned at last, their clothes torn and their faces full of disappointment. Cass pulled herself up to her feet but not before Rowan saw her.

The stag had not appeared again, nor did Cass think that it would.

'I was certain it was a sign,' Rowan said, full of frustration, as they remounted their horses.

As Lily cantered off ahead and Rowan turned her horse's head for home, Cass saw her pause and look back at her, a slight frown on her face.

They went home empty-handed. But Cass's mind whirled and her heart was full.

Chapter 18

Dancing lessons began in earnest as the November rain set in. For days, grey sheets of water sluiced the manor. The meadow became a bog and outdoor drills were cancelled in favour of long afternoons watching intricate demonstrations of swordplay and poring over complicated diagrams of melee positions and tactics until the tapers had to be lit and the light was too dim to continue.

Every morning the long tables were moved to one side of the hall and straw bales with targets pinned onto them were brought inside, so that the squires could range themselves at one end of the hall and practise their archery.

Arrows whistled down the length of the hall, occasionally

straying off course. Lily dissolved into a fit of hysterical giggles when the newest squire, a timid little thing named Nell, accidentally loosed an arrow before she was ready. It soared upwards and lodged itself in the nostril of a stuffed stag's head mounted above the fireplace.

'Not bad,' Cass remarked, climbing on a table to retrieve it. 'It's a sensitive target, the nostril, I'll give you that.' And she gave the little squire an encouraging clap on the back, realizing with a start that she wasn't the newest or least experienced member of the fellowship any more. The girl smiled bashfully and fitted her next arrow more carefully, and Cass felt an inch taller, even though her own arrows still quite often sailed wide of the mark, even now.

'You're feeling better,' Rowan remarked casually, after Cass had handed back Nell's arrow. Cass flushed a little.

'It was only a quick ducking.' She shrugged.

But Rowan's eyes searched hers a little too deeply for comfort, and that little frown played across her forehead beneath her close-cropped hair. Cass smiled and returned to her bow, but she could feel Rowan's eyes on the nape of her neck as she pulled back her bowstring, and the arrow sailed wide of the target and clattered uselessly to the floor.

In the afternoon, the squires sat, entranced, legs dangling off the wooden tables, and watched as Vivian and Angharad sparred and feinted, darting backwards and forwards in a routine so intricate it seemed at times more like a dance than a fight. Cass watched them closely, noting the way that Vivian switched her sword into her left hand for one strike, throwing Angharad off her rhythm. She saw the flash of understanding and the twinkle of laughter in Angharad's eyes as Vivian took advantage of her momentary distraction and lunged in to claim a point, the blunted tip of her sword resting for the briefest moment on Angharad's collarbone. And when Vivian stepped back and frowned, her left knee twisting when she put too much weight on her old ankle injury, Angharad was already there, lunging onto one knee, her hand out to gently support Vivian in the small of her back, helping her upright again and then whirling back to meet her so that their swords never missed a beat.

Cass knew then it was more than swordplay she was watching, and she ached for a moment without loneliness, and with the loss of Mary, the only other person who had known her body as well as she knew it herself.

She also missed Lily's solid, reassuring presence in the dark hours after the candles had been blown out and Sigrid's snores vibrated from the next room. She turned the images she had seen in the water over and over in her mind and drove herself almost to complete torment obsessing over what they could mean. She wished she could ask Mary if she remembered that day when they had collected the firewood, if she remembered the woman, the golden eyes, the way she had looked at Cass. Could she have imagined it, even then?

She could have asked Lily about it. Indeed, she was coming to feel that Lily was almost as much of a sister to her as Mary: more so, in some ways. When Cass thought about the choice she had made to ride away from the possibility of a loveless, unchosen match, and contrasted that shadow future with the close, loving kinship she had found here, with Lily and the others, she knew with absolute certainty that she had made the right choice that morning at the edge of the orchard. And yet something held her back from telling Lily what she had seen in the surface of the pond. The forces that sometimes seemed to take over her body were so powerful, so frightening in their intensity, that she couldn't say herself whether they were something to be celebrated or feared. What if revealing the truth scared away the closest friend she had ever had?

Most nights, just before she fell asleep, she managed to convince herself it was all in her mind, the excitement of a child's memory. That she really had slipped and stumbled into the pool as she followed the stag, that her brain was playing tricks on her. But then she saw the antlers again, protruding disgustingly from her head, and overlaid on the image was the memory of Mordaunt's shield, the silver antlers shining on his regalia and his squire's tunic, and she tossed uncomfortably in the bed and turned until the image shook free and all she could see was darkness again.

Lily pulled a pan full of popped corn from the edge of the fire and started to throw it at Cass's mouth, laughing as she missed and it caught in her hair, and Cass let herself be distracted, let herself slip back into the alluring pull of life at the manor.

The feeling of missing Mary was constant, inescapable, as if she were wearing only one glove. But the exhilaration of being in control of her own destiny was greater still. Yes, she was exhausted, working harder here than she ever had on the farm; yes, she officially had a mistress now, a hierarchy in which she was at the bottom, where before there had technically been none. But the weight of the expectations (or lack of expectations) that had been lifted from her was immense. The openness of choice and possibility for her own life and what it might look like. The joy of feeling power in her newly muscular limbs, the supple arch of her bow in her hand, the sword in its scabbard always at her side. The knowledge that she could make her own choices, determine her own fate. That nobody could choose for her.

She picked the kernal out of her hair and popped it in her mouth, laughing. Settling cross-legged and moving closer to Lily, she cupped her chin in her hands contentedly and leaned forward to watch as the next pair of knights took the floor.

Every evening, in the space cleared at the centre of the hall, they joined hands and circled, curtseyed and whirled back and forth, accompanied by Rowan's vielle and the instruments of a few of the other squires. Blyth, who had declared that 'somebody has to stay with the horses and keep out of trouble', had been excused from attendance at the feast, and sometimes appeared in the doorway, crunching an apple and watching with open enjoyment as Cass and the others stumbled over one another's feet. Their dance moves were as awkward as their combat was well-oiled, and more than one of them would inevitably end the evening swearing or sitting out the practice at the side of the hall with a bruised elbow or a swollen ankle.

Lily was in her element, spinning gaily from Susan to Joan, accidentally elbowing Elizabeth in the eye as she passed, loud yelps following her wherever she went as she inevitably trod on her partner's toes in her excitement. Angharad was a passionate teacher, moving with a mesmerizing grace, and, by the second week of lessons, even Cass was beginning to feel more confident in the steps.

One, two, three, Lily mouthed silently at Cass as they faced each other across the hall, stepping forward then turning and bending a knee as they walked back to their original positions.

'You couldn't call us graceful, exactly, could you?' Lily grimaced as they sat together, taking a break with a bowl of warm roasted nuts between them.

'Not unless you were comparing us to Rowan,' Cass replied under her breath, giggling as Rowan started the round with the wrong foot for the third or fourth time, sending all the other dancers in the circle toppling in the wrong direction. 'In which case we'd be elegance personified.'

Rowan, overhearing, threw a plum at Lily, and the session descended into chaos as the squires began to play-fight and tease each other.

But later, when the wine had been flowing for a little time, when Angharad crossed the room and sank into a deep bow before Vivian, extending an arm draped in dark amber silk and taking Vivian's hand in her own, a hush fell over the hall. They moved as if they were part of the music, as if they could feel each other's thoughts, fluid and emotional. Eyes closed, bodies bending and swaying together like trees in the wind. And like any other court their knights and the other members of the fellowship watched them with reverence and pride.

Then they all came together again, hands joined, voices raised, the warm glow of the firelight shining out brighter than the dark and the rain could press in. The rainbow hues of their silk dresses created a dazzling display as they danced, noisy and defiant, the scene in the hall unlike anything Cass had ever seen before. As the music grew louder and the dancing faster, the stamping of feet and the clapping of hands crescendoed into a beautiful frenzy, and Cass and Lily collapsed together, cheeks flushed, eyes alight, laughing so hard they clutched at their stomachs.

Nobody heard the knocking, or noticed that the great, solid oak doors had swung quietly open. No sentries had run from the gate to warn of his coming, for when the evening grew late, they had all gathered to the dancing and the warmth of the fire.

So the knight stood in the doorway, unobserved for a moment, taking in the extraordinary scene. He wore a mail shirt beneath his tunic, and an elegant, gold sheathed sword hung at his belt. Under his right arm he carried a helmet topped with an eagle feather, and his tightly curled red hair and beard dripped with rainwater. He was stocky, his face square and ruddy, his eyes small and close-set, his stance wide. And the expression on his face turned from amazement to confusion to guarded courtesy as he watched the women in the hall become aware of his presence and scramble to collect themselves.

'Welcome, sir,' Angharad cried, moving towards him, her green eyes flashing, her cheeks flushed. She swept into a deep curtsey, taking hold of the situation as the squires around her scurried about in confusion.

'You must excuse our merriment,' Angharad laughed lightly, extending her arm to the hall. 'My maidens make their own entertainment these long, cold evenings, as the dark draws in, for our menfolk are away, as you see.'

'It is a welcome sight, for I have seen no other soul in three days,' the stranger answered courteously, taking the fingertips Angharad extended to him and touching them briefly with his lips.

'You ride alone, Sir . . . ?' Angharad's voice was polite, yet Cass could hear the note of wariness beneath it, knew she was calculating, probing for information, thinking of their safety, always.

'Sir Beolin,' he supplied, with a courteous inclination of his head. 'I ride from Ceredigion, with correspondence from King Ceredig for Sir Mordaunt and other lords and lesser kings of Northumbria and Mercia.' He held up a batch of parchment envelopes, each sealed with red wax, stamped with the insignia 'CR'. The seal matched a heavy gold ring that glinted on his swollen, ruddy finger.

Angharad eyed the envelopes curiously and looked up at Beolin from under her eyelashes.

'Your correspondence must be of great urgency, I am sure,' she murmured.

'We seek their help in repelling the war boats of the sea wolves that threaten our coastline. Just as the men of the Teifi Valley and beyond have helped them when the Picts harried their borders, now we ask them to come to our aid in return.'

Angharad, who Cass could tell was carefully taking in this information, gave a girlish smile. 'Of course, I know nothing of such matters, Sir Beolin, but you are warmly welcome here. Please let us offer you our simple hospitality, a seat by the fire and a plate of food, and we will prepare a bed for the night. I will send for someone to stable your horse.'

He nodded, but all the while Angharad was speaking, Cass could see his little piggy eyes sweeping the hall, evaluating and probing.

He stalked over to the bench Angharad indicated and sat heavily, letting his helmet fall onto the table beside him with a clatter.

'It is strange,' he murmured, as he took the glass of mead she offered him without thanks and gulped at it, 'to see such a gathering, and so few male attendants here.'

'They travel with my lord,' Angharad replied calmly, as if there were no significance to the question, 'though those left behind, of course, have retired already, heavy as their duties are.' She passed Sir Beolin a plate of roasted chicken and he took a piece, grease smearing his fingers and beard as he tore into it hungrily.

179

'My maidens and I allowed ourselves this evening of frivolity, so rare is it for us to be together without any other company. And of course it is a pleasant diversion from the absence of my lord and his men,' she lowered her eyes, with a little sigh.

'Of course,' Sir Beolin said with an oily belch. 'Still, it is strange your seneschal has not been roused by a gatekeeper, is it not? Should you wake him, so that I may speak with him about the business I have with his liege?'

At that moment, Rowan, who Cass had not seen quietly slip out of the hall at Beolin's arrival, stepped in from the direction of Angharad's chambers, her smart tunic and hose buckled with shining precision, short hair neatly swept back beneath a squire's cap.

'If I may, my lady,' she said gruffly, and whispered briefly with Angharad.

'My page informs me that the seneschal has taken to bed with an attack of gout,' she said presently. 'He sends his regrets and hopes to be well enough to break fast with you in the morning.' She nodded at Rowan, who quickly disappeared.

'That is well,' Beolin answered after a pause, but Cass could see that his frown had deepened, Rowan's intervention not having fully allayed his suspicions. 'Still, it does seem rather . . . irregular.' His eyes slowly raked Angharad's body, taking in her translucent skin and flushed cheeks, the long, dark red curtain of hair that fell round her shoulders, lingering on the laced bodice of her dress. 'Strange for a group of women to be left with so little escort, or—' he paused, leering, little pieces of chicken skin quivering between his top front teeth – 'defence.' And the threat in the word was naked, even before he smiled and added, 'It would be of grave concern, it strikes me, for others nearby to become aware of the vulnerability of your situation, would it not?'

The room was very quiet now, the musicians long since having put down their instruments. A log sighed and subsided into the fire with a hiss and a shower of sparks. The squires were frozen, their eyes on Angharad. But Vivian jerked her hand beneath the table, towards the sword Cass knew was hidden there, her face tight with rage. And Angharad met her gaze and gave the slightest, imperceptible shake of her head, as she closed her eyes very briefly and then covered Sir Beolin's hand with her own.

'Perhaps,' she murmured, 'you will allow me to show you to your bedchamber personally.' They rose together and as he followed her, hungrily, wiping the grease from his fingers on his hose, he gave a great laugh, mumbling something about hospitality and understanding. And Angharad's fingers brushed Vivian's shoulder for the briefest moment as she swept past her, her other hand firmly clenched in Beolin's sweaty paw, and exited the hall.

Chapter 19

When Cass awoke before dawn the next morning she felt sick for a moment without knowing why. Then she remembered. The music in the hall had stopped and the light had seemed to drain out of the room, leaving all the colour and brightness that had so recently enriched it somehow lost and forgotten. The knights and squires had drifted off to bed, feeling helpless and lacklustre. The wild abandon with which they had danced seemed like a flimsy illusion. A pretence of being in control, nothing more. Nothing any of them could do to help Angharad, to help Vivian, without endangering the whole fellowship.

Cass was glad to be assigned to check the snares and traps

for small game that morning, glad of the excuse to leave the manor behind and stride away the walls that suddenly seemed oppressive and looming. Glad to feel her heart begin to pump and her lungs fill with the chill autumn air as her feet crunched across the frost-laced leaves. The sun's first rays were just beginning to penetrate the mist that hung heavy over the manor walls and she felt them on her forehead like a salve.

She hadn't meant to eavesdrop, not seeing Angharad and Vivian until she was almost upon them, and as she moved forward to greet them, their raised voices and the expressions on their faces killed the words in her throat.

'—didn't have to put yourself through that. Put me through that. There were other ways.'

'There were not. And there was no time. I will not apologize, Vivian, for doing whatever I had to do to protect my people. He will cause us no trouble now.'

'And if he comes again, and expects the same *hospitality*?' Vivian spat the words, cold with anger.

'Then we must bear it, my love, as we have borne so much more these past four years.' Angharad's voice was fraught with raw emotion. She caught up Vivian's reluctant hand and pressed it to her cheek. 'And with your love I could bear it a hundred times over. Because in my mind I could escape to you. As I have done so many times over.'

183

'I could have dispatched him. I could have run my sword through him as he lay in your bed. I have done it before.'

'Aye. And left us in enough danger.'

'Would you have had me take another course? Sit back and watch for years more while your husband abused and despised you, humiliated you and robbed you of every form of sovereignty over your own body? Would you have had me play the dutiful lady-in-waiting for years longer, and block my ears in the antechamber?'

'No. Of course not.' Fingers pressed to lips. A brief kiss. 'But the circumstances were not the same. Beolin was better neutralized than removed. This way he leaves – satisfied – and will not endanger us. His lust will attract less attention than his disappearance. He posed no immediate risk.'

Vivian's response was sharp. 'Then our notion of risk is very different.'

'No, sweetheart. It was a high price to pay. But one I paid willingly and would again for the sake of our lives here, together. All of our lives. We can no longer afford to risk drawing attention to ourselves. Eboracum was too close to disaster for comfort. We must get through Mordaunt's feast without misadventure. This is a time to be cautious.'

'I will not break fast with him,' Vivian answered at length, and her voice was ragged. 'I will be out riding Bessie.' And she turned away from Angharad and made towards the stables without looking back. Angharad sighed deeply and returned to the manor.

Cass stumbled unseeing through the woods, her heart in her throat. Did anybody else know? Sigrid? Rowan? Lily had told her Angharad's husband was dead, but not the manner in which he had died. But she had said it had happened while he was away on a trading expedition. Had she been lying to Cass, or was she, too, ignorant of the truth?

She fought to make sense of it all, to decide how she felt about it, but she could not. Clearly, Angharad's husband had been a threat to her, had abused her. And had Vivian, now Angharad's lover and second-in-command, not stood to gain greatly from her lord and master's death? Could it truly have been a selfless act of defence on behalf of her mistress, when the situation was really a lot more complicated than that?

Cass walked on, neither noticing nor caring that she had strayed from the path.

But then . . . how different was this really from Sigrid's cold-blooded murder of a man on the day they had met? Hadn't Cass justified the act to herself as punishment for the man's misdeeds?

Her thoughts roiled unpleasantly as she almost tripped over the first trap, a well-hidden snare at the foot of an ancient chestnut tree. The ground was littered with the shells of the tree's bounty, the brown kernels broken and soiled, half-eaten by squirrels, their shine faded to dull brown. The shells were curled and brown at the edges, the smooth creamy interior beginning to rot.

There was a dead fox in the trap, its leg mangled and bloody where it had struggled to free itself. Its eyes were dull and glazed, its mouth crusted with flies. Cass knelt down, choking back a sob as she drew a dagger from her belt and started to hack at the fox's leg. She should have been able to loosen the snare to release it, but the animal's thigh had become so swollen the loop of the trap was embedded deep in its flesh. She sawed horribly through sinew and bone, until there was a dull crack and the carcass was released. She gathered it into her arms, not caring that the blood stained her tunic. The fabric of her face mask was hot and damp. She was about to get to her feet when she felt the point of a sword at the back of her neck.

'Stand up slowly, and don't turn round.'

She did as she was told, chest tightening, heart racing. As her fingers closed round the handle of the dagger, her mind returned to Sigrid's practice room.

'Drop it.'

She hesitated. The pressure of the sword-tip increased uncomfortably at the base of her skull. She dropped the dagger. It fell with a soft thud into the earth at her feet.

'And the animal.'

She let the fox carcass slip to the ground, her hands raised in cautious surrender.

'What are you doing here?' the voice asked.

And perhaps it was the sense of frustration and betrayal after what she had witnessed that morning, perhaps there was a part of her that could not be so easily overruled by yet another dangerous man, but without thinking, she snapped, 'What does it look like?'

A beat. A tone of mild surprise. Amusement, even?

'It looks like you are stealing our game.'

This was not what she had expected.

'Yours?'

'My master, Sir Mordaunt, owns these lands. You are poaching. It is illegal.'

She almost laughed in relief. She remembered to keep her voice low. Her hands steady.

'It is a misunderstanding. I have much on my mind and have strayed off course. I meant to check my own traps, and have come across one of yours by mistake. I apologize for the misunderstanding and will take my leave.'

She waited. Silence. Slowly, slowly, she began to turn on the spot. The pressure of the sword receded.

A young man, perhaps twenty or less. Light brown hair, swept back from a square forehead. A stubble-lined jaw. Full lips, twitching. Thick eyelashes. Sword still pointed at her chest. He regarded her evenly.

'You are in a hurry to take your leave, young man? You will not stop to introduce yourself?'

Cass was keenly aware of his scent; sweat mixed with something sweet – hay, perhaps. She had never been alone with a strange man in such proximity before. She noticed the tension along his jawline, the way his grip made the muscles of his forearm stand out.

'My name is of little consequence.'

'Yet still I would like to know it.' His eyes met hers, searching, curious, and she held herself quite still, willing every particle in her body not to betray her.

'Unlike the fox,' she said lightly, forcing her voice to remain level, 'it is not yours to command.'

He chuckled, crinkling lines appearing at the edges of his light hazel eyes. 'That is true, youth.'

She waited, perfectly still, their gazes still locked.

'Then perhaps you will allow me to win it?' And he brought his sword to his side, taking up a sparring stance.

Cass's mind whirred. To turn and run would invite suspicion, capture, even. To refuse was to risk angering him, escalating a friendly sparring match into a real duel. To show weakness or fear was to risk exposure.

She drew her sword. For a moment, he caressed its tip with his own. Then he lunged, quick and direct. She remembered her training. Don't try to block, dodge instead. Faster than him. Lighter. Quicker. Not stronger. Don't engage. Don't try to take the full force of a steel sword on one half-made of tin. Frustrate and tire them out instead. She feinted left, then darted right, leaving him wrong-footed. She ducked and jumped, making swift little jabs and strokes of her sword, its tip making contact with his thigh, his ribs.

He smiled and those crinkles appeared again at the corners of his eyes, reassessing. Another bout, the two evenly matched, their swords rarely meeting. A clash of the tips, the briefest stroke of her blade before she stepped neatly to the side, allowing his sword to slide harmlessly off the end of hers. She turned, misjudged it, found herself pressed into his body, her back against the firm ridges of his torso, his breath suddenly on her cheek. They both froze, the moment stretching out between them.

Then: 'No!' she burst out, and she brought her heel down, hard on his foot and streaked away as he jerked backwards in surprise, leaving him half laughing, half cursing.

'None too courteous a technique,' he called after her, as she darted into the trees and made for the thickest cover. As Cass ran, she heard his laughing voice fading with distance. 'Your name will have to wait, then. Until our next meeting.' And her heartbeat did not slow, even when she reached the safety of the path.

Chapter 20

In the coldest part of winter, Angharad and her household kept a tradition of riding to the nearest villages with gifts and food. She travelled with neither disguise nor weapons, and invited Cass and Lily to join her.

Pebble's breath formed great steaming clouds as they made their way down overgrown lanes where thrushes feasted on blackthorn berries and crows called to each other across stripped, frost-clad branches.

Cass felt strangely exposed in her silk dress and thick wool cloak, and she realized with a smile that women's clothes now felt almost as unfamiliar as her squire's outfits had at first. She rode side-saddle, frowning in concentration as she gripped the pommel tightly, pressing her knees together uncomfortably. It was ironic, she thought, that this technique, supposedly much more ladylike and creating less unseemly exertion than riding astride the animal, in fact required much greater skill and strength.

Trotting beside her, Lily peeked into her horse's saddlebag with glee, counting the food packets and bundles of warm clothing.

'This is my favourite time of year,' she confided, her heart-shaped face glowing with excitement above the fur-trimmed collar of her cloak.

Ahead of them, Angharad's back was straight and proud, her slender form elegantly poised in Star's saddle. But Cass eyed her uneasily, the picture of graceful charity with her red hair cascading round her shoulders and her saddlebags packed with gifts and sustenance for the villagers. Here she was playing Lady Bountiful, yet she was complicit in the murder of her husband. She had covered it up, brazenly entered into a relationship with his murderer. The word echoed uncomfortably in Cass's mind. Less than a year ago, the idea that she would ever use it of someone she knew would have seemed absurd. And now here she was, thrown into this world where everything was different, heightened, and moral boundaries seemed so much more complicated than she ever could have imagined. Murder was different, somehow, in this world where life was so much more disposable, where bandits and ruffians and sea wolves were like villains in stories, justifiably vanquished by the heroes. But she wasn't used to those heroes being heroines. Nor women she actually knew. Still less those she was actively choosing to follow and learn from. What did that make her?

The villages were nothing like Cass had imagined. She had always thought of her own upbringing as simple and unvarnished, but the sturdy, spacious farmhouse and land surrounding it were luxurious compared to the miserable little clusters of wattle-and-daub buildings they approached, straw roof huddled together, some of them rotten and leaking into the dingy dwellings beneath.

As they entered the village, the horses' hooves squelched in streets turned boggy by heavy rain. Children ran out into the mud to greet them, exclaiming at the sight of the horses. A little boy of about two with an unruly cowlick sticking up at the front of his sandy blonde hair reached out towards Cass, babbling nonsense words. She carefully reined in Pebble so that the child's mother could lift him up to pat the horse on the nose, giggling in delight as Pebble flared her nostrils. Cass patted the cob's neck reassuringly and smiled at the mother, a girl of about her own age with flaxen plaits coiled round her head, simply clad in a cotton dress the colour of honey and a kitchen apron, a tattered grey shawl around her shoulders.

Cass pulled a wrapped package of oats, vegetables and flour from her pannier, offering them shyly to the young woman.

'Thank you,' she said, dropping a clumsy curtsey. The boy was still clinging to her neck as she struggled to manage both child and food parcel. 'We don't like to accept charity, but I don't know how else we will survive the winter.' She gestured to the common plot of ground at the centre of the ring of houses, where a few stunted pumpkins straggled across the mud and some feeble patches of beetroots looked almost ready for harvesting. One side of the patch was trampled into muddy turmoil, with bruised and discarded vegetables strewn on top of the soil, their leaves withering. Next to the plot lay the broken remains of a fenced enclosure, the wooden planks now twisted and splintered on the ground. The metal door of a rudimentary pigpen swung in the breeze.

A short man with a sun-browned face put a comforting hand on the woman's arm. 'We could not pay the rent Sir Mordaunt demanded,' he told Cass quietly. 'His men said this would be the only warning.'

'But how do they expect us to eat without the pigs?' a woman broke in, tears in her eyes. 'They did not take them for the meat, but in spite. Destroyed the enclosure and slapped them on the rump so that they ran off into the forest.' Her voice cracked softly.

The little boy tugged his hand free of his mother's grasp and ran to play in the mud, thrusting his hands joyfully into the sludge with a loud squelching sound.

Lily shook angry tears from her eyes. 'It is not just,' she railed furiously, turning to Angharad as if to demand she right this wrong immediately.

'Why don't others help?' Cass asked Lily, her heart racing with anger at the unfairness of it. 'Why don't people rise up against them?'

'They tried to, at first,' Lily choked out. 'But after Mordaunt slew two of the neighbouring landowners for trying to step in, claimed their lands and left their wives and children penniless and homeless, nobody else dared to try.'

Angharad shook her head sadly. 'We will bring you what we can,' she said, removing her own cloak and wrapping it round the shoulders of an elderly man who had hobbled out of his hut on bare feet and stood shivering outside his front door. 'But we dare not cross Sir Mordaunt.'

'What kind of shameful, cowardly, inadequate . . .' Lily muttered passionately under her breath as they rode on towards the next village.

'Anything else you'd like to add, Lily?' Angharad asked, her lips twitching with amusement, as she rode up swiftly behind the girls.

'I just mean . . . that is . . .' Lily flushed but stuck her chin out stubbornly. 'What do we stand for, if we will let this lie?' she asked her mistress defiantly.

'Who said anything about letting it lie?' Angharad asked smoothly. 'You must learn to let your cooler head prevail, my firebrand, or your hot head will get you into more trouble than your sword can get you out of. Valour is not just leaping into the fray without thinking. There is courage, and wisdom too, in waiting to act at the optimal moment.' And she trotted on along the path, leaving Lily and Cass to exchange mystified glances as they followed in her wake.

'Bit rich for someone with such a quick temper, isn't it?' Lily grumbled. 'Last Eastertide Leah beat her at dice and she cast the things into the fire and overturned a bench!'

Ahead of them, Angharad was studying the path closely, scanning from side to side.

'What is she doing?' Lily asked curiously.

'I think she is tracking them,' Cass murmured, and looking at the muddy path she could see fresh hoofprints suggesting a group on horseback had recently passed by.

Abruptly, Angharad veered off the path and into the undergrowth, leaving Cass and Lily to follow. They soon came across a group of Sir Mordaunt's knights, recognizable by their black armour and the silver antler symbol, slumped in a clearing, their horses hobbled nearby. They were sharing a loaf of bread and a slab of cured meat. As the women approached, the one who seemed most senior, by virtue of the black feather in the helmet that lay beside him, hacked a great chunk off and speared it on the point of a richly jewelled dagger.

'Good day,' Angharad murmured politely, her eyes lowered, as she rode into view.

The man chewed noisily, wiping his dagger on his sleeve and replacing it in his belt. He belched.

'You are far from home, my lady.'

'An invigorating ride with some of my maidens.' She smiled. 'They are over-young to be cooped up in the manor all winter, and their young bodies require exercise and fresh air.'

The man grunted and Cass became uncomfortably aware that two of his companions were smirking and talking quietly behind their hands, their eyes baldly assessing her and Lily, travelling blatantly up and down their bodies. It was only in the shock of the discomfort that it occurred to her how long it had been since she had felt like that slab of meat thrown on the forest floor to be shared out and hacked off as a group of men saw fit.

Suddenly she felt the freedom she had enjoyed from such discomfort in the past months, each time she had ventured out in her boy's clothing or her armour. Plunged back into the heat of unabashed male scrutiny, she felt exposed and vulnerable, as if her clothes had been peeled away. She remembered the feeling of eyes on her as she walked into the village with her family, as she stood at their stall on market day, as she walked past the boys who helped in the fields at harvest time. The effect of the men's gaze, and their expressions, was abrasive, as if her skin were being blasted with sand the way Iona used a grit wheel to hone the edges of her blades in the forge.

At home, she would have felt humiliated; shamed by their leering. Mary would have grasped her arm and pulled her quickly away, chided her for catching their eye or somehow not exuding sufficient chastity to dissuade them. Standing here, in her new body, she felt nothing but anger and superiority. Who were these pigs to make her feel small? Cowardly thieves who had stolen from villagers who owned so little. She felt the heat rise into a burning point on each cheek and Lily laid a warning hand on her arm.

'My lords,' Angharad began respectfully, 'we have just witnessed a scene that disturbed us deeply.' She drew a square of silk from her bodice and dabbed her eyes delicately. 'A poor couple unable to feed their family, their hogs having been most ungently turned loose and their vegetable garden destroyed.' She paused, innocently. 'You have not come across the creatures who would have stooped so low?' And she allowed her gaze to rest, just for a moment, on the horses' mud-drenched fetlocks and the men's dirty, scratched hands.

Cass felt a sudden, overwhelming urge to laugh out loud, to clap and cheer. In spite of everything, she still couldn't help but admire Angharad's brazen courage in confronting these men. Could she really blame her for being glad to be rid of her lord, if he had been like these brutes, or worse?

'You would do well to ride closer to home, lady,' one of the men sneered, getting to his feet and drawing himself up to his full height, the silver emblem on his chest flashing slightly. He pulled his sword from its sheath and fingered it with studied nonchalance. 'It would be so terribly sad if any accident were to befall you.' He took a step closer to Lily and allowed the blade to rest on her knee. 'Or one of your gentle maidens.'

Angharad's lips were drawn into a thin line. 'Of course,' she replied tightly, turning her horse. 'How silly of me to attempt to interfere. Thank you, sir, for your advice.' And Lily and Cass turned reluctantly and followed her out of the clearing.

No sooner had they reached the path than Angharad swung her leg astride her horse and kicked her into a canter, hitching her skirts up round her waist so that her thighs clung to Star's sides. Cass and Lily exchanged exhilarated glances as they did the same, eagerly shifting their riding positions.

It soon became clear that Angharad had no intention of letting the matter rest. She did not ride onwards towards the other villages they had intended to visit that day, but retraced their journey to the manor, riding as if wolves were on her tail. When they arrived, she called Blyth to water the horses and leaped from her saddle, turning to Cass and Lily.

'Put on your armour and helmets quickly, and meet me again here. You will need your swords.'

The girls rushed to change, fingers trembling with excitement as they fastened each other's buckles and laces.

When they returned to the clearing, dusk was beginning to fall and the knights were kicking dirt over the embers of their fire and saddling their horses. This time, Angharad wasted no time on courteous greetings. She rode past the first knight, unsheathing her sword and giving him a great smack on the arse with the flat of it as he bent to shoulder his pack, so that he toppled forward, his face plunging into the mud.

He leaped up with a great roar of surprised rage, scrambling for his helmet and sword and swinging himself onto his horse.

'You shall not take me unprepared again, discourteous knave,' he yelled, cantering after Angharad.

Left in the clearing, Cass and Lily, still on horseback, began to slowly circle the other two knights, who had been slower to rearm and now found themselves separated from their armour and their weapons.

'We want no trouble,' one of them stammered, looking up at the silent knights, with their visors lowered and swords drawn.

'We are returning from a charitable visit to a village of our lord's tenants,' the other explained, opening his pack to show it was nearly empty. 'We carry no valuable goods, for they had little to offer, and we did not force them to pay.'

'Ah, that's so touching, isn't it?' Lily asked Cass conversationally, her voice deliberately low and rough inside her helmet. 'I might shed a tear.'

As she continued to circle the men, she carelessly allowed her sword to dangle a little lower, so that it scratched the backs of the men's necks as she passed them. One winced and put up his hand to the injury.

'Why do you treat us so, when we have shown you no insult?' he demanded indignantly 'We are all knights, after all.' Lily remained silent, but Cass suspected she was smiling inside her helmet. Then these bullies were getting a taste of the fear caused by unprovoked intimidation. Good.

They heard the sound of galloping hooves and at that moment Angharad rode back to them, sword in hand, and Cass immediately saw that the tip of the blade was red. One of the men at her feet let out a cry.

'Come,' Angharad commanded, and Cass and Lily left the cowering men and followed her. They did not speak until they were well into the homeward ride.

'Is he . . .'

'He will live,' Angharad said grimly, raising her visor. 'But his arrogance will be reduced considerably,' she added, with a satisfied smile.

'What did you do?' Lily asked, her voice tinged with awe.

'I gave him a choice,' Angharad replied, as if it were the simplest thing in the world. 'When he begged for mercy, I told him he could decide: lose his life or swear fealty and submit to the nameless knights. Return by sundown tomorrow to repair the damage to the village and bring three of Mordaunt's fattest piglets to replace the missing livestock. Then return to his snivelling master but wait for the day when his oath would be called upon and he must do the bidding of the nameless knights. Or die on his knees in the mud like the hogs he stole.'

Lily gave an exhilarated whoop, and Angharad laughed and spurred her horse on.

'It is not how quickly you act,' she called over her shoulder, 'but how greatly you care that matters most.'

'I only wish,' Lily panted, as they cantered after Angharad, 'that we could have removed our helmets. I would like those men to know who schooled them today.'

Cass understood what she meant. But for her, it was enough that they had changed the course of events. That they had been able to help, that she, Cass, had played a small part in protecting those villagers. For the first time in her life, she had power – power great enough to bend the will of grown men. And her body quietly buzzed with the thrill of it, all the way back to the manor.

That night, she dreamed of the pool again – there in the forest, dressed only in her thin cotton nightgown, shivering as her bare toes touched the water's edge. But something was pulling her onwards: she knew she had to look at the surface again, had to know the meaning of what she had seen there before – the visions of herself, her sister, the stag.

But this time it was Vivian's face that rose from the depths towards her, at once familiar and unrecognizable, her eyes dancing with flames of rage and lust. She reached out towards Cass, the blade of a dagger flashing in her hand.

Her voice was a hiss and a shriek and a keening moan. 'Stupid girl. Did you think you could learn my secret and live?'

In the moment that the blade slid agonizingly between her ribs, Cass awoke, panting and sweating. She did not sleep again that night, but lay awake, staring unseeing into the dark.

Chapter 21

One winter morning, Cass was woken by a shriek and a thump as Lily flew across the threshold of her chamber and launched herself into Cass's bed at breakneck speed. 'Whasshappened?' Cass mumbled, still half asleep. The tip of her nose was freezing and she tried to snuggle back into the warmth of her fleece blanket. 'Too early,' she moaned, as Lily burrowed in beside her, placing her ice-cold feet between Cass's calves to warm them.

'Ask me what the news is,' Lily squeaked, positively trembling with excitement. Cass reluctantly opened her eyes and laughed at the sight of her friend's infectious smile. She propped herself up on one elbow, yawning and kicking Lily's cold feet away.

'What's the news, Lily?'

'The battle of the squires is happening in the spring!' Lily squealed with excitement and kicked her legs, sending the blanket flying.

'Careful!' Cass jumped out of bed to retrieve it, wincing as her bare feet hit the freezing stone floor. 'The what?'

'The what?' Lily looked shocked. 'You are NOT telling me you've never heard of the battle of the squires?'

'Lily, until I came here I barely knew what a knight was, let alone a squire!'

'Fine, fine.' Lily let out a dramatic sigh and rolled her eyes. 'I'll enlighten you. But let me tell you right now that the appropriate reaction to this news is screaming, jumping up and down and possibly weeping with excitement.'

'I'll bear that in mind,' Cass laughed, climbing back into bed.

'The battle of the squires is a legendary tournament that only takes place every three or four years. It's like a regular tournament, but squires are allowed to compete alongside newly made knights. They come from the length and breadth of Britain to have the opportunity to compete. And those who acquit themselves most courageously stand a chance of earning their knighthood on the battlefield.'

Cass sat up straight.

'Aha, now I have your attention.' Lily smirked.

'Is there jousting?'

'YES!' Lily cried. 'And Vivian is going to start teaching us today!'

'Why is the tournament only held every three or four years?' Cass asked curiously as she pulled on her tunic.

'Oh, just because of how many squires lose their lives,' Lily replied airily with a dismissive wave of her hand.

'What?'

'Well, they can't really afford to have it more regularly than that, or there would be a shortage of squires,' Lily said matter-of-factly. 'And squires are valuable: they take a lot of training – you should know. Are you ready? Come on!'

Cass hurriedly washed her face and dressed before they clattered down the stairs to the hall together, grabbing a warm roll each from the dining table on their way past as they raced out to the meadow.

Pebble, Lily's pony Elise and the other squires' mounts were ready and saddled, with Blyth waiting beside them. There was excited chatter amongst the squires. Even little Nell, a squat, earnest-faced girl who had barely begun her training, was on the field, excited about learning to joust.

Jousting, Cass quickly learned, was as much about horsemanship as weaponry. Before they could even approach the pile of brightly painted lances Vivian had assembled, they first had to master the art of riding one-handed, even at a gallop, which was no easy feat. But the long autumn days of training and the many rides out through the woods had served Cass and Pebble well – they had developed a strong bond of understanding. The plucky little horse now responded as much to Cass's movements and the tension in her legs as to her touch on the reins. Looping the leather straps between her thumb and little finger, her other hand resting on her thigh, she was soon racing round the meadow in exhilaration, Pebble's tail flowing, her hooves crunching the crisp, frost-veined blades of grass underfoot.

Galloping beside her, Lily gave a carefree grin and Cass, urging Pebble onwards to keep up with her friend, the cold air slicing into her in great, exhilarating lungfuls, thought for a moment that she had never been happier.

The lances were heavy: great, sturdy wooden poles the length of two horses, their ends sharpened to a point but capped safely for the purposes of practice.

'Hold it here,' Iona instructed, demonstrating the correct position of the hand behind the conical wrist guard, 'not in front, unless you want to lose your lance backwards and give away a finger or two into the bargain.'

'These lances are a little lighter than traditional ones,' Iona went on, weighing one up in her right hand, 'because I've hollowed out a section at the rear, but we can't lose too much weight without diminishing the force of the blow on contact. And you're already at a weight disadvantage compared to your opponents.'

Cass frowned. This had not occurred to her. Swordplay was one thing, when the women's superior agility and skill could offset male knights' greater physical strength, but how would they manage in a contest that basically amounted to using the greatest possible amount of power to knock your opponent off their horse? She chewed on her lip, and really thought for the first time about what it would mean to have a fully grown man with the speed of a horse beneath him crash deliberately into her torso with a massive pole.

Lily nudged her in the ribs. 'Don't look so glum. If we get seriously injured just think how long we'll have to laze in bed and talk without any chores,' she sang cheerily, her voice taking on a dreamy note. 'No shovelling horse dung for weeks if we break a bone . . .' Her smile widened. 'Maybe even months if we puncture a major organ!'

'Is that supposed to be encouraging?' Cass whispered, as she took the lance Iona offered her, which was painted a bright cornflower blue and striped with yellow. She baulked at the sheer weight of it.

'It'll get easier, I promise,' Iona told her, smiling. 'You'll couch the lance in your armpit, and the balance will help take some of the weight. A poorly balanced lance is much more difficult to carry, but luckily for you I made these myself, and the point of balance is—' she paused, and demonstrated, her palm flat beneath the lance as it balanced perfectly horizontal – 'perfect.'

'See how it feels,' Vivian encouraged, and the squires obediently heaved their lances into horizontal positions and set off round the meadow.

'Give each other space,' Iona yelled, 'otherwise—'

It was too late. Joan turned slightly in her saddle to check how the girl behind her was managing and her lance spun round like a windmill's sail and swept the other girl directly backwards off her horse.

Lily giggled and Cass struggled to keep a straight face.

Riding with the lance felt more natural than she had imagined. As she circled the meadow she tried to picture herself approaching a foe, and she jabbed the weapon forward instinctively as if to strike them.

'No, no, no,' Vivian shouted. 'Never uncouch the lance from your armpit, particularly not before the moment of impact.' She demonstrated, holding her arm out in front of her. 'If you extend your arm to strike, the full force of the blow will go straight through your wrist, shattering it if you're unlucky. But if the lance is tucked firmly beneath your arm,' (she demonstrated, clamping her elbow tightly against her ribs), 'then the force of the blow is directed down through your body and into your horse, who is much better able to withstand it than you.'

'Poor old Elise,' Lily murmured, giving her horse a little pat.

Blyth grinned. 'She won't feel it, not like you would.'

Cass was staring at Vivian, trying not to see that stabbing motion she had made with her wrist again and again in her mind's eye. Trying not to imagine her with a dagger in her hand and Angharad's bloodied husband at her feet. She shuddered and shook her head as if she could physically clear her mind, and Pebble snorted and stamped her feet.

Iona was wheeling a great metal contraption into the middle of the meadow. A tall pole, with another metal bar affixed horizontally across it, a large shield nailed onto one end of the cross-beam and a heavy metal ball hanging from the opposite end by a chain.

'What is *that*?' Cass asked apprehensively.

'A quintain,' Lily replied, her voice full of excitement. 'You have to ride and strike the broader side with your lance, whereupon the force will cause the whole thing to swing round, and if you make the mistake of stopping, or fail to ride on swiftly enough, the metal ball will swing round from behind and unhorse you.'

'That's ridiculous,' Cass deadpanned. 'There are no metal balls trying to knock you off your horse in a real joust. Who on earth looked at a competition in which people try to unseat one another with sharp sticks at top speed and thought, "I know what this needs, some added peril"?'

'It's to train you to follow through,' Vivian answered crisply. 'One of the most common mistakes made by inexperienced knights is to pull up their hands at the moment of impact, when the force knocks you backwards in the saddle, and you automatically jerk the reins as a result, unintentionally stopping your horse. But you must maintain your forward momentum. If you stop your horse just at the same moment somebody's lance lands squarely in the middle of your shield you are going to find yourself on your back in the mud faster than you can say knighthood.'

'So you need to remember,' Blyth said, 'lower the reins and move your hand forward just before your lance makes contact. That'll prevent you from accidentally stopping, and let your horse know you want to follow through fast.'

'Oh right, no problem,' Lily mumbled, 'just keep the incredibly heavy wooden pole horizontal, ride with only one hand, hit a small, *rapidly moving* target, make sure your own shield protects you from the tip of your opponent's lance, drop your reins and encourage your horse forward. Simple. No idea why we're training really, I could do this in my sleep.'

'Go on, girl,' Vivian commanded, ignoring Lily's mutters. 'You're first up. Tilt at the quintain.'

Lily took a deep breath and squared her shoulders, cantering down the meadow. She held her lance steady, her aim was true, and for a moment it looked like it would be a triumphant first attempt. But then the lance struck the target, with a great echoing clang, the force of the blow took Lily by surprise, throwing her backwards in the saddle, she completely forgot the warnings about the reins, jerking them up as she fought to steady herself, and Elise came to a sudden halt. The quintain spun round and the metal ball whipped through the air and caught Lily full in the small of her back, sweeping her forward over Elise's neck and onto the ground.

There was a long moment of silence, then Lily's peals of exuberant laughter rang out across the meadow. Elise snorted disapprovingly, unimpressed with this new activity, and Lily laughed even louder, clutching her ribs.

'This is the most. Fun. Ever. Can I go again?'

Chapter 22

Yuletide brought flurries of snow that lay deep around the manor walls. In the courtyard, Blyth and the squires brushed and shovelled it into great heaps, clearing pathways from the main gate to the entrance to the great hall, from the kitchens to the stables, where Cass and Lily brought Blyth frequent cups of hot spiced cider to ward off the cold. They covered the horses with thick sheepskins, forked piles of straw into their stalls and sat amongst their warm bodies, playing knucklebones, laughing, sipping the hot cider until their fingers and stomachs tingled with warmth and enjoying the respite from training that the snow had brought.

Though her sessions with Sigrid had decreased as her

form improved and jousting practice paused for the Yuletide celebrations, dance practice was the one form of training that continued apace. The Yuletide season would climax with Twelfth Night, the date of Sir Mordaunt's feast, and so all cosy celebrations at the manor were tempered with wariness about the upcoming gathering and punctuated with dancing at every opportunity.

'You will be expected to behave like the young ladies of any other estate,' Angharad reminded them, her forehead wrinkled with worry, after another circle dance had ended in chaos, with Rowan and Lily gallivanting out of formation and off round the room together, arm in arm, before collapsing in a laughing heap by the fire. 'Most young gentlewomen would be used to dancing and participating in such celebrations. We must not give Mordaunt any reason to suspect we are different.'

Vivian slid her hand into Angharad's. 'Let them have their merriment,' she said gently. 'They have worked hard. All will be well. Mordaunt has no reason to suspect us.'

But still the worry remained on Angharad's face, and it gnawed at Cass too. At least some of the girls had attended feasts and festivities before. But this was the first manor house she had ever set foot in, and the idea of comporting herself appropriately in an even grander setting, surrounded by lords and ladies she had never met, filled her with dread.

She would rather have met them a million times on the battlefield, where her confidence with lance and sword was increasing with every passing day.

But there was plenty to distract her. They staged a great snowball fight in the courtyard one crisp, sunny morning, knights and squires alike cavorting in the freezing air, pelting one another with close-packed handfuls of snow until they were all breathless and the tips of their ears turned bright red and ached with the cold. The squires gathered round the outer gates to hear mummers who emerged from the woods one evening carrying sticks with lanterns that swayed and flickered, briefly lighting the trees before the shadows swallowed them up again. Cass recognized the village woman with the braided hair and pressed some beeswax candles and a jar of honey into her hands as the mummers left, still singing their festive folk songs as the light gradually faded into the trees.

In the long, dark afternoons, when the sun set early and the hall was the only warm room in the manor, they would gather to mend dresses and make new traps, trading battle stories and bad jokes. Even Alys would join them, bringing sticky, clove-spiced toffee apples to share. And the squires spent a whole, high-spirited day preparing a play with much hilarity and innuendo in which each took on the guise of her mistress, using their armour to disguise themselves and exaggerating their mannerisms. They presented it in the hall that evening to raucous applause, Lily striding confidently about giving orders and commanding her knights in Angharad's brown breastplate, Cass imitating Sigrid's barking laugh from within her helmet, and Rowan even perfecting an uncanny imitation of Vivian's slight occasional limp when her ankle wound was troubling her. The knights enjoyed it immensely, with even the normally stoic Sigrid cracking a smile. Cass felt full of joy in those evenings, with no thoughts of the nightmares that still occasionally woke her, nor of the heavy secret about Sigrid that she was keeping from Angharad and the rest of the knights.

On the eve of Twelfth Night, Cass was huddled by the great fire with Lily, listening to Rowan singing a melancholy winter tune, and roasting chestnuts over the fire. She was thinking about Mary that night, and wondering what her first winter in her new home had been like. Had she celebrated the season alone with her new husband in a warm glow of newly married bliss? Had they gone back to their parents' house, to the festive chaos of the little ones tumbling around, shrieking and laughing and squabbling over spinning tops and trinkets? Were the little ones taller? Had they missed her? Was Mary's husband kind?

'Here,' Lily said, nudging her and passing her a small

wooden box with a 'C' carved roughly into the lid.

'It's – um . . .' Cass searched for a complimentary way to describe the slightly splintered offering.

'My whittling isn't exactly expert,' Lily laughed, wincing as she showed Cass several cuts on her fingers. 'But it is what's inside that matters.'

Cass opened the box and found a delicate silver chain with a horseshoe pendant inside.

'For luck,' Lily said. 'Or secure horseshoes. Which amounts to the same thing, really.' Cass enveloped her in an enormous hug, feeling a warmth that had nothing to do with the fire or the ale.

The following morning the manor was abuzz with the thrill of expectation as Cass asked Lily to fasten the new necklace round her neck. Their silk dresses complimented each other, Lily's a soft rose and Cass's fern green, and Lily paused for a moment and slipped her hand round Cass's waist as they stood in front of the glass.

'It's not that I miss being trussed up and put on display like a turkey,' she began, dimpling. 'But . . .'

'But we look pretty spectacular,' Cass laughed, giving her friend's waist a squeeze. Lily's hair hung in shining ringlets, crowned with a wreath of holly, the bright crimson berries contrasting with the creaminess of her complexion. Cass's own mane had been partially tamed thanks to her friend's efforts with olive oil, and most of it wrestled into a long, glossy plait. Lily had presented her with a simple garland of ivy, which she had pinned across the crown and then worked all through the plait, so that flashes of green burst out unexpectedly amongst the brown.

Riding side-saddle, it took them until mid-afternoon to reach Sir Mordaunt's lands. As they neared his manor, they traversed vast fields covered in a thick blanket of snow and Cass saw great orchards crowded with hundreds of fruit trees, their winter branches stripped bare. She was struck by the contrast between the richness of these lands and the barren poverty of the nearby villages.

'His father commandeered the richest land and displaced the serfs who lived there,' Rowan said bitterly, seeing Cass's face. 'Forced most of them out with promises of rich pastures elsewhere which never materialized and, so local whispers have it, killed the ones who refused to leave. So Mordaunt inherited a divided estate, with rich lands but desperately poor people. And instead of giving them access to the land that could get them back on their feet and create more bountiful rent, he refuses and grinds them further into poverty but expects the same levels of rent regardless.'

She gave her horse a particularly vicious kick in the ribs and it snorted crossly. 'Sorry,' she muttered, patting it on the neck as she continued to glower into the dark.

As she spoke, they emerged from a thick swathe of woodland onto the lower slopes of a hill. A golden glow appeared in the darkness, growing brighter and more splendid every moment. It was a great manor, almost as grand and fortified as a castle, sitting atop the slope with a commanding view of the countryside all around. The wooden edifice was surrounded by crenelated stone walls, with flaming torches blazing from the ramparts. It was encircled by a deep, algae-clogged moat where a sturdy drawbridge lay open to allow their passage. On either side of the drawbridge a wicked barricade of sharpened branches bristled like a gaping mouth of menacing teeth. The effect was daunting. As they crossed the drawbridge towards the main entrance, a vaulted stone archway embellished with carved roses and miniature statues, Cass thought it was the most dazzling sight she had ever seen.

Smartly attired stable hands with silver antlers on their tunics took their horses' reins and ushered them towards the inner courtyard, which was decorated with hundreds of fir trees, their branches draped with strings of fluffy popped corn and jewel-like cranberries, and lit with dozens of wax tapers. The effect was enchanting and Cass actually gasped out loud at the sight.

'Like walking into fairyland,' Lily breathed. 'If fairyland

were the domain of a heartless tyrant, obviously,' she added under her breath.

They joined a stream of people making their way through the miniature forest towards the doors to the hall, where light spilled out in a great flood. There were men in rich velvet and silk tunics, their edges hemmed with gold and silver thread, with shining buckles on their leather shoes, their beards carefully oiled. The women wore sweeping gowns, their waists encased in jewelled belts, their arms encircled with twisted golden rings. Sparkling stone pendants hung round their necks and many of them wore silver or gold circlets in their hair, some adorned with pearls and precious stones.

Halfway across the courtyard, the queue seemed to pause and cluster, with soft exclamations and gasps, as people passed something Cass and Lily could not yet see. When it was their turn to approach the place, they saw a curious sight: the pommel of a sword, inset with a dark crimson ruby, its blade buried up to the hilt in the stone floor, so that only the handle was visible, the red jewel burning like a flame as if lit from within. There was a little raised stone frame round the handle, as if to highlight or protect it, and Cass heard the people around them murmuring that it had been there since before the manor was built and that superstition had caused the masons to build the courtyard round it without disturbing it.

'It is rumoured to be the sword of the great King Constantine, lying where it fell from his hand as the lifeblood ran out of him when he was stabbed by a Pict,' whispered one woman excitedly.

'I heard his warriors tried to retrieve it, but none could remove it from where it fell,' another man nodded enthusiastically.

'Nonsense, it is a trinket placed there to ignite the admiration of idle gossip-addled fools,' declared a second man pompously, and he strode quickly forward and grasped the handle, straining with all his might. He frowned and put two hands to the job, using his foot for leverage as he heaved, but the handle did not move an inch, and the crowd murmured round him.

'Oh hogwash,' the man spluttered, his face colouring. 'I doubt there is a blade there at all – merely a hilt with most likely a false stone fastened into the floor with mortar to give the place an air of mystery and superiority.' And he tossed his cloak over his shoulder and stalked quickly onwards as if that were the last word on the matter.

Finally the girls approached the vaulted stone doorway, guarded on either side by malevolent-looking gargoyles that jeered down at them with hideous gaping mouths. Cass grasped Lily's hand. They took a deep breath and stepped across the threshold together.

Chapter 23

Walking through the doors was like entering a shimmering kaleidoscope of colour, scent and sound. Torches lined the walls and every surface was clotted with great clusters of beeswax tapers, so that the light dazzled the eyes. The room was enormous, bigger and grander than anything Cass had ever imagined. One half was left clear, the space surrounded by instruments and clearly intended to be used for dancing. But the other half of the hall steamed with the most delicious spread Cass had ever seen. While the Yuletide feasts at Angharad's manor had been plentiful, here the tables groaned under the weight of steaming meat pasties, sausages and black pudding, whole baked fish with herbs and wild garlic, stuffed fowl of every size studded with apricots and raisins, and great trays of roast meats steeped in their own rich juices. Cass could not imagine anyone needing the amount of food on display here.

At the end of the hall on a raised dais sat Sir Mordaunt in a splendid chair of finely wrought metal covered with rich furs. He wore an extravagant blood-red tunic that fell to his feet, embellished finely with brightly coloured silk thread, gathered at the waist with a black leather belt and silver buckle, and adorned with gold-striped sleeves.

Mordaunt drained his goblet, his eyes ranging constantly across the crowded hall, and Cass caught her breath and stepped back a little, her eyes lowered, as his gaze briefly rested upon her. As he turned to his left to reach for a joint of roasted venison, Cass saw that the back of his richly fur-lined cloak was embroidered with a gigantic, sparkling pair of silver antlers, their tips decorated with delicate silver whorls and curls.

Harpists and lute players lined the hall, playing gentle, lilting music that Cass knew would later give way to the quicker tempo and livelier notes of the dances they had been practising for so many weeks. Her fingers tightened involuntarily round Lily's at the thought.

'Courage,' Lily muttered. 'Let's get some food. No point dancing on an empty stomach.'

Cass bit into a soft, flaky pastry filled with succulent meat and fragrant juices, gently spiced and sweetened with stewed prunes. She closed her eyes, savouring the flavour, very much aware of the fact that she might never taste food like this again. With each bite there was a slight bitterness, as she saw in her mind's eye the reproachful, hungry stares of the little boy and the flaxen-haired village girl, standing with the others over their ruined crops.

The guilt prickled at her as they filled their stomachs with slices of rich smoked ham, crisp roast potatoes steeped in goose fat until their outsides were crunchy and succulent and their insides as fluffy as clouds, and fine, soft bread slathered with butter.

As they ate, Lily entertained Cass with what scant information she knew about the assembled crowds. 'Lady Alice over there is said to prefer to allow her hounds to sleep in her bedchamber and send her husband elsewhere,' she whispered, pointing discreetly to a woman in a sweeping midnight blue gown, 'and there he is, in the corner, already drunk. I think I'd choose the dogs as bedfellows too, wouldn't you?'

'That's Sir Albinor.' She nodded towards an elderly man with a long white beard, sitting quietly at a table with a handful of older knights in rather faded tunics and a lady next to him in a simple gown, her white hair swept back from a high forehead. 'His land neighbours Mordaunt's. He's a good man. He used to be able to challenge Mordaunt and stand up for some of the local people in disputes over land and property, but as he has grown older he is less and less able to exert any influence: he and his knights keep themselves to their own estates now. It is widely expected that Mordaunt will try to absorb Albinor's lands into his own territory upon Albinor's death,' Lily whispered, 'and his wife knows it.' Cass saw how the white-haired lady's fingers shook slightly as she buttered a roll, how her eyes flicked repeatedly up towards Mordaunt's dais and her mouth worked as if she were concealing the expression that it wanted to make.

'Look,' Lily whispered, jerking her head towards the corner of the hall. Cass craned her neck and saw Sir Beolin, his stocky body swathed in a rich cloak of dark green velvet fastened at the shoulder with a gold rosette brooch. His oily red curls were smoothed close to his head, his beard trimmed and waxed. He was standing in the corner of the hall, deep in conversation with two taller knights whose bodies bore the rangy, tightly muscled appearance of those who rarely saw a soft pillow at night or a period of rest from fighting.

Lily gripped Cass's hand. 'See their insignia?' Each knight's tunic bore three gold coins on an azure background, and their white cloaks featured a bright red dragon, clawing fiercely upwards as if in the moment of attack. 'Those are Arthur's knights, of the Round Table,' Lily hissed. 'The sea wolves must be gaining ground fast if they have come this far north to join Sir Beolin in recruiting support from Mordaunt and others.'

As they watched, Beolin moved closer to Angharad, Vivian and Sigrid, who stood clustered together beneath a blazing torch. Vivian and Angharad were at least wearing painted smiles, inclining their heads occasionally in greeting as others passed them. Sigrid stood stiff and straight as a lance, her midnight blue dress hanging still. Angharad wore a dress of deep violet silk, her flame-red hair tumbling from a gold circlet decorated with bronze leaves.

As they watched, Beolin paused behind her and moved his head a little to slowly breathe in the scent of her neck. Cass saw Angharad's shoulder blades stiffen, saw the anguish on Vivian's face before she quickly turned away. Then Beolin moved past, to greet another knight, and she saw Angharad's knuckles whiten as she briefly clasped Vivian's hand.

She turned to Lily, to see if her friend had noticed, but she was watching Mordaunt's knights who moved amongst the crowd with an air of pompous superiority. A crowd of them were gathered round the dais, laughing uproariously and picking their teeth with small jewelled daggers. Their seniority, Lily explained, was indicated by the decoration

LAURA BATES

of their tunics, with the most experienced knights wearing sleeves fully embroidered in gold and silver thread, while the novices wore just a single ring of silver edging. And as Cass watched, Mordaunt looked in her direction, frowned intensely and beckoned his squire to him.

'Look,' she hissed at Lily, 'Mordaunt's squire.' The boy with the straggling lip-caterpillar was listening intently as Mordaunt murmured in his ear.

'He'd better not be coming over here,' Lily seethed as he began to saunter towards them, 'or he'll get a second beating worse than Eboracum . . .'

'Shh,' Cass hissed out of the corner of her mouth. 'We are polite, sheltered young ladies, remember?' She felt goosebumps crawl up her neck as the boy made a beeline for them. Had he recognized her? Her fingers tingled as she remembered the sensation that had overcome her as she faced him on the edge of the tournament field: the exuberance of power seeming to flow through her and into her sword, the exhilaration at seeing the smile fade from his smug face. But now she felt nothing but hot fear. If he knew it was her, everything was over.

'I'll give him a reason to shelter his gonads,' Lily responded hotly, and Cass elbowed her in the ribs, just as Mordaunt's squire greeted them, oily and obsequious.

'Young lady,' he said, and it was not Cass he addressed,

but Lily. In fact, he barely glanced at Cass at all.

He gave a low bow, the effect slightly damaged by the fact that a piece of congealed egg dropped from the front of his tunic and landed next to Lily's shoe. 'My master has taken notice of you and would be pleased to speak with you,' he announced, smirking a little.

Lily started and the colour that had rushed to her cheeks as the squire approached faded a little.

'Oh. Well, I . . .' She looked to Cass for help but Cass, who until last week had never been alone with a man except for relatives, and was trying very hard to pretend that the meeting in the forest had never happened, had no idea what to say and could provide no help at all.

'I am honoured, of course,' Lily gabbled, 'that your master has taken the time to notice anyone amid such spectacular . . .' she gestured feebly at the hall, 'er, arrangements, but I must remain near my . . . sister,' she grabbed Cass's arm, 'who I have promised to keep company, and so must sadly – uh – decline this most courteous request.' Cass brought her hand to her mouth to hide her smile at Lily's attempt at courtly language.

He grinned nastily. 'My master doesn't request, sweetheart. He commands.' And without any further discussion he unceremoniously grasped Lily by the wrist and moved off towards the dais, dragging her with him.

Cass watched helplessly as Lily was pulled through the crowd, her panicked eyes throwing an imploring look back at her friend.

The squire pushed Lily into a seat next to Mordaunt and Cass saw how the lord leaned uncomfortably close as he began to speak to her. Lily was cringing away from him a little even as she seemed to be making an effort to smile and nod politely. Mordaunt's knights apparently saw nothing unusual in this: they nudged each other and laughed salaciously.

Cass cast her eyes round the room, looking for Sigrid or Angharad, but just at that moment a rotund girl in a white cotton gown plumped herself down next to Cass and introduced herself. 'I'm Rosemary.' She smiled. 'It's so exciting, isn't it? It's my first time, and I've been to Twelfth Night celebrations before, of course, but nothing like this, and—' and she rattled along in full flow for the next five minutes, giving Cass no opportunity to interrupt or politely excuse herself.

She was relieved when pages approached with dishes of custards, tarts adorned with bright berries and plates of nuts and sweetmeats dusted with icing. As they placed the dishes on the table, Cass seized her opportunity and slipped away, weaving through the mass of bodies, looking for Angharad. She moved faster and faster, worried that Lily might need help, frantically scanning the crowd. Suddenly a page bearing a heavy tray laden with candied fruit crossed her path and she stumbled and twisted, knocking into one of Mordaunt's black-clad knights, his tunic edged in a single line of silver. A novice knight. He steadied her, his hand on her back, hazel eyes narrowed in concern.

The young man from the forest. The one who had sparred for her name.

'I'm so sorry . . .'

'Are you all right?'

They both spoke at once, then Cass flushed and laughed.

'Forgive me, I was looking for my friend and didn't see . . .'

'Excuse me, I was not paying close enough attention . . .'

He broke off, his eyes fixed on hers, narrowing slightly in recognition.

'Have we met before, my lady?'

'Oh, I do not think so,' Cass gabbled, already starting to back away.

She was keenly aware of how close their bodies had been in the forest, how their eyes had locked together through the slits of their helmets. The hazel was flecked with little specks of gold. His eyes were instantly recognizable. Were hers? Would he recognize their unusual mixture of blue and green, or perhaps the way they were frozen wide in panic now, just as they had been that day in the forest? She hastily lowered her eyelashes.

'Please, forgive me for my clumsiness . . .' She trailed off, realizing she did not know his name.

'Sir Gamelin. And there is nothing to forgive.' He glanced down at her hands, noticing that her fingers plucked nervously at her silk gown. 'You are newly come to court?' he asked gently.

'Yes,' Cass answered, instinctively knowing that the closer she stayed to the truth, the more convincing her half-lies would be. But it was difficult to concentrate when those gold-flecked eyes were fixed so earnestly on hers, when her whole body seemed acutely aware of how close he was standing. 'My family is from the countryside,' she murmured, 'so all this is . . .' She gestured around her at the opulence and excess, her voice trailing off.

'To me, too,' Gamelin said kindly, his eyes crinkling as he smiled at her. 'I served my squirehood with my uncle in Wessex, and my duties were more composed of catching escaped hogs and bringing in the cows for our elderly neighbours than jousting or attending glittering balls.'

Cass laughed. 'Escaped hogs?'

'Oh yes,' he said seriously, but with a twinkle in his eye. 'Swineherd-in-chief, at your service.' And he gave her a mock salute. 'Once I slipped several times during the chase and came home so thoroughly coated in excrement that my aunt would not allow me in the house until I had been thoroughly dunked in the rainwater butt.'

She let out a snort.

'My mother would do the same to me when I turned up covered in mud after a day climbing trees in the orchard,' she laughed, then immediately wondered if she had said too much. 'That was before I came to Lady Angharad's household, of course,' she added quickly.

But Gamelin just smiled and nodded.

'It must have been a great adjustment', he said sympathetically, and Cass felt a lump form in her throat.

'When I came of age and they sent me here to be knighted by Sir Mordaunt, it was . . .' He hesitated, and his eyes flicked to the other knights with silver-edged tunics nearby. 'It was a very different life from what I imagined knighthood to be,' he finished quietly.

At that moment there came the great clang of a gong. It reverberated through the air, and the hall fell silent.

'Thank you all,' Mordaunt's voice rang out, though Cass could not see him through the thick crowd, 'for joining us on this most festive night.'

Suddenly a pair of arms grabbed Cass's waist from behind and she gasped, whirling round. It was Lily, grinning that dimpled grin of hers. Cass hugged her in relief. 'What happened?' she whispered, as Mordaunt continued to drone on. Out of the corner of her eye she saw Sir Gamelin moving away, and she felt her shoulders unclench in relief. Relief and the slightest hint of disappointment.

'Well, Mordaunt claimed to want to ask me about my favourite walking routes in the local countryside,' Lily grimaced, 'but his thigh was pressing against mine under the table and his breath . . . ugh!' She shuddered. 'I heard one of his knights laugh and say to his neighbour: "She is neither rich nor titled, but she might be good for a tumble in a hayloft."'

Cass put a protective arm round her friend's shoulders.

'So I told him I had my monthly courses and thought I needed to visit the privy lest I experience an unfortunate leak, and enjoyed watching all the blood drain from his face in horror before I skipped away,' she finished gleefully.

Cass didn't know whether to be delighted or horrified by this. 'Lily!'

'I know, I know. But, Cass, just think of the list of things I would choose over being "tumbled in a hayloft" by Sir Mordaunt: pulling my own brain out through my nose with a darning needle . . . mucking out the stables with my bare hands every day for three years . . . cleaning the privy with my tongue . . .'

Her last words were drowned out by the polite smattering of applause that indicated Mordaunt had finished speaking, and there was a great surge of bodies in the direction of the dance floor, while a cacophony of notes sounded as musicians tuned their instruments and prepared for the festivities to begin in earnest.

'This is it,' Lily muttered apprehensively, as they shuffled their way towards the open flagstone dance floor, carried along by the crowd. 'This is where we either blend in or fall on our arses and put everything Angharad has built at risk.' She grinned. 'Good luck.'

Chapter 24

Cass joined the circle with Lily on her left and a shy, thin man old enough to be her father smiling nervously on her right. The music began, louder and more complex than anything they had experienced at practice, but the rhythm was the same, and the steps simple enough. She frowned fiercely at her feet, focusing every bit of concentration on moving left and right at the correct time, stepping backwards and then forwards, turning to the left, weaving between the other dancers, coming to a stop and facing into the centre of the circle again.

The tempo increased, the dance livelier and lighter. People were beginning to smile and laugh, nodding across the circle as they danced, and Cass was smiling too, her feet falling into the patterns they had paced so many times over the past month in the manor hall. It was going to be all right. Across the circle, she could see Angharad, a careful smile on her lips, swaying and bending in perfect time to the music. She spotted the knight they had bested in the forest and noticed that Angharad was careful always to dance away from him, keeping her distance, her eyes respectfully lowered. Sigrid was nowhere to be seen, neither in the dancing circle nor amongst the spectators clustered round the edges of the hall, and Cass suspected she had removed herself before the dancing began, just as she had said she would.

Cass scanned the circle as dresses whirled and rustled around her, bright tunics flickering in and out, side to side. And then suddenly she saw him.

At first, Cass thought she might be mistaken. The softly curling hair was not unusual, nor the weakness of the chin. But then the dancers turned, and she saw the scar immediately, unmissable across his cheek. And beneath it, the silver antlers of Mordaunt's livery. Her breath caught in her chest and she stumbled a little, losing her place. Angharad's eyes snapped towards her, and she heard Lily give a slight gasp. With her blood rushing in her ears she forced herself to breathe, to step, to fall back in sync. The middle-aged man next to her gave her a reassuring little smile and she tried to smile back, as if it were nothing, as if she had merely missed a step. The music continued. The dance went on and the moment passed, mercifully without any further disruption.

But as soon as the dance ended and the musicians struck up gentle interlude music to give the guests time to refresh themselves, Cass backed politely away and escaped into the cool chill of the outer courtyard, her thoughts racing. Why had Sigrid been meeting with a member of Mordaunt's court? Why in secret, at night? Had she betrayed them? Were they plotting to take the manor? Was Sigrid a spy? Her feet paced as quickly as her mind was speeding until she found herself in a secluded corner, surrounded by the firs, the candles long since blown out, and only the light of the moon falling on the feathered branches.

'Lady.'

Cass jumped and spun round, her soft green dress catching on a branch and tearing a little.

A man stepped out of the shadows. A knight of Sir Mordaunt's court, his sword carefully polished and hanging at his side, his black hair oiled and slicked back. His chin was flanked with prominent jowls and his eyebrows were wild and bristly.

'I'm sorry,' Cass stammered, assuming she had transgressed some rule. 'I should not have presumed – I thought perhaps the courtyard was open to guests.'

'It is indeed, madam. And I was pleased to respond to your invitation.' He moved closer, breathing heavily, his voice thickening.

'My – sir, there has been some mistake.'

'You are a tease, lady.' His fingers began to trace the bare skin of her neck and collarbone. Cass froze, her skin crawling, frantically running through her options. To run or to fight would cause a commotion she could ill afford. 'I saw how frequently you looked in my direction. How you glanced back at me before exiting the hall.'

'You mistake me, sir, I assure you.' Her voice was high, her breath coming quickly. 'I had no other purpose but to cool myself.'

His hand closed round her shoulder, the tips of his fingers digging uncomfortably into her skin.

'Stand still, bitch. Do you think I do not see you for the goose girl you are beneath the silk and jewels? Do you think your voice does not betray you for the low-born country wench you are?'

Cass's whole body turned to ice. She jerked backwards, out of the man's grip, but came up against the rough, solid trunk of a fir tree. He grabbed her wrist in a vice-like grip, fingers white with pressure.

'Do you think you can come into my home and toy with me, wench?'

Cass struggled wildly, her free hand reaching towards the silver dagger she had hidden in her underwear.

'Sir Leogrand.' The voice was sharp, furious.

The grip on Cass's wrist loosened. The man released her, turning.

Another of Sir Mordaunt's knights stood behind them. He stepped forward, and the moonlight illuminated his face. Sir Gamelin.

'What is happening here?' He spoke with venom, eyeing the other knight with barely concealed disgust.

'This young lady became disorientated amongst the trees,' Sir Leogrand answered smoothly, not looking at Cass. 'I offered to help, naturally, and was just about to guide her back inside.'

'It did not look like you were helping her.' He turned towards Cass, his voice softening, and offered her his arm.

'May I escort you inside? The dancing is about to resume.'

Cass straightened her dress, her hands still shaking. She blinked tears out of her eyes. She needed to remain calm. She must not draw attention to herself, must not cause a scene, must not put Angharad and the others at risk. She took an unsteady breath and forced down the lump in her throat.

'Thank you,' she said simply, and slipped her hand through Sir Gamelin's arm. They walked away without a backwards glance at Sir Leogrand.

She could smell that scent, the hay and something rich and earthy. She concentrated on putting one foot in front of the other, feeling his concerned gaze on her.

'Are you sure you're all right?' he asked.

'Yes,' Cass whispered, still battling the tremor in her voice. 'Thank you.'

His hand was soft and reassuring on hers. With a gentle squeeze and a courteous bow, he left her at the doorway. She stood there, blinking in the light. It was as if time had not passed. The guests were smiling and picking at sweetmeats.

The music resumed, and she felt her feet numbly, dutifully, carrying her back in the direction of the circle. She let herself be swept round, forwards and backwards, like a piece of driftwood on the tide. Outwardly, she smiled and nodded her head and touched her fingertips to those of the other dancers and followed all the right steps. Inside, she felt scorched, as if she had come very close to a great heat and only narrowly avoided being engulfed by the flames. But they had burned her nonetheless. She felt ashamed, deeply ashamed, and angry at the same time.

Why had she let herself be fooled into believing that it was possible for somebody like her to assume a position of such power, such control as that of a knight? What did it matter if they dressed up and played pretend with their swords and their horses, if the moment she slipped back into a pretty dress a man could treat her as his plaything, shake her like a rag and toss her away? If the other knight had not intervened . . .

Her eyes swam with tears, the dancers swirling like a smudged rainbow, the candlelight distorted into bright beams.

And it was in that moment, dancing, disassociated, moving without knowing where she was going, that Cass chose the sisterhood. Chose Angharad and Vivian, no matter what they had done, no matter if there were blood on their hands. She understood what would make a woman act in the way they had. She could still feel his fingers gripping at her collarbone, smell the stench of his breath on her neck. And Angharad had endured so much worse. For so long. While Vivian, who loved her, had to watch. She tried to imagine what she would have done if it had been Lily there, against the rough bark of the tree, if she had been standing nearby, her sword at her belt. Could she honestly say she would have stood idly by, listening, and let her sword lie?

At last, the music ended, and Cass found that Lily's arm was round her waist, that they were leaving, and finally that Pebble was beneath her, warm and comforting and solid.

'Come on,' Lily said, looking at her with concern. 'Let's go home.'

Chapter 25

There was no opportunity to confront Sigrid about Sir Mordaunt's knight until the following evening. By the time they arrived home it was almost dawn, and Cass gratefully unclenched numb fingers to hand Pebble's reins to Blyth, who searched her face with a worried glance but asked no questions. She hobbled stiffly upstairs, her legs aching from the cold and the long ride, collapsed into bed and fell asleep without even undressing. When she woke in the morning, Sigrid had already ridden out.

So it was not until they gathered in the hall that night for the evening meal that she saw Sigrid, wearing the leather armour that seemed so much more comfortable to her than a silk dress, striding in from outside and skirting the edges of the hall as usual. She nodded to Angharad and the others and made quickly for the stairs to her chamber. But Cass pushed back her chair and crossed the floor, reaching the doorway first and blocking Sigrid's path.

'Good evening,' Sigrid said curtly. 'Please excuse me.'

Cass folded her arms. 'No.'

Sigrid looked at her in surprise, her sharply defined eyebrows narrowing. 'No? Is that any way for a squire to talk to their knight?'

'Yes,' Cass replied calmly. 'It is, when that knight is a traitor meeting secretly with a member of Sir Mordaunt's retinue.'

Sigrid's face contorted. She looked round the hall, checking that nobody had overheard, and grabbed Cass by the elbow, pulling her through the doorway and onto the stairs.

'You don't know what you are talking about,' she growled.

'Then tell me,' Cass pleaded. 'I have no wish to betray you. But I saw you in the woods, meeting with a man, and then saw him again at Sir Mordaunt's court. What was I supposed to think?'

They both stiffened as footsteps clattered down the stairs and waited awkwardly while a young squire darted past them and into the hall, giving them a curious look over her shoulder.

Sigrid's anger gave way to weariness. She sighed and

reached up to loosen the tight knot that confined her hair. 'Come with me,' she said, and led Cass up the staircase past torch brackets that sent shadows leaping round its spiral and into their own chambers.

'I am not a traitor,' Sigrid began, sinking heavily into a carved chair before the fire. 'I told you that I would have followed my twin to the ends of the earth. Well, I cannot follow Jonathan to where he is now,' she said with a miserable smile, spreading her hands as if it explained everything.

Cass looked instinctively down to the sword at Sigrid's waist, the simple silver pommel engraved with the letter 'J'.

'Yes.' She smiled bitterly. 'It was his. Until the day Mordaunt killed him in his sleep.'

Cass sank into another chair, aghast. For a minute the only sound was the soft hiss and crackle of the fire.

'He was a man of principle, my brother. He saw everything in black and white, with no grey areas, at least not where right and wrong were concerned. We were born and raised in the east, in the fenlands. Jonathan was apprenticed to a blacksmith, but he dreamed of becoming a knight and eventually persuaded a travelling knight named Sir Pyrland to take him on as a squire. He was sixteen. He travelled with Pyrland to the estate of his lord and became part of the household there. I did not see him for many years, until he sent word that he would take part in a great tournament, with the chance to prove himself and earn his knighthood.'

'The battle of the squires?'

Sigrid nodded. 'He was so excited. I met him the night before the tournament and it was like no time had passed. We spent the whole evening together, talking, eating, exchanging news about our lives the past four years. Our parents had both died, and I was the only family he had left to share that night with.' She sighed. 'I had never seen him so happy, so full of life. Everything he had dreamed of and worked for was within his reach.'

'What happened?'

'He distinguished himself.' She smiled proudly. 'He was knighted there on the field and remained a loyal member of his fellowship. He proved himself many times in battle, as his lord became part of King Uther's war host, driving back the Saxons at Verulamium.' Her face darkened. 'He never failed to send me word of his whereabouts, his well-being. And though I was left in the fens, alone, running our parents' smallholding, I lived through him. Learned with him. Considered tactics and manoeuvres and weaponry. I was beside him, always.

'Many years later, he sent me word that there was a tournament in Cair Grauth, just a few miles from our childhood home. He had returned from the wars and was full of boasts and merriment about his performance: how I must attend and see him among the knights he had always dreamed of, shining and victorious. How we would be a family again, at last.'

Sigrid was silent for so long that Cass wondered if she had thought better of disclosing any of this. It was clear from her expression that she was not used to speaking so personally or so openly, and that it was costing her a great deal.

'What happened?' Cass whispered eventually.

'There was a stupid quarrel. Mordaunt accused my brother of cheating in the tournament. My brother's horse had been killed in battle and the replacement he rode that day was young and inexperienced – the noise of the crowd startled it and it set off down the lists before the signal was given. Mordaunt made no complaint until after Jonathan unseated him. Jonathan tried to explain, offered to begin again, but Mordaunt was livid, his pride wounded. He lashed out and Jonathan answered angrily, smarting at the accusation of dishonesty. They were separated, but Mordaunt bore a grudge.

'That night, after we had been reunited, Jonathan was resting at his lodgings. When he fell asleep, I left to fetch supper for us both. When I returned, I saw Sir Mordaunt leaving. His exit was furtive and hurried and he did not notice me. I thought perhaps he had come to make amends, to reconcile, but . . .' She paused and closed her eyes for a moment. 'When

I entered, Jonathan was dead. Stabbed through the heart in his bed as he slept. The blood was . . .' her voice grew hoarse, 'everywhere, just everywhere.' She shook her head and sat with her face turned to the fire for a long time.

'It is hard to explain what it means, being a twin. I am one half of a whole. We were not siblings, not in the normal way of it. We knew each other's thoughts before they were spoken. We were each other's everything. Each other's home. We lived in a world of our own making, spoke a language only we knew. So half of me died that day. And all that is left of me is an open wound that will not heal.'

Sigrid stood and threw another log onto the fire. It sizzled and roared, sparks flying up the chimney.

'The only thing that has kept me alive since that day has been the promise I made to Jonathan that night. That I would find Mordaunt and avenge him. I returned to the tournament field that night, but Mordaunt had already ridden for home. Jonathan's young squire was distraught when I told him what had happened and vowed to join me in my quest for revenge. He was young, but could not be dissuaded.

'So we began training together, him teaching me the sword and I sharing all I had learned from Jonathan about strategy and tactics. We travelled north, towards Mordaunt's stronghold, and spent months camping in the forest, learning what we could about his estate and his household from local peasants and tavern gossip. He was too well protected, the manor too well fortified to risk an attack. But I met one of the young pages from Angharad's household in the market one day and she let slip a little: not much, but enough to rouse my suspicions. I began to learn all I could about Angharad and her fellowship. I realized that this was the opportunity I needed: a place to gather my strength, to form allegiances with other fighters, and to watch and wait for my opportunity to exact revenge.'

'Do they know? Angharad and Vivian and the others?'

'No. And nor must they, until the time is right.'

'But why? Surely they would support you?'

'Mordaunt is their nearest neighbour and therefore the greatest threat to their secrecy. They cannot afford to be directly complicit in a plot to kill him. But I will not act without their blessing. I will explain all to them, but not yet. I cannot risk my position.'

'And the young man in Mordaunt's court? The one you met in the woods?'

'My brother's squire, a little older and wiser now but still a rash young man. He joined Mordaunt's company as a means to get close to him, to provide me inside information that would be invaluable to me. But he is hot-blooded. I was meeting him that night to try and calm him, to urge him to wait until the moment was right to attack. Acting too soon could cost us everything. We must be prepared. We must be certain of success.'

Cass shook her head, bewildered, trying to take it all in. Her heart was torn between aching sympathy for Sigrid and anxiety about the risks to which her vengeance could expose the rest of the court. Should her greater loyalty be to her mistress or to Angharad, the woman who housed, fed and clothed her? Could she even believe any of what Sigrid had said? And yet even as the question occurred to her she knew in the pit of her stomach that it was all true. There was no fabricating such grief, least of all for a woman so unused to showing emotion of any kind.

'Can I trust you?' Sigrid's voice was humbler and more hesitant than Cass had ever heard it.

'Can I trust *you*?' she replied at length.

'Yes. I came here because it suited my purposes, I admit. But I have come to admire and care deeply about this place and the people in it. I will not betray them.'

Cass nodded, and they retraced their footsteps down the spiral staircase and back into the hall.

The meal was almost ended, and Cass slipped into a seat on a bench between Rowan and Lily, hungrily helping herself to a slice of cold meat pie and some boiled potatoes.

'You have interrupted an argument,' Lily said hotly, glaring at Rowan.

'It is not an argument,' Rowan responded coolly, draining her cup of wine. 'It is simply fact.'

'It is not!' Lily replied. 'They were not both cowards!'

'Well, they were neither of them heroes,' came the curt reply.

'Who?'

Lily looked embarrassed. 'We were discussing your . . . misadventure yesterday evening. In the courtyard.'

Cass shifted uncomfortably in her seat and shot Lily a hurt look. She had not thought, when she confided in her on the ride home last night, that she would have to ask Lily not to mention it to anybody else. She had simply assumed.

'I'm sorry.' Lily bit her lip, looking ashamed. 'It slipped out. But I was expressing my admiration for the valiant knight who came to your aid.'

Rowan gave a tiny snort and refilled her cup.

'He showed valour,' Lily insisted stubbornly. 'How can you possibly argue otherwise?'

'There is a low standard for "valour",' Rowan replied, 'if preventing an attack is the measure of it. Does he deserve great praise simply for being a better man than the other? Or shall we ask why he didn't act sooner, if he knew what a bastard the other knight was? I'd consider it valour if he kept him on such a short leash he was never alone with women in the first place, instead of swooping in to play the hero after some damage had already been done.'

Lily clicked her tongue in frustration but Rowan was in full flow.

'You would have rescued yourself had he not intervened,' she appealed to Cass, frustrated. 'Yet now he is named a hero, while you are a victim.' Cass winced. 'Not in my eyes,' Rowan added hurriedly, 'but the eyes of the world. Why should men achieve holiness through valour and action, and women only through passivity and surrender?'

She struck the table angrily with her fist. 'Why shouldn't we show our deeds to the world, and receive the glory we deserve? We should ride to tournaments with our heads uncovered, and damn the consequences. People would soon learn to fear us, as they have Mordaunt's men. Why shouldn't we do as we please equally? We have the skill.'

'Do you not think he showed valour, Cass?' Lily pressed, turning her back on Rowan.

Rowan shrugged, dipping the crust of her bread into the juices of a pigeon pie and tearing off a great hunk with her teeth.

'I—'

At that moment, the door of the hall crashed open, sending the light of the torches and candles skittering wildly up the walls. For a moment a great figure seemed to loom in the doorway, shadowed and distorted in the leaping light. A storm was starting outside, and the wind howled mournfully. As the light settled, the figure emerged: a woman, seated on a mare, swathed in a thick woollen travelling cloak. Her hair was bundled into a long, thick plait that hung halfway down her horse's flank and she wore a fine gold circlet that seemed to shine and twinkle in the firelight. A square-cut emerald was set into its centre. Fine eddies of snow whirled in round the horse's hooves, and the hall felt suddenly cold. Blyth stood behind the stranger, motioning with a helpless shrug towards Angharad as if to say, 'I tried to stop her.'

Then the stranger spoke.

'I have heard tell of this place,' she said hoarsely. Her face was lined with exhaustion. Her shoulders drooped and she looked as if she might slip from her horse at any moment. 'And have ridden days without pause to reach you.'

The woman faltered for a moment, looked as if she might say something else, and then fainted, her eyelids fluttering closed as she slid from the saddle and into the arms of a very startled Blyth.

And as she slipped sideways her cloak fell open. Lily gasped at the protruding belly that revealed she was with child.

'That,' remarked Rowan quietly, 'is valour.'

Chapter 26

The talk amongst the sisterhood for the next few days was all of the new arrival and her circumstances. It didn't help that the storm raged on for days and nights without abating, so that there was little distraction to be had outside, leaving rumour and hearsay to spread like flames amongst the occupants of the manor.

At breakfast one day, a whisper seemed to travel round the hall, faster and quieter than a ripple.

Elaine. Elaine.

'It cannot be,' Joan argued indignantly 'Elaine is dead. Her body washed ashore in Camelot – everybody knows it.'

'She died of her love for Sir Lancelot, they say,' young Nell chimed in eagerly. 'And he was so grieved at her passing that he paid for her rich burial with all honour and ceremony.'

'I heard she was the most beautiful corpse anyone had ever seen,' Elizabeth sighed.

Susan nodded earnestly. 'I heard they wept at the banks of the river for her.'

'But I heard she wore a circlet of gold with a square emerald,' the girl with freckles added in stubbornly. 'And her golden hair fell below her waist. And—'

'She had left instructions, knowing she was dying,' Joan interrupted, 'for her body to be laid in a barge draped in black samite and a letter placed in her hands telling of her love for Lancelot, and lilies all around her body, and the barge drifted down the river from Astolat, all the way to Camelot,' she finished, her face wistful.

There came a loud and distinctly unromantic snort.

'Women have died of stomach sickness, of fevers and bloody flux,' Sigrid called loudly, across the hall from the head table, her honeyed voice rough with scorn. 'They have died in childbirth and died of apoplexy and ague and grippe and starvation. But no woman has ever died of *love*.' And she barked her great, loud laugh.

Next to Sigrid, Angharad smiled politely.

'Perhaps we should afford our visitor the dignity of privacy, instead of speculating about her over our kippers.'

The freckle-faced girl looked suitably chastised and returned to her porridge, but another squire objected plaintively, 'But how can it be Elaine, when so many saw her body in Camelot? So many spoke of it that the tale has spread to all corners of the kingdom!'

'Did you see her there, girl?' Sigrid asked, grinning. 'Do you personally know anyone who did?'

'Well – no, but—'

'Let me tell you something about stories,' Vivian cut in quietly. 'Those who write them hold power. They can change the truth and shape the way the world sees them for ever, no matter what really happened. And once a story begins to spread there can be no stopping it. It becomes a living thing, with a journey all its own.'

'But, Vivian,' Sigrid protested in mock indignation, 'what possible motive might a knight of Arthur's court have to spread the story that a lady heavy with child had died pining for his unrequited love?'

Nobody heard the newcomer pad in on bare feet, or noticed her until she laboriously and deliberately lowered herself onto a bench and began to spoon honey onto a piece of cornbread.

'What motive indeed,' she said softly, not raising her eyes from her task. 'Except perhaps that a dead woman is less troublesome than one got with child and abandoned with no further ceremony. A woman dead for the love of a man makes him a romantic hero, not a lying wastrel.' Her voice was steely. 'And a dead woman's child claims no birthright, because he does not exist.' She placed one hand lightly on the top of her protruding stomach and lifted the bread to her lips with the other. Then she paused, the bread hovering in front of her mouth, and looked up at the squires staring at her open-mouthed over their breakfasts.

'BOO!'

They started, the freckled girl almost falling backwards out of her seat, and Elaine let out a peal of laughter that rang round the wooden rafters of the hall.

'Then again, perhaps I am a ghost.' She took a large bite of her bread. 'And maybe I haven't finished haunting yet.'

When the squires assembled in the meadow a few days later, after the storm had weakened and given way to milder days of thawing snow and watery winter sun, they were surprised to see Elaine already there, her swollen stomach swathed in a man's woollen tunic, measuring fifty paces from the target before she turned and drew back her bowstring.

When the arrow shot straight to the heart of the target, Angharad raised an eyebrow. 'Your father taught you?' she asked, and Elaine smiled and nodded. 'This is no reason to get out of practice.' She shrugged, caressing her stomach as she went to retrieve the arrow.

'You might share your expertise with our squires while you are here,' Angharad asked, and Elaine nodded, shooting her a look of gratitude.

As she bent over the target, Elaine winced, putting her hand to the small of her back. 'It's just backache,' she said dismissively, seeing concern on Angharad's face. 'To be expected at this stage, especially after so long a journey.'

'Why did you choose to ride to us now?' Angharad asked, her voice lowered, so that most of the squires, except for Cass, who was setting up her target nearby, would not hear.

'It had become unbearable at home,' Elaine replied quietly. 'Not just the rumours, but being treated like a ghost. My own voice was not loud enough to drown out the story someone else had created for me. But it was the shame also. It grew with the child. I needed to be somewhere safe, somewhere without judgement. Before my time came.'

'You are safe here,' Angharad said firmly. 'For as long as you choose.'

'Cass,' she called, and Cass jumped guiltily and tried to look as if she had not been eavesdropping. 'Go to Alys and ask for a remedy to soothe back pain.'

So Cass relinquished her bow and set off for Alys's hut. She found her sitting cross-legged outside next to her herb garden, her face turned to the sun's scant rays as she carefully skinned a lithe young rabbit carcass.

She wiped her bloody hands on her apron when Cass explained her request and made her way inside, indicating that Cass should follow. The little hut was bursting with ingredients and remedies as before: carefully arranged ceramic pots containing various salves and syrups, baskets of dried seed pods and mushrooms, and, new since Cass's last visit, a shelf lined with the delicate skulls of what looked like rodents or other small mammals of some kind.

'Will you have some tea?' Alys asked in her direct, easy way, lifting a kettle that had been hanging from a metal hook over the fire and taking down a pot filled with dried petals, leaves and fruit peel.

Cass took the steaming drink gratefully, cupping it in her chilled hands, inhaling the calming herbal scent. She closed her eyes.

'You are troubled?' Alys watched her, assessing, while she pulled down an earthenware jar and began to mix together various oils and herbs inside it.

Cass sighed. There was something about the feeling of separation from the manor here, something about the soothing smell of the tea, perhaps, that gave her clarity.

'Not troubled, exactly. More . . . uncertain.'

'Uncertain of what?'

Cass smiled. 'Of almost everything. Do I belong here?

Am I pursuing a life of purpose and honour? Or am I a deluded and ungrateful daughter who doesn't know her place and should return home?'

She brooded into her tea, watching a chamomile flower drifting gently across the surface.

'Is there a future for me here?'

She had chosen to trust Sigrid: she hadn't told anyone, not even Lily, about the knight's twin, her spy in Mordaunt's court and her true intentions in joining the sisterhood. But how long could she continue to live under Angharad's protection and enjoy the community of the sisterhood she had created, while her silence felt like betrayal? What if Sigrid's fury and grief over her brother's death put them all in danger? What if she did something rash and catastrophic and Cass were partly to blame because of her silence?

And yet none of these were the questions that really plagued her, or kept her awake late into the night. It was those returning dreams – the pond, the woman in the water, the stag. And the yellow eyes she had seen years before.

She shrugged, and took a sip of her tea. It was not as if she could ask Alys: *Am I special? Did the woman in the forest that day when I was a child see something in me, or was she just a desperate beggar trying to charm me? What is it that I feel inside myself when I take up my sword? What was the vision I saw in the pond? Was it all my imagination?*

What does it all mean?

Alys regarded her evenly. 'Often,' she said, gently grinding the herbs with a pestle, 'the most difficult questions we face are the ones that nobody else can answer for us. Either we have to find the answer for ourselves, or we already know the answer, and must find the courage to face it.'

Cass sighed heavily. She drained her tea and pushed the cup across the table.

'Thank you.'

Alys nodded, looking down at it, then froze, her eyes fixed on the muddle of herbs and leaves at the bottom of the cup.

'Is there something you have not told us about where you come from, Cass? About who you are? Your bloodline?' Her voice was urgent, worried, and there was a note of near awe in it.

Cass felt her face warm. 'No. Nothing!'

'But . . .' Alys paused, turning the cup carefully and looking up again at Cass, searching her face as if it might reveal some secret. It seemed as if she were struggling with herself, as if there were something she badly wanted to say. She bit her lip and stood up abruptly and pulled Cass into her arms, embracing her tightly. 'We will be beside you, Cass, wherever your path takes you. And I think perhaps you already know it will not be an ordinary journey.'

As Cass walked back to the manor with the remedy

for Elaine, her thoughts tumbled and whirled. There was something inside her that exhilarated and terrified her. A small, trembling part of her, deep in her gut, had known it since the first moment that she raised a sword against Sir Mordaunt's squire.

She wasn't sure she ever wanted to know what it meant but she knew it was real. She felt quite certain that something was happening to her, or coming for her, something so great that her mind couldn't even grasp the enormity of it. And it had always been there – she could see that now. The same part of her that had always known she needn't twist the apple stalk to find her husband's initials. That she wouldn't be following Mary's path. That the woman in the forest that morning so long ago had been the first person in her life to see her for what she really was.

Chapter 27

The Yuletide festivities had subsided into the endlessly cold days of the new year, when the frost crept in to coat bedstead and bathtub each morning and the simple act of getting out of bed required a long, uncomfortable period of anticipation and then a sudden surge of courage. When bare toes almost froze to flagstones before the fire could be kindled and even with the great blaze roaring in the fireplace their breath rose milky before them in the great hall.

The days were drab and unchanging, with low-hanging, metal-grey clouds and cold so biting that they had to break the ice on the horses' water troughs each morning. Cass, Lily and the other squires spent most of their time huddled round the fireplace to keep warm, Angharad deeming it too cold to be training outside. The summer supplies were waning, and the menu dwindled to salt pork and bean stew and thick pease pudding, day after day. The cows' milk faltered and then gradually dried up altogether with the freezing weather and so the morning porridge had to be made with water: an unappealing, lumpy, grey sludge.

The younger members of the sisterhood were restless, frustrated at the lost training time with the battle of squires looming in the spring. The older knights were preoccupied, and took to whispering in draughty corners of the manor with drawn, worried faces as the cold snap dragged on and their supplies grew increasingly scant. Elaine was keeping to her chamber, spending the long, frigid days in bed to conserve her energy and prepare for the personal battle that lay ahead of her.

One morning, Cass rounded a corner to find Angharad and Sigrid arguing in a corridor. Sigrid was gesticulating animatedly and Angharad was pressing her fingertips into her temples as if to soothe a pounding headache.

'—cannot spare you, Sigrid, not to the risk of a foolhardy wild goose chase that will more likely than not see you trailing home empty-handed.'

'Well, if nobody rides out it will soon be of little

consequence, as we will all have starved anyway,' Sigrid snapped.

They quietened when Cass approached, but the strain was apparent on both their faces.

Cass often wondered afterwards if what happened later might never have come to pass had such stress and discord not already been present in the manor that day.

It was late afternoon when the knock came.

Cass and the other squires were sitting near the fire, half-heartedly playing yet another game of cards. Neither the trenchers and dishes from breakfast nor those from the midday meal had been cleared away, so bone-weary did the squires and pages feel with the numbing, relentless cold, and the hall was dark and squalid in the gathering dusk. Even the torches seemed to smoke and smoulder reluctantly, refusing to leap into crackling life, for the damp and the frost had crept into every piece of wood in their stores, just as it had into each woman's bones.

There could be no lookouts in this weather without the risk of finding them stiff and frozen at their posts, so there was nobody to greet him, or to foretell his coming. But with training suspended it had been days since they had worn their riding gear or sharpened their weapons, so he came upon them weary and lethargic, but properly dressed, at least, and with no evidence to betray their secret.

Sir Beolin walked into the hall, bandy-legged like one who has spent too much time on horseback, and surveyed the scene in the manner of a herdsman looking out across his flock.

'What squalor is this?'

'Sir Beolin.' Hastily summoned by one of the squires, Angharad swept into the hall in a long, pale yellow silk gown. 'What a pleasure and an unexpected surprise to see you again.' Cass was impressed at her skill in pretence. She genuinely did sound pleased to see the visitor.

'My business with Sir Mordaunt is concluded,' he said proudly. 'I will soon be raising a band of men, with his support, and we will march west together.' He paused, his eyes roaming the hall, taking in the dirty plates and disorganized tables, the girls grouped awkwardly round the fire. 'I am surprised your lord permits your household to neglect their duties so wantonly,' he said, foregoing the traditional greetings in his disapproval at the state of the hall.

'Alas,' Angharad flushed, 'you must forgive our unkempt state, as we had expected no visitors in this cold spell. My lord has been called away most urgently to settle a matter at the trading post in Mercia, and in his absence the younger girls grow remiss.'

Beolin gave an oily smile. 'A strong hand is needed here in your lord's absence, I can see.' And he made straight for Angharad, putting a hairy-knuckled hand on her lower back. 'Perhaps we should discuss these matters in private, my lady,' he said, practically licking his lips, and Cass saw the briefest flicker of panic in Angharad's eyes before she smoothly assented and led him out of the hall.

The mood only darkened as the day dragged on and neither Angharad nor Sir Beolin reappeared. Vivian emerged in the early evening, swathed in a thick woollen cloak, and disappeared into the courtyard. A few moments later the swish and thud of the axe came faintly into the hall, as she vented her feelings on the neglected woodpile.

There was a sombre silence around the fire that evening. After the onion soup and slightly stale bread had been eaten, nobody had the heart to bring out instruments or games. The fire smoked fitfully and the atmosphere was brittle and ill-tempered. Rowan roared at Joan like a lion with a thorn in its paw when she accidentally stepped on the back of her cloak, bringing her crashing to the floor. Joan retreated in tears to her bedchamber and within a short time the others had one by one sloped miserably off to bed.

Cass stayed to damp down the dying embers of the fire and convey some baked potatoes from the ashes to Blyth outside, for warmth through the frosty night.

As she walked back inside, the manor seemed cold and strange, and her candle threw long, twisted shadows in front of her. She tried to imagine how different it must have been just a few years ago, when Angharad and her husband had lived here: a 'normal' household with maids and pages. She strained to picture Angharad sitting placidly beside the fire, her head bent diligently over a detailed piece of embroidery, or bringing her husband his travelling cloak and the stirrup cup to speed him on his journey. She thought of Vivian, curtseying and taking orders from her master, watching the way he treated his wife, seeing all but saying nothing. She wondered if Angharad had known, even then, or if Vivian's monstrous act had revealed her true feelings for the first time. She shook her head a little and moved across the silent and deserted hall, making for the stairs at the opposite end.

Before she reached the stairs, there came a faint cry, and a loud clatter as of some heavy metal object falling onto a stone floor. Cass froze, the hairs rising up along her forearms. She strained her ears to listen, her heart bumping against her ribcage in the darkness. There was silence. She waited, alert like a fox that scents the night air, as the hall around her grew colder and the shadows lengthened. And just as she had decided that she must have imagined the noise, or that it had simply been Blyth knocking over some tool in the stables, it came again, a heavy thud and a rattle as if something were being dragged across the floor.

Cass turned, dreamlike, and followed the noise to the opposite end of the hall, to a small exit and a narrow staircase that led upwards towards Angharad's chambers. She blew out her taper and left it on the bottom stair, then crept upwards, her fingers feeling their way along the stone walls as she felt for the edge of each uneven stair with her toes. It was not until she was almost at the top of the stairs, the great, iron-bolted door looming ahead of her, that she began to hear more. A strained panting that sounded almost more animal than human: a noise that somehow leaked with sweat and hot breath and motion. It came rhythmically, rising and falling, sometimes building to a sharp intake of breath, sometimes falling away to a low grunt.

Cass stood frozen, her stomach curdled. The noise was intimate, visceral: already, standing as she was, she was intruding on something vulnerable and grotesque, something that was not her place to hear. Very slowly, she felt backwards with one of her feet and began to descend the staircase again, one chill step at a time.

But even as she did so, the noise began to build again, the rhythm quickening, the gasping more urgent and strained, the voice crying out, sharp, twice, and then a horrible, gurgling wail of anguish, another great thud, and then silence.

267

Cass stood frozen to the spot, her eyes trained in horror on the door's black metal studs, her fingers digging painfully into the crack between two stones. She tasted blood and realized her lip was between her teeth. She would retreat, in a moment, when she could move again.

Except that was when the door opened. And Angharad stood in the doorway, her silhouette lit brightly and unnaturally by the full moon streaming through the window behind her, her hair wild and dishevelled, her cotton undergarments torn, her face pale with shock and fury, and her right hand bright scarlet.

Dazed, she raised it to her forehead where it left a smudge of blood. Then she looked down at it as if it were somebody else's and frowned, seeming confused, rubbing her palms together. The blood smeared horribly onto her left hand too – she wiped it across the cotton, making a vivid stain beneath her belly. Her eyes, wide and staring, seemed to lock onto Cass's as if she both did and did not see her. She showed no surprise to find her there.

'He would not finish,' she said matter-of-factly, as if she were describing a rodent in the pantry or discussing a leak in the roof. Then a sudden, eerie, burbling stream of laughter escaped her lips. 'He would not finish and let me be.'

Cass heard footsteps behind her and she turned to see a candle bobbing slowly up the stairs. As it came closer it illuminated Vivian's round, worried face. Cass watched as Vivian's expression clouded, then passed through shock and terror. Her eye widened in horror and fixed on the scene in the chamber behind Angharad.

Sir Beolin's armour, his chainmail, his fine gold sword and eagle-feather-topped helmet lay abandoned on the floor.

The tapestry that hung on the wall behind Angharad's bedstead was spattered with red.

Sir Beolin's partially clothed body was hanging half off the bed, his legs and feet tangled in the sheets, his arms thrown out wildly to the sides, his neck twisted unnaturally towards the floor. Cass felt the shock of the sight like a physical blow to her gut. There was a heavy silver candlestick on the floor. Cass retched, and the bitter liquid splattered the steps.

Wordlessly, Vivian pushed past her and gathered Angharad into her arms like a child, sinking to the floor with her back against the door. Angharad allowed herself to be drawn down onto Vivian's lap, where her body was as limp and floppy as a ragdoll. She let her head loll onto Vivian's shoulder, her eyes open and staring, sightlessly, at the door.

'She is in shock,' Vivian said sharply, turning to Cass. 'You will need to help.'

'Me?'

'Do you see anybody else here?' Vivian's eyes snapped

angrily, as if she held Cass to blame for being there and not stopping it, for daring to intrude on this spectacle of horror. Then she saw that Cass's chin trembled as she wiped the bile from her lips, remembered, perhaps that she was seeing a dead body for the first time, having never fought a real battle.

'Shh,' she commanded, gently but firmly, her gaze intense. 'Listen now.' And she spoke in a tone that was low and wary, her hand out in a placating gesture as if approaching a wild colt that might bolt or kick out at any moment. 'You can do this, Cass. We will take care of you. You have a home here, a life, a mistress: but all that will be gone if anybody finds out about this.'

Her voice changed, cajoling, pleading almost. 'Nobody needs to know. He was not a good man – he was forcing her, she had no choice – you know that.'

Cass trembled, feeling sweat lining her top lip. She felt like she was in a dream. She could not move.

'It is not the first time,' Vivian gabbled, becoming more desperate. 'You know her as the great, fiery leader she is now, but you did not see her before, see what her husband did to her. She almost died, Cass, so many times over.' Angry tears spilled down Vivian's cheeks, and she did not wipe them away. 'I watched her almost die, again and again. Until I couldn't take it any more. And eventually, I snapped. Just like she did tonight. Because there are certain things that human beings cannot endure. Everybody has their limits. She is innocent, Cass. She is the victim here.' And Vivian's face convulsed in anger, as she looked down at Angharad's limp form. She let out a scream that was hoarse and raw and horrible, and she grabbed the poker that sat next to the fireplace and hurled it towards Beolin's body. It bounced off the side of the bed and clattered to the floor.

'I would kill him again for you. I would do it instead of you, love,' she choked, and she bent her forehead to Angharad's and sobbed.

Cass stood there for what felt like a very long time, looking at the two broken women whose strength and kindness and generosity she had grown to know, and the battered body of the man who had hurt them both. Then she stepped forward, over Vivian's outstretched legs, pulled a sheet from the bed and began to wrap it round the corpse. The legs were an easy enough matter, and the arms too, though she shuddered when his fingers brushed momentarily across her hand as she heaved them across his torso. The weight was surprising, like a great joint of ham, and she embraced the idea gratefully, imagining herself simply wrapping up portions of meat for winter salting in the barn at home. Just a shoulder of pork. A side of beef. Until she looked down and there was a clump of hair in her hand, and then she began to sob.

But she did not stop. She carried on, wrapping the sheet tight, though the tears ran freely down her cheeks. And when Vivian rose to help her carry the body downstairs (after setting Angharad tenderly down on the sheepskin before the fire like a little child) her eyes were full of gratitude. But they could not manage it, not alone. They half-dragged, half-pushed it down the staircase, but when they came to cross the floor of the hall it was too heavy, even with both of them straining together. Then they heard footsteps and froze in horror.

Sigrid swept into the hall, her travelling cloak pulled up round her face, striding purposefully towards the entrance doors. Vivian and Cass's eyes met for a moment, then Vivian croaked, 'Sigrid.'

She wheeled round, checked herself in surprise at the sight of them, the heavy, unwieldy bundle slumped on the floor between them, taking in Cass's distraught, panicked expression and Vivian's tight, white lips. For a long moment the three of them looked at each other. Then Sigrid moved towards them, wordlessly, and heaved up the mid-section of the bundle under her arm, so that Vivian and Cass could take the two ends, Vivian leading the way.

They carried the body out through the postern door and into the forest, heaving and panting and occasionally stopping to readjust their grip. Once, Cass stumbled on a tree root and their load fell to the ground with a sickening thud and a crack, but she gripped the sheet again with grim determination and together they dragged it onwards. It wasn't until they had been walking in near total darkness and silence for some considerable time that it occurred to Cass that Vivian had not faltered once, nor paused to think. She knew exactly where she was going.

They were deep in the forest when they neared the pond, and the eerie sense that Cass was in a dream only increased when she saw the crooked black silhouette of the hawthorn tree and knew where she was. But there was no vision tonight, no reflection in the dark surface as they tied heavy rocks inside the sheet and heaved it unceremoniously over the bank so that it slipped quietly under the black skin of the water.

Vivian turned without a word and began to walk back through the trees towards the manor, and Cass followed her silently, ears ringing, fingers numb. It was only when they had nearly reached the outer walls that she realized Sigrid had melted away into the darkness. She suddenly felt the cold, and seeing that her feet were bare, began to shiver uncontrollably.

Chapter 28

By the time the snow thawed, and the morning light had begun to creep over the threshold before Cass awoke in the mornings, her room had become a prison. She barely recognized the girl with the matted hair, heavy bruised shadows under her eyes and thin, hollow cheeks who looked back at her with dull eyes on the rare occasions she glanced in the glass. Her nails had grown long and dirty and there were angry red scabs along her forearm where she had picked at it until it bled.

At night, she saw his body. She felt his fingertips brush across her arm and she awoke, scratching at the place where she had felt them, screaming silently into the dark. Time passed strangely, in lumps and clots. There was a plate of food, cold and congealed, then three plates, outside the door. The porridge was lumpy and sticky. She retched, and pushed it outside, shutting the door again.

Sigrid was gone, riding out the moment the first thaw came. So Cass was left alone. Vivian came, those first few days, knocking at the door and calling, but Cass kept the bolt drawn across, and did not answer.

She slept little, and fitfully. Again and again her dreams would lead her back to the pool in the forest, but there was no white-clad arm, no reflection, no glimpse of Mary. Just Beolin's body, bloated and swollen, floating face up with his mouth lolling horribly open and his eyes staring blankly up into the starry sky.

Cass did not think that there was a way back into the sunshine for her. But she had not accounted for Lily.

Lily did not stop coming. At first she laughed and joked, sang and cajoled, then sulked and shouted. And when the silence continued, she simply came. She sat outside the door for hours, quietly, with her fingers just underneath so that Cass could see them. She brought her meals upstairs and sat there on the other side of that slab of oak, sometimes whispering snatches of gossip about the other squires, sometimes describing the growth of the colts in the stables, the taste of the tincture Alys had brewed for her sore throat.

Always, she described the outdoors. So that, even as Cass's skin grew paler and her muscles weak from lack of use, she knew that, little by little, the air grew warmer outside. She knew that the brook had begun to trickle again through the trees at the far side of the meadow, that the purple crocuses were opening their golden throats and the redwings and bramblings had started to return from their long winter absence.

And one day, she opened the door.

Lily looked up, got to her feet and slipped an arm round her waist, as if she had just been waiting a few moments for Cass to fetch something from her room. They walked outside together, and Lily supported her, as her eyes flinched from the bright sun and the colours overwhelmed her and her legs felt strange and unreliable.

They only walked for a few minutes, that first day, and said nothing. But Lily came back the next morning, and waited, and Cass opened the door again.

It was the day before Candlemas when they stopped in the woods and Cass sat on a soft carpet of moss and told Lily everything.

The poison that had been choking her and holding her hostage seemed to seep out of her along with the words, and Lily held her tight and said nothing at all. And that night, for the first time, Cass slept soundly until morning.

Very slowly, she began to come back to herself. She started to train again in the meadow, and the baton felt good in her hand. She returned to the stables and buried her face in the sweet, verdant smell of Pebble's mane. She began to taste food again, and found, to her surprise, that her appetite slowly returned and that the sensation of filling a hungry stomach could still be pleasurable.

She passed Vivian and Angharad in the hall and though they never spoke of it, she was able to meet their eyes. There was a new measure of trust and respect between them that had not been there before, and something else, that was a kind of kinship. And though she was not and would not be the same girl who had walked up the stairs towards Angharad's chamber that night, little by little Cass realized that another girl would go on living, and only a small part of herself would be left behind.

But the respite she had finally found from endless thoughts of Beolin and his body would be short-lived.

One unseasonably warm spring day, after training under the brightest blue sky, with a brisk breeze chivvying wispy feather-clouds along, Lily and Cass left the manor together to ride to the first market of the season. They took empty panniers to fill with produce and for the first time since the frost thawed it was warm enough to need no cloaks. As her silk dress streamed out over Pebble's hindquarters, Cass let the fresh, floral scent of spring fill her lungs.

They stopped on the way for lunch and Cass lay in the sunshine that filtered down through the delicate unfurling new leaves and buds, her head in Lily's lap, and sighed contentedly, closing her eyes.

'Just think of it, Cass.' Lily stroked her hair absent-mindedly. 'If we were both to be knighted at the battle of the squires, we would return to the manor as full members of the sisterhood, sit at the knights' table, move into apartments of our own . . .'

Cass laughed. 'Is that what you're most excited about? Where we will eat and sleep once we become knights?'

'No.' Lily flicked her forehead playfully. 'But think what those apartments would represent! We will be able to come and go as we please, ride out together on journeys and adventures, follow our own destiny! We will have squires of our own, Cass, just think of it! No more polishing armour and mucking out stables! Just honour and glory! Tournaments and treasure!'

'I like mucking out the stables!'

'Then you can come with me and shovel Pebble's poo while I'm collecting prizes and winning accolades.'

'Excellent deal. And I'll be there to rescue you when you find yourself captured and thrown in a dungeon.'

'Oh, using your excrement-covered shovel to do battle with the guards?'

'No, I will carry my sword with me too, just in case.'

'Oh, good.'

'Or I'll use yours, since you probably dropped it when you were taken prisoner.'

They subsided into contented silence and Cass enjoyed the gentle warmth of the sun on her forehead and nose, while daydreams of wild adventures with Lily and Pebble played pleasantly across her eyelids.

When they rode into the market in the early afternoon it lifted Cass's spirits still further to see the huddle of stalls beneath vibrant fluttering canopies. The smell of freshly baked bread and pastries filled the air and the whole scene was alive and pulsating with bustling commerce. There were farmers shouting their prices in good-natured competition, and women from villages for miles around gathered to laugh and talk over their baskets, enjoying each other's company after the long winter separation. And there was only one brief moment, when Cass saw a girl sitting on the back of a cart loaded with produce, her bare feet kicking in the air and her hair loosely braided, that she wondered how her father was managing, and who was sitting on the back of the cart at home. But she could pull herself out of those moments more easily now. Her feeling of belonging in this new life was so much stronger than it had been before.

Cass and Lily purchased everything Alys and Vivian had instructed them was needed for the manor's stores. Cass left the bargaining to Lily, who proved to be a shrewd negotiator.

'It's your dimples,' Cass teased, as they walked away from a stall with half a pound more salt than they had really paid for. 'They see those sweet ringlets and that smile and they never notice the cut-throat haggling coming until it's too late.'

'What can I say?' Lily grinned, but then her voice trailed off. Cass followed her gaze and saw a pregnant woman leaning against a stall, smiling as her little one reached up eagerly towards the vegetables. She recognized the sandy hair with the unruly tuft and saw that it was the mother they had met in the village during the Yuletide charity visit. Lily hurried over and pressed the few remaining coins they had into the woman's hand.

'How are you?'

The young woman beamed and pulled Lily into an unexpected hug, pregnant stomach and all. 'Thanks to you, we survived the winter. I don't know how you convinced those men to replace the hogs but we would not have managed had it not been for your visit that day, and for your kindness. Thank you.'

'We will tell our mistress,' Lily said, blushing with pleasure.

They returned to where they had picketed the horses, Cass gratefully accepting Pebble's reins from a scruffy boy who had seen to it she had water and a bag of oats. But while they busied themselves with loading their panniers, there was a commotion behind them.

'Have you never learned to tie a knot, idiot boy?' The voice was loud, rough and angry.

Cass turned and saw the two knights of the Round Table who had attended the Twelfth Night feast, and a third burlier man, similarly dressed, but somewhat shorter and plumper than the others, his face framed by a pudding-bowl haircut. He was returning from retrieving his horse, a fine bay mare, which had loosed itself from the picket, and was berating the stable boy, his cheeks puffed out with annoyance while his fellows rolled their eyes at each other, clearly used to such outbursts.

'The knot is still tied,' Lily pointed out, never one to hold her tongue, while Cass elbowed her. 'So it was the peg that slipped, not the knot.' She nodded towards the boy. 'You owe him an apology.'

'And who do you think you are, girl, to give orders to a knight of Arthur's court?' The man swung himself into his saddle, and trotted over towards Cass and Lily, causing Elise to paw the ground nervously.

'Your horse has the same effect on other animals as I

imagine you have on women,' Lily muttered angrily, as she quieted her mount, and Cass tried to stifle a giggle.

'I'll have you know I have bedded any number of women of higher breeding than you,' he retorted pompously.

'Oh, really?' Lily feigned polite interest. 'And had these women no sense of sight or smell?'

'Sir Kay!' One of the other men intervened, hailing his companion. He was tall and thin, with a neatly clipped blonde moustache and kind eyes. 'We must ride north, our business cannot wait.' Then he looked more closely at Lily, seeming to recognize her.

'You are one of Lady Angharad's maidens? From the Twelfth Night festivities?'

Lily nodded warily, and Cass wondered how often she was picked out by men in a crowd, used to being the face they took notice of and remembered, just as Mordaunt had.

'It is fortunate we have met with you,' the blonde man said, nodding politely. 'My name is Sir Elyan.' Then he indicated the other tall man, who sat quietly in his saddle. His green eyes studied Lily and Cass keenly, though his expression remained neutral. His skin was acorn brown and his bare forearms were powerfully muscled though the reins lay loose in his hands. 'This is Sir Safir, and I see you have already met Sir Kay.'

'We must ride northwards, but we seek Sir Beolin, a

knight I believe to be well known to your mistress. He is working with us to amass a war host, and we must return to Ceredigion with great urgency. But he did not meet with us as expected to ride on the next phase of our journey, and so we have lingered here longer in hopes of reuniting with him.'

Cass's ears rang, as if a great bell were chiming and chiming and could not be stopped. She put a hand to Pebble's mane and tangled her fingers there, trying to keep herself from sinking to the ground.

'We thought perhaps he might be visiting your mistress before departing?' Sir Safir spoke slowly, his voice low and direct, those piercing green eyes searching. 'We had heard they were great friends.' He put undue emphasis on the last two words, and he looked directly at Cass and Lily, with a meaningful expression.

'No,' Lily said quickly, tossing her head. 'No, we have not seen him since before the night of the feast. Indeed, we have had no visitors since the frost set in, have we, Cass?'

Cass shook her head mutely, and she saw Lily's eyes widen with alarm as she took in her pale, slack face.

'We must hasten, Cass,' Lily gabbled, practically throwing her friend into the saddle and mounting herself. 'Or darkness will fall before we reach home.'

'One last thing,' Sir Elyan called after them, his voice

light and pleasant. 'One of our comrades seeks news about a lady. He tried to help her but she seems to have vanished and he is deeply concerned for her well-being. She is heavy with child.'

Cass stiffened in the saddle, grateful for the fold of her hood falling across her face, shielding her from the men's gaze.

'Oh, dear me, no, we have seen nobody like that in these parts,' Lily replied, lightly and dismissively. 'I do hope he finds her.'

She waved pleasantly to the men, as if their query held no significance. Then she kicked her heels and grabbed Pebble's reins, pulling Cass along with her as she trotted quickly back towards the road. But Cass glanced back and saw that Sir Safir was watching them closely as they rode away.

Chapter 29

Over the next few days, Cass tried to shake off the heavy sense of foreboding that hung over her like a dark shadow. She threw herself into training with Lily and the other squires. They were all now spending the time from dawn till dusk in the meadow, tilting at the quintain and practising their hand-to-hand combat in anticipation of the upcoming tournament.

'Nothing will come of it,' Lily panted, as they sank down into the grass to rest after a particularly lively bout of sword fighting. Their skill had changed subtly in the time Cass had been at the manor, so that they were now much more evenly matched, though neither of them mentioned it. What Lily lacked in accuracy, she more than made up for in sheer enthusiasm, but she would never have the pinpoint precision, the fleetness or the fluid, dreamlike quality Cass was learning how to channel.

'They have no proof. All they know is whatever bawdy boasts he made about Angharad. So Beolin visited here. So what?' She gazed around at the teeming activity of the meadow: girls letting arrows loose and grunting in victory or frustration as they landed, horses cantering round the perimeter, the steady clang and screech of the quintain being struck and creaking into action. 'Nobody else knows. And nothing is going to change that. You're safe.'

'And Elaine?'

Lily did not answer.

They had warned Elaine, of course, visiting her in her apartments as soon as they returned home from the market. They found Alys with her, carefully examining her stomach in front of a gentle fire, using a strange, conical instrument to listen at intervals.

'A strong heartbeat.' She smiled, and Elaine clasped her hand tightly.

'I did not know you had the skill of midwifery,' Cass said, a little surprised.

'It isn't something you crow about,' Alys said drily, 'when giving life can be enough to risk your own, if there are superstitious folk around.'

They told Elaine everything, and Cass waited to see her cry out, or her face drain of colour. But instead she flushed with anger and leaped to her feet despite her extra load.

'Let them find me,' she snapped, and the flames seemed to leap higher in the fireplace behind her. 'And I will tell the world what a true *hero* their great Lancelot is.' Her voice dripped with sarcasm. 'It will not be to my shame, but his,' she said defiantly.

And Angharad had been defiant too, though Vivian's forehead had creased with worry when Cass told them about the exchange with Arthur's knights. 'We have been careful,' she said, stroking Vivian's back with a reassuring hand. 'They might speculate, but there is nothing for them to find.'

They rose from the grass again and Cass tried to let Lily's comforting words in, tried to wrap them round herself like a shawl against the cold, but her fear found the gaps and crept in to nip at her skin.

She felt an anger swelling inside her. She picked up her baton and approached a dummy, a heavy sack of grain mounted on a wooden post, used for target and combat practice. She felt the anger swelling, an uncomfortable, hot knot in her stomach that pushed its way upwards and outwards, into her sword arm. Anger at how Elaine had been treated. She swung at the dummy. Anger at Sir Beolin for forcing this situation upon them. She hit it again. Anger at

Angharad for losing control, at Vivian for drawing Cass into their trouble by forcing her to dispose of the body. Strike, strike, strike. And above all at the situation that had brought them here in the first place, the way that women were so powerless to prevent men from having sway over their lives. None of this would have happened had Angharad been able to openly rule the manor on her own, or had her husband not abused her in the first place. Cass's strikes rained down faster and harder, and she felt herself losing control as the rush took over her, like someone else was acting through her, like something else was telling her body what to do.

Dimly, she was aware of other squires murmuring, of the sound around them faltering and stopping, of a crowd forming, but still she could not stop. It was as if a release had been granted and all the heat and the pain of the past weeks was pouring out, faster and hotter than she could control.

The sackcloth was becoming battered, the grain bursting out and pouring to the ground, the post beginning to buckle, and Cass heard her name being called, over and over again.

Then there were arms, pulling her back, pinning her hands to her sides as she screamed, and then as the fury drained from her and she let herself be dragged backwards, away from the meadow.

'Shh. Shh.' And when Cass's sobs dwindled to great, heaving gulps, she looked up and saw it was not Lily or

Rowan who was holding her, but Elaine, her heart-shaped face creased with compassion, her heavy braid hanging down to the ground. Her eyes were a dark blue that reminded Cass of still, calm waters, and when she smiled there was a gap between her front teeth that made her look younger than her years.

She put her hands on Cass's shoulders and breathed deeply, her eyes closed, in through her nose and out through pursed lips, until Cass began to breathe with her and the heaving slowed.

'I know a little something about holding rage inside yourself,' Elaine said wryly. 'But we have a choice. To be consumed by it, or to fight on in spite of it.'

And then Sigrid was there, nodding quietly at Elaine and taking her place beside Cass. She did not speak at first, simply standing beside her, letting the pounding of her heart subside, watching as her fists gradually unclenched.

'One day,' she said quietly, 'you will feel that rage inside you on the battlefield and know it has built the warrior you are. So breathe. Focus. And know that your fury can be a strength, not a weakness, but only if you have the self-control to wield it wisely.'

The next two days passed in a whirl of packing and preparation. Oiling and shining their armour, preparing the horses, gathering and wrapping rations and clothing they would need for the journey. The tournament would take place at Tamworth, the closest Cass had been to home since she left it on Mary's wedding day the previous summer. As she rubbed her dark chestnut breastplate to a rich shine, she tried to imagine how she would have responded in the orchard that day had somebody told her that she would be returning, less than a year later, in full armour, on horseback, with a sword at her side. Her lips twitched. She would have told them they had lost their senses.

Elaine was at the gates to wave them off, her bow in her hand. She was largely confined to the manor now as her time approached, but she insisted on taking guard duty every few days. 'I've got to earn my keep,' she smiled gently, 'and it is better to be purposeful and distracted than to simply contemplate the battle to come.' And her gaze flickered downwards.

The journey was not a long one. It was a warmer and more pleasant experience than the cold ride to Eboracum, and Cass marvelled at the memory of the scared girl who had spent that journey terrified of what was to come. She was different now. Prepared, strong and excited for the battle ahead. As if reading her thoughts, Pebble snorted and tossed her head enthusiastically, straining at the reins.

Tamworth was bedecked with bunting and streamers for

the occasion and the streets were thronged, King Pybba having given all the townspeople a two-day holiday for the festivities.

'It's rumoured that King Pybba's desire to host the battle of the squires is hardly selfless,' Sigrid noted sardonically, 'what with him having twelve sons all keen to prove themselves.'

They found lodgings at a small inn, where the landlady paid little attention to a group of knights in town for the tournament, only showing interest in the coins they paid her and the cleanliness of their shoes.

Lily and Cass slept that night in the same bed, whispering their hopes for the next morning late into the dark.

They rose at sunrise and breakfasted in their room, then helped each other to arm. Cass paused, her mother's silver locket in one hand and Lily's delicate horseshoe necklace in the other, then quickly slipped the horseshoe over her head and tucked the locket inside her leather boot. They fetched their horses from the stables and left for the tournament field before the others had awakened, keen to be the first to see it.

It was smaller and less grand than the expanse at Eboracum, a farmer's field cleared specially for the occasion, with a ramshackle old barn and a few pigsties at one end. There were no grand wooden stands here, but pretty canopies with fluttering pennants had been set up along one side of the field and the spectators would be expected to find themselves spaces to sit or stand. Many had already arrived and were milling around or laying down blankets and cloaks to claim their spot with a view of the field.

The lists were already set up, with a series of gold-painted wooden rings glinting in the sunshine along the top. The first round would be a test of skill and precision, with the competitors tasked with collecting as many gold rings as they could on the end of their lance.

Next would come the sword fighting, and finally the jousting. When all was finished, one competitor would be named the champion, but the greatest prize, for any squire who attended, would be what happened afterwards: recognition from their lords that they had distinguished themselves sufficiently to earn their knighthood.

As the sun rose higher the atmosphere grew increasingly feverish. The crowds swelled, with parents holding excitable children on their shoulders and groups of young people chattering excitedly as they thronged the canopies. Knights, and squires dressed as knights, arrived, and gathered in groups around the field, their horses bedecked in bright regalia, their armour gleaming and glinting.

Just before the tournament was due to begin, a blast of trumpet fanfare heralded the arrival of King Pybba, a portly man whose face was ruddy with fine blood vessels, his fingers swollen with gout and heavy with twisted and bejewelled gold rings. He wore a thick, plain gold band round his head, and his dark blue cloak was trimmed with white fur. Servants carried a cross-legged chair and a dais that they hastily set up in prime viewing position, exactly level with the centre of the lists, elevated behind the crowds of ordinary spectators. As he settled laboriously into his chair, the king was shouting instructions to a gaggle of young men in shining silver armour, their wealth paraded in full-length chainmail, their dark blue shields decorated with white crowns. But for all their regalia, Cass thought they looked like rather poor specimens of chivalry: the smallest was nursing a dripping nose, the tallest, with a long, mournful face and hollow cheeks, kept stumbling and dropping his helmet, and two more were bickering over a sword with an emerald set into the pommel.

Sigrid and Angharad ushered Lily, Cass and the rest into a group, checking their buckles and fastenings, helping them to saddle and prepare their horses.

Cass noted a group of Arthur's knights, Sir Elyan among them, urgently whispering last-minute instructions to their squires. She saw with a jolt that Sir Safir was mounted, the bright red dragon emblazoned on a proud shield buckled to his left arm, and remembered that the youngest and newest knights, who had less than three years' experience, were also allowed to compete.

At the far corner of the field were a group of knights wearing Mordaunt's immediately recognizable black, the fine silver antlers shining sharp across their shields as if it had been cut there by a sword.

Cass swallowed and looked away, trying to focus on everything she had learned over the past few months. Trying to clear her head of the swirling fear and confusion. Trying to remember what was at stake: freedom, and the choice to live life on her own terms.

Angharad passed Lily a buttercup-yellow lance and she tucked it carefully beneath her elbow.

'Why thank you, sq—'

'If you are about to call me squire you may find you do not have a home to come back to tomorrow,' Angharad warned, her tone sharp but her eyes twinkling. 'Now go and make me proud.'

Cass watched, shielding her eyes from the bright sun, as Lily snapped her visor shut and confidently trotted to the beginning of the lists. Ahead of her, a short little squire who could not have been older than thirteen lurched nervously down the course, missing four of the five rings entirely and knocking the last one wildly into the crowd with the side of his lance. There were peals of laughter from the spectators and Cass saw him withdraw in tears, throwing his helmet to the ground and giving it a petulant kick.

Lily was next, holding Elise under tight control, her lance straight and true. As she trotted confidently forward, Cass knew the exact expression that was on her face even though she couldn't see it under the shining silver helmet: her eyebrows drawn into a V, her mouth twisted to the side, her lip sucked in a little in intense concentration. She had watched her friend rehearse for this moment a thousand times and she held her breath and clenched her fists as she watched.

Riding beautifully, Lily deftly hooked four out of the five rings onto the end of her lance, only missing the last one because a man in the crowd sneezed loudly, startling Elise so that she tossed her head and caused Lily to raise her arm momentarily, swinging her slightly off balance. The crowd groaned at the interruption and cheered Lily enthusiastically as she rode back down the lists, her lance raised in triumph with the four gold rings shining along its length.

One of the Round Table squires was next, swaggering confidently to the lists but only managing to retrieve three of the rings, then one of Mordaunt's young knights confidently swept a clean field with every ring glittering along his lance. There followed three indistinguishable brothers from Pybba's brood, each of them less inspiring than the last, their posture slouched and their technique sloppy. But their horses were of thoroughbred stock and well trained, and they each scooped a few gold rings, to loud applause from the back of the crowd.

And then it was Cass's turn.

'Find that thing inside yourself,' Sigrid said to her quietly, 'and let it out.'

Cass breathed slow and deep, remembering everything she had learned. Time seemed to slow down as Pebble trotted dutifully forward, then waited for the signal. The flag dropped and they set off, the drumbeat of hooves and the drumbeat inside Cass's chest seeming to thrum in perfect rhythm. The first ring slipped onto her lance almost without effort, then the second and the third. It was as if she weren't even thinking about it, as if she were watching herself move slowly down the field in a dream. She threaded the tip of the lance smoothly through the fourth ring and surged towards the next, her eyes flicking towards the crowd for just the briefest moment as the sunlight caught a girl's brooch.

Then time stopped. Because it wasn't just a girl. It was Mary. Mary laughing, arm in arm with her husband, her belly swollen and round, hardly even glancing at the knight riding down the lists, not knowing that it was her the eyes were locked on through the helmet slits as the lance slipped and fell out of the gloved hand, thudding to the ground.

Chapter 30

igrid's sigh of disappointment, Lily's swift look of concern, Angharad's surprise, the jeering of the crowd as she missed the final ring, all of it bounced off Cass as if she were locked inside a bubble. Mary was the only thing that mattered, the only thing she could think of. Seeing her had been like a physical blow, and even now she felt it, as she stood with the others, holding Pebble's reins, watching the next squire take his turn. Her chest throbbed, her legs trembled and her throat ached with a lump that she could neither swallow down nor let out in a cry of anguish.

Mary's face was the same and yet she was so different: older, confident, grown-up suddenly, like somebody else entirely. A grown woman, a *wife*, with a child on the way, taking in the tournament with her husband. A day out. A holiday. Why had it not occurred to Cass that this might happen? She knew they were in Mercia, knew the battle of the squires was a rare day of entertainment, yet this belonged in the here and now, in her new life, and there was no part of her mind that could process it overlapping with all that she had left behind.

Seeing Mary reignited everything: her doubts, her guilt, and the aching, yearning loss that yawned open inside her again where she had tried to force it shut. She wanted to run to her, to throw her arms round her, to push the stranger beside her away and reclaim her rightful place at Mary's side. She wanted Mary to know, to see everything she had become, everything she knew she could be. She needed her.

She needed Mary to understand. To give her blessing, somehow, to the path Cass had chosen.

There was time.

The four rings had been enough to secure Cass's place in the next round of the competition, but the sword fighting would not take place until the afternoon.

'It was just a slip,' Lily coached her encouragingly, while Cass gazed into the stands. 'You lost concentration, that's all. And you're even better with a sword, Cass, you know you are.' But Sigrid looked searchingly at Cass, her face clouded with disappointment.

As the rest of the squires and knights waited for their turn to tilt at the rings, Cass pulled the locket from her boot and wrapped it in a handkerchief, her fingers trembling, feeling sweat trickle down her neck inside her helmet. Before she could change her mind or talk herself out of being so reckless, she cornered a young page and pressed the locket into his hand, along with a silver coin, pointing Mary out and whispering her instructions. Then, while Sigrid and the others were focused on cheering for Joan, who was trotting nervously towards the lists, she slipped away to the little barn on the other side of the field and waited.

The barn was quiet and dark, with the only light filtering weakly through one broken wooden shutter. The noise of the tournament was muffled here, the atmosphere strangely calm. A few strands of rotten straw remained in the manger fixed to the wall. There were iron rings set into the stalls where the animals had once been tethered. It smelled rich and earthy, reminding her of Blyth and the stables and helping her to ground herself. Still she strode back and forth, back and forth, while she waited for what seemed like an eternity.

The door creaked open and Mary set one foot uncertainly inside, the other still outside as if she were poised to run. And Cass choked out a laugh that was half a sob, because Mary had always been so cautious, and it was exactly the same position she had used to adopt when they were children, playing hide-and-seek in the attic, setting just one foot inside, ready to run if anyone jumped out and scared her.

She threw off her helmet and stepped forward into the shaft of light. Mary gasped 'Cass . . . is that . . . is that you?'

Cass could only nod mutely and the door banged shut as Mary threw herself forward into Cass's arms.

They stood like that, shoulders heaving, as Cass cried hot, happy, guilty tears into Mary's neck, as she felt the strange bulk of her stomach pressing between them.

Then Mary took her by the shoulders and held her gently at arm's length, searching her sister's face. And Cass saw how her eyes wandered from the freckles across her cheekbones to the new muscles and the lithe, strong body that had replaced the softness of the little sister she remembered.

It took Cass a long time to explain. She was rushed, painfully aware of how easily they could be interrupted, and how dangerous it would be if they were. Long, precious minutes crawled by, while Mary's face passed through shock and relief to anger and then bewilderment. The words tumbled out in the wrong order. Cass rubbed her temples in frustration, trying to explain things for which even she had not been able to find an easy explanation herself.

At last she stopped, and stood there, her helmet under her arm, the man's clothing and armour that had come to feel so natural suddenly seeming ridiculous and clownish before her sister's gaze.

'You did not come home.' There was resentment and anger in her sister's voice, but above all there was such hurt that hot needles sprang to Cass's eyes. 'You were not prevented, and yet you chose not to. I thought you were dead, Cass. I have been in such pain.' She stopped, shaking her head.

And all Cass could say was, 'I am sorry,' over and over.

Mary's eyes travelled over her slowly, resting longer on her sun-browned face and muscular thighs than the helmet or breastplate. And at last she asked, 'Are you happy, Cass?'

And slowly, Cass nodded. 'I think I will be.' Then they were in each other's arms again, and Cass was gently exploring Mary's belly with wonder and awe and Mary was crying again, and there came a voice outside, calling.

'Mary? *Mary?*'

'It is Thomas,' she said in alarm. 'We are leaving soon – we only came for the morning, he cannot leave the forge longer—'

She gripped Cass's hand, neither of them ready to let go.

'I will let our parents know you are well, Cass, but your secret is safe with me. Your place was never going to be in some farm kitchen or alehouse, and I think we both knew it. I cannot pretend to understand, but I love you. I love you.'

The door banged shut and she was gone.

Cass had thought that seeing Mary might break the spell, somehow. It was only now, as she emerged, blinking, into the sunlight again that she realized how afraid she had been that allowing herself to reconnect with her old life would extinguish the spark she had discovered inside her. Like admitting she was not the person she was now pretending to be. But seeing Mary seemed to have had the opposite effect. It was as if her sister's blessing had lifted some barrier she had not known she was holding tightly round herself, as if it had shattered some internal blockage like water bursting through a dam.

When she stepped forward later that afternoon to meet a young squire of Arthur's Round Table in combat, Sigrid spoke to her sharply, her words stinging a little.

'I expect better from you, Cass, because I know you have it in you.'

And Lily nodded encouragingly at her as she passed, hands clasped at her chest in nervous excitement for her friend.

But they need not have worried. The liquid power that had been sporadic and elusive since that day at Eboracum now came at her bidding, flooding into her more potently than ever before. The flickering moments and sparks of brilliance that had sprung from her during her training with Sigrid were outshone by this outpouring, and from the corner of her eye she saw a look of sheer triumph on Sigrid's face. Her sword took on a grace and speed she had never yet mastered, her feet flew out of reach of her opponent and her shield was like lightning, deflecting every blow without ever seeming to feel their impact. She saw the surprise in the eyes between the helmet slits, saw the squire's sword falter as he realized he was outclassed, heard the gasps of the crowd as the spectators surged to their feet in excitement. Instead of adding to her nerves it was like these things fed her, carrying her forward, lifting her higher, filling her with warmth and light and strength.

Then the squire lay dazed at her feet and the bout was over. And Cass felt dazed too, as if she had experienced some precious, private vision, and she stumbled from the field, vaguely aware that the crowd were chanting, and Lily was jumping up and down. Somewhere, briefly glimpsed just as her husband guided her away, Mary was looking back over her shoulder, beaming in pride and disbelief. Standing beside Sigrid, Angharad's expression was one of surprise and admiration, but Sigrid, who had always known, gave Cass a look of pure pride that meant more to her than any prize.

Cass made her way across the field, past the crowds and the other squires who reached out to thump her excitedly on the back, through the narrow streets, across the river that surged and roiled beneath the bridge, through the holiday crowds that thronged the alehouse, and into the chamber she and Lily had shared the night before. She lay down on the straw mattress, took off her helmet, and cried.

Chapter 31

When Cass awoke the following morning, Lily had crept in without waking her and wrapped her arm over her ribcage and under the soft part of her stomach. She smiled, and lay still in the quiet of the morning, watching the dust swirl and dance in the light that shone through the gaps in the wooden shutters and enjoying the warmth of Lily's sleeping body. A calm and a sense of purpose settled on her in that still, quiet morning, of a kind she had not felt in months. She was ready.

Lily awoke, and as they splashed their faces in the frigid water from the wash bowl, she excitedly described for Cass, blow by blow, the fight she had won to earn her place in the final round. There were just six competitors left in the running: Cass and Lily were the only silk squires remaining. One of Pybba's middle sons had made the cut, Lily told Cass, as well as Sir Safir of the Round Table squires, and a junior knight of Mordaunt's court. They would each joust against two different opponents, and the most successful and skilful rider would win the tournament.

'It is hardly a fair fight, if King Pybba is the judge,' Cass complained, 'with his own son in competition for the title.'

'It isn't Pybba's decision alone,' Lily reassured her, 'he has brought his witan, and they all have an equal vote. And I hear they are none too keen to see the middle sons gain any more popularity than they can avoid. People say Pybba is old and weak, and there are enough wolves on the witan who would like to take his seat themselves, instead of see it pass to a popular son.'

'How do you always manage to know the juiciest gossip of a place less than a day after we arrive?' Cass shook her head in laughing admiration.

Lily grinned. 'Because I know that the people to ask are the ones nobody else notices!'

The last six competitors met at the field later that morning and were summoned to pay their respects to the king and the witan. Cass nervously fiddled with the straps of her breastplate and pulled her helmet down more firmly on her head. Although she knew the armour would protect her from being recognized, knew that nobody would ever suspect the truth, still she felt reckless as she walked boldly towards the dais and sank onto one knee like the others.

Pybba was doddery and bloated: his watery eyes seemed to widen in surprise as if he had not expected to see them there, and Cass, exchanging a glance with Lily, thought she understood why the members of his council were so concerned with succession.

'My noble Lord Arthur sends you his greetings, lord,' the squire of the red dragon proclaimed loudly, and Pybba nodded vaguely, his eyes fixed on his own son.

'This is a great opportunity to show your worth and mettle,' he wheezed, waving his hand uncertainly in the direction of the field. 'May fortune favour you. Godspeed.' And he slumped back in his chair, clearly dismissing them.

'I am Sir Gamelin,' a pleasant, low voice came from beside Cass as they rose to their feet and began to walk back towards the lists, and she turned and found herself looking straight into those hazel eyes, the crinkled smile always hovering at their edges, the full lips parted a little, dark stubble shadowing the square jaw.

He smiled expectantly, waiting for her to respond. Cass panicked, feeling sweat spring out onto her upper lip inside her helmet. His eyes met hers through the slit in her helmet and she saw a faint frown flicker across his face, a moment of confused recognition. She lifted a hand in acknowledgement of his greeting and stumbled hastily and wordlessly away, leaving him gazing curiously after her.

'The boy you've been swooning over since you met him in the forest? The one who rescued you at the ball?' Lily fizzed with excitement as they checked their horses' bridles and stirrups. 'It's fate, Cass!'

'I have *not* been swooning!' Cass hissed indignantly, already regretting having opened up to Lily about Gamelin. 'And he did not "rescue" me, he was simply in the right place at the right time. I could have fought that knight off myself if I had needed to, just like Sigrid said.'

'Sure,' Lily nodded mischievously, 'but you didn't have to, did you, because Prince Dreamy arrived . . .'

Cass batted her with the gauntlet she was about to pull back on. 'Not a prince. Not dreamy.' She looked across the field, her eyes following the black shield with the silver antlers. 'Just another novice knight to beat on the way to winning this tournament.'

'That's the spirit.' Lily grinned, her dimples flashing. 'But you'll have to put your gauntlet on the right hand if you're going to do that.' And Cass flushed and quickly pulled it off again.

The sky began to darken as Lily trotted to the end of the lists for her first joust, where she had been drawn to face

King Pybba's son. Angharad looked up at the swollen clouds rolling towards them across the huddled roofs of Tamworth and frowned. 'The ground may be muddy and churned up by the time you ride, Cass,' she cautioned. 'It will be harder for your horse to keep her footing. But you can use it to your advantage too. Your opponent will be less able to keep tight control of his mount, so last-minute adjustments will be difficult.'

They all watched as Lily sat poised in her saddle, her lance straight and still, her pure white shield ready. At the other end of the lists, Pybba's second-eldest son, the one who had squabbled with his brother over the emerald-set sword, saluted his father as he pulled on his helmet and raised his lance to indicate he was ready.

The flag dropped and the two raced towards each other just as the first drops of rain began to fall. Lily's helmet lowered as she urged her horse onwards, her lance travelling smoothly forward, until the moment of impact, when it caught her opponent with exact precision in the centre of his shield, knocking him backwards so that he rolled off his horse without ever managing to make contact with his own lance at all.

'YES!' Cass punched the air and jumped up and down, cheering along with Sigrid and Angharad, as well as the other squires who had come to support Lily despite having been knocked out of the tournament themselves.

Lily returned, her face flushed beneath her raised visor, and Cass hugged her tightly.

But there was little time to celebrate. It was Cass's turn. Her whole body began to tingle with anticipation as she lowered her visor and mounted Pebble. 'We can do this,' she whispered fiercely into the little horse's ear. 'We can do it together.'

She checked for a moment, pulling gently on the reins, as Sigrid came to hand over her lance.

'I am proud of you. No matter what the outcome,' Sigrid said gruffly and unexpectedly, before turning abruptly away and marching back to the other spectators, leaving a lump in Cass's throat.

She swallowed hard and proceeded to the end of the lists, then lowered her visor, protecting her face from the drizzle that had begun to fall lightly from a tight, iron-grey sky. At the opposite end of the field, the confident squire of Arthur's fellowship was preening a little, allowing his horse to prance back and forth to the delight of the crowd. When he turned and raised his clenched fist to indicate he was ready, the crowd roared its support.

Cass closed her eyes for a moment, blocking them out, narrowing her focus to her own body, to her connection with Pebble and her single forward trajectory. Then she opened them and squeezed her calves together hard, her heart leaping joyfully as Pebble streamed forward, their bodies moving in perfect harmony. Her lance was ready, her shield gripped firmly in preparation for impact. And as if they were standing quietly right next to her, she heard Angharad, Sigrid and Vivian's voices as clear as birdsong on a windless day.

Aim for the upper-right quadrant of the shield.

Lower the reins at the last moment.

Carry the momentum forward, and do not check your horse.

Her body responded to the training, smoothly repeating the movements she had practised over and over and over again in the meadow behind the manor.

Just before the moment of impact, she saw Arthur's squire bring his lance forward, his confidence bursting out of him, and she knew, before she even felt it, that the blow would be glancing: he had not couched his weapon and the force would ricochet through his wrist, twisting him sideways. And precisely as all this happened, her own lance struck his shield, bold and true, exactly where it was supposed to, and his already twisting body was tossed like a doll out of his saddle and into the softening ground.

Then the roars of the crowd swept back in as if suddenly Cass could hear again, and she was hugging an ecstatic Lily and being heartily applauded by the older knights and burying her face in Pebble's mane, and there was a look of pride on Sigrid's face that was sweeter than all the rest of it put together.

They watched as Sir Gamelin in his black tunic and Sir Safir in blood-red faced each other from opposite ends of the lists, Safir's magnificent, jet-black stallion pawing its hooves in anticipation. But though Safir bore down on him with the speed of a hurricane, Sir Gamelin, smaller, slighter on his piebald mare, lifted himself slightly out of his saddle just at the moment before they met, so that Safir's eyes widened in panic as his lance slipped harmlessly beneath his opponent's shield and Gamelin took him in the centre of the shield, his lance shattering, and knocked Safir beneath the frantic hooves of his horse.

Cass saw Sir Elyan race forward, the blood draining from his face, desperate to calm the horse and lead it aside, and the sheer, immense relief in his expression when Sir Safir climbed shakily to his feet and limped from the field.

'Then there were three,' Lily said dramatically. But the smiles disappeared from both of their faces a moment later when the steward announced that in the next round of combat the two knights of the white shield must ride against each other to determine who would proceed to the final round.

Chapter 32

'I won't do it.' Lily was striding back and forth, her fists clenched. 'They cannot make us ride against each other, it is not fair, I will simply resign from the tournament.'

'I won't let you,' Cass gasped, close to tears. 'You have been training as a squire far longer than me – if anybody should resign it should be me.' And she tasted the bile of disappointment, even as she tried to smile encouragingly at her friend.

'Neither of you may resign,' Angharad hissed angrily. 'Not without arousing unnecessary suspicion. No man would shy away from a fight, even if it were against one of his own fellowship. The lances are blunted, the course is safe and there is too much at stake for either of you to give up now.'

Lily looked rebellious, shaking her head vigorously. But before they could protest any further, the trumpets sounded and as if in a dream, Cass felt herself being boosted up into her saddle, her lance thrust into her hand.

'I will feint,' she whispered urgently to Lily, as their horses' heads turned in opposite directions. 'Take my shield in the centre, I will let my lance travel too far to the left so it does not touch yours, and you will unseat me.' And before Lily had the chance to object, to say anything else at all, she kicked her heels and Pebble cantered towards the far end of the lists.

The rain had begun to fall in earnest now; heavy, large drops plopping onto Cass's helmet and tracing uncomfortable, cold trails down her neck and back. She shivered, and readjusted her grip on her lance, squinting down the field to see Lily hunched miserably over her shield, her helmet drooping, lance held limply beneath her arm.

'Come on, Lily,' Cass muttered under her breath. 'Don't let your nerve fail you now.'

The flag fell and they both began to trot forward, their horses seeming to sense their hesitation, reluctant to break into a canter. Cass urged Pebble onwards, ready to slip her lance sideways, ready to give her friend the victory, braced for the impact of the fall.

And then something took over. Cass felt it invading her, filling her, the warm, golden light that had come to her for the first time on the edge of that tournament field in Eboracum. And she tried to fight it, tried to push it away or force it down, because she didn't want it, not now! She wanted to fail, wanted to give Lily the gift of her defeat.

But something inside her would not allow it. It took over her limbs and her lance and forced them into formation, then burst out of her in a perfect blow that smashed into the white shield with shattering force, not only leaving her lance splintered and ruined but battering her best friend so powerfully that she flew backwards out of her saddle and rolled over and over in mid-air before she hit the ground with a sickening crash and lay still.

Cass could not breathe. Pebble ran automatically the rest of the length of the field, with no check or signal from Cass to stop her. She raised her visor and sat there for a moment, gazing out across the farmland beyond the field, stunned, as if the blow had been to her own head, not to Lily's shield. Then her limbs unfroze and she was sliding, tumbling frantically out of the saddle and running across the grass, her feet slipping and slithering in the wet mud kicked up by the horses' hooves, skidding to her knees beside the still body in the cross-hatched leather armour.

Angharad and Sigrid were beside Lily, lifting the visor,

and seeing the eyelids fluttering beneath Cass cried hot tears of relief as together they lifted her and carried her off the field.

Lily was alive, she knew that much. 'Likely just stunned,' Sigrid told her, bluntly, but there was no time to take it in, no time for Cass to do any more than squeeze her friend's hand and fiercely whisper, 'I am sorry,' into her ear, before she was thrust unwillingly back onto her horse, gripping a new lance, back in the now-driving rain, riding to the lists for the final round.

Sir Gamelin rode past the crowd as was customary for the last pair of challengers, his helmet under his arm, his light brown hair swept back from his forehead, his lips curving into a slightly bashful smile. Cass remembered what he had told her of his background at the feast, and wondered if all this felt more overwhelming to him than he let on. The crowd rose to their feet, clapping and shrieking for him, a great roar of sound pushing him onwards. Cass did not follow him but numbly let Pebble carry her to her place at the end of the lists, turning to face her opponent as he gave her a respectful nod and smile and pulled on his helmet.

Cass felt sick and weak. The fire inside her seemed to have flickered and gone out. The idea of becoming a knight suddenly seemed distant and absurd without Lily's encouraging presence beside her. She wanted to abandon the field altogether, to run back to Lily's side. This didn't matter. She shouldn't be here. But she heard Angharad's stern voice in her head – she couldn't give up and risk arousing suspicion.

The first pass was fast and brutal. Gamelin's horse was fleet and his aim was perfect. But even in her worried state, Cass's muscle memory took over, Pebble remembered her training, and the lances met their shields at exactly the same moment, both splintering, both pushing the other backwards in their saddles, but neither quite unseated. The shock of it was like a pail of freezing cold water being poured over Cass's head. She gasped and struggled upright, grappling to regain control of Pebble's reins. Her neck ached and her arm throbbed, almost vibrated with pain, but she had not been unseated. She was still in this.

She turned to face Sir Gamelin again while great, billowing sheets of rain flew across the field so that her vision was almost obscured.

'She lives. She will recover fully.'

It was Sigrid, bearing a new lance and news to make Cass's heart leap within her breast. Squinting through the rain to the edge of the field, she could see that Lily was sitting up, supported by Angharad, and that she was talking. A burning relief the like of which she had never felt before spread through Cass's veins like liquid fire.

She turned and galloped straight for Sir Gamelin, her

heart on fire, thighs gripping tight to Pebble's sides, her lance clasped beneath her arm with all the strength she had. But Gamelin was a shade faster, his lance seeming to fly through the air towards her, unstoppable. With the sheer force of the blow its covered tip ricocheted off the top left-hand corner of her shield and smashed into her left shoulder, forcing her backwards again before her own lance could even make contact, sending a shooting pain through her body that felt like a bright, clean, searing flash of light.

But she was not unseated. By some miracle she hung on grimly, her right foot still tangled in the stirrup, even as the rest of her body sprawled helplessly down Pebble's left flank like yolk dripping from a smashed eggshell.

Then Sigrid's hands were there, meeting her, supporting her, pushing her back upwards, and with a gargantuan effort she regained her seat, though her body felt as though it were vibrating with pain and exhaustion. Her shield drooped from her left arm, but her lance was still firm and steady, and as the rain pounded down around her, Sigrid shouted words of encouragement and advice and slapped Pebble's rump so that she charged back into the fray.

Gamelin's body was pressing forward, his horse scenting victory. Cass was shattered, throbbing with pain and barely able to see through the driving rainstorm. As they drew closer, she began to prepare herself for the blow, the impact, the inevitable fall.

But at the last moment, she remembered Angharad's words. *'Last-minute adjustments will be difficult . . . Use it to your advantage.'*

With a final, gargantuan effort, Cass checked her horse at the last possible moment, doing everything she had been taught not to. Pebble hesitated in surprise, Cass saw Gamelin's lance jerk upwards in panic as he tried to readjust his trajectory, but his horse skidded in the slick mud and he twisted sideways, missing Cass altogether. In the same moment she kicked her heels hard into Pebble's flanks and flew forward, striking her opponent in the centre of the shield, knocking him backwards. But Pebble's hooves were slipping now in the same boggy ground that had undone Gamelin's horse, and in horror Cass felt herself lurching unstoppably forward, tumbling with Gamelin over the flank of his horse and into the mud.

It was a terrifying tangle of limbs and splintered weapons, crashing hooves and hot, panting breath. Cass rolled clear and jumped to her feet, her heart pounding as she saw that Gamelin had immediately drawn his sword. She reached for her own, automatically, and it leaped into her hand as if keen to be used, sending a jolt of that warm certainty down her arm and into her stomach.

'After the third bout, if both knights are unseated, the matter is decided by the sword,' came a booming announcement from the seneschal.

'Ready?' Gamelin gasped, as squires rushed forward to lead the panting horses away. Cass gulped and nodded grimly, gripping her sword tighter.

He and Cass circled each other, swords held ready, each wary, each trying to catch their breath, each waiting for the other to make the first move. The rain was like a physical curtain between them, so thick and distorting that it felt as if she were doing battle with a ghost.

Gamelin swooped, his sword slicing through the air and forcing Cass to bring up her shield to meet it. She gasped as the motion sent a stabbing pain racing through her shoulder. The blow was deflected, but at a high cost. Her shield drooped lower. The knight paused, his sword still raised, and lifted his visor.

'Are you all right?' he asked, without relaxing his stance or lowering his sword, so that no casual viewer would have known that he spoke. But his gentle golden hazel eyes were creased with concern. 'There is no shame in retiring, if you are wounded. I don't want to hurt you.'

Cass shook her head fiercely, heaving her shield arm back up, gritting her teeth to ignore the tearing pain. It felt as if the very fibres of her muscle were shredding, and she screamed silently inside her helmet. The fight would have to be over quickly. She would not last much longer.

She allowed herself to droop, seeming to falter, her shield suddenly lowered. And when he leaned forward worriedly, lowering his own shield, as she had known he would, she took her chance. She leaped forward, dropping her shield altogether and taking the chance to make a great stabbing blow, the point of her sword finding the join between his breastplate and his pauldron. She felt the flesh yield, felt the slight resistance give way to spongy softness, and he screamed and jumped backwards, his black tunic darkening further with the wetness of blood.

Dimly, through the tumult of the downpour and the shrieking of the wind, she heard a surge of noise from the crowd and knew that they were baying for blood, hoping for another blow that would finish it.

'So it will be that way, will it?' he panted angrily, and he smashed her sword aside with his shield, advancing on her where she stood, shieldless now and unprotected. Cass felt fear then, as she had not allowed herself to feel it since that very first night at the manor in Lily's bed. She saw the gleam of the blade, and imagined it slicing through her skin, cleaving muscle and bone. At the very last minute, she ducked and twisted, the sword whistling a finger's width from her cheek, and she turned backwards and stumbled right into him, just as she had in the forest, her body pressed against his, her helmet crashing against his breastplate.

For a single breath the rain seemed to hang suspended in the air before her, weightless, as she flashed back to that day in the quiet glade and the smell of him. 'No!' she burst out, exactly as she had before. She heard him gasp. Then her body took over and she raised her foot, to stamp it down on his exactly as she had before.

'Not this time,' he shouted, kicking out to sweep her other leg from under her at the very moment she lifted her foot, so that she fell down, through the rain and into the now-swirling river of mud underfoot, his sword raised to claim victory, and in the fall and the confusion and the clash of their armour her helmet caught on his gauntlet and was wrenched from her head, pulling the leather thong from her hair with it, and she lay in the mud, pelted with the deluge of rain, her face and hair exposed, her secret revealed, her mouth open in horror.

For a long moment he stared down at her, while her stomach filled with lead and the heavy curtain of rain wrapped itself round them, hiding the spectators from view. She watched, helpless, as the shock of recognition crossed his features. 'You are not just the youth from the forest, but also the girl from the feast.' Then shock was replaced by indecision, even fear, as he glanced towards the crowds, where already onlookers were getting to their feet, threatening to press closer in an attempt to see what had happened.

He took off his helmet and bent closer, his body obscuring her from their view. His face was so close to hers that she could feel the roughness of his chin, see the amber flecks in his eyes. Rivulets of rain ran down his forehead and dripped onto her chin.

'Please know,' he whispered, his breath warm on her lips. 'Not all Mordaunt's men are of his ilk.'

And without knowing exactly how or why she did it, Cass raised her head, the slightest fraction, so that their lips met, wet with rainwater and salty with sweat. He did not move away, and for a long, suspended moment, she felt the kiss through every aching muscle of her body, every freezing, soaked patch of skin.

There were shouts of frustration from behind them and the splash of approaching boots in the mud.

'Quickly,' he urged, and he seized her helmet in his hands and gently lifted her head, slipping it back on. Then he took his sword and pressed it into her uncomprehending hands, pulling her to her knees.

A moment later, they were overtaken, surrounded by onlookers and competitors and members of the witan, all shouting and quarrelling at once.

'Chaotic . . .'

'Outrageous!'

'Demand to know . . .'

'My lord.' Sir Gamelin spoke calmly, his voice raised above the storm, looking past all of them. King Pybba had risen and made his way falteringly across the boggy field, his defeated sons trailing sullenly behind him. He gazed on the scene, discombobulated, leaning heavily on an elaborately carved wooden staff, its engravings coated in gilt.

'My lord, I must forfeit the battle,' Gamelin spoke directly to the king. 'As you see, my opponent has relieved me of my sword.' He gave a bitter laugh. 'And as victor, I believe he has earned the right of anonymity.'

Cass was beginning to understand: she struggled to her feet, an objection in her throat, but Gamelin turned, for the swiftest moment, and shot her a warning look.

'Very well,' the king sighed, waving them all away as if the thing had become tiresome to him. He looked down at his feet and seemed to see for the first time the sticky, oozing mud that coated his shoes and clung to the fur lining of his cloak. He clicked his tongue in irritation and gestured to summon his attendants. 'Let us get out of this damned storm.'

Chapter 33

It was a muted homecoming. Lily was bruised and pale, but well enough to ride. She drooped in the saddle, never once turning her head in Cass's direction. And for her part, Cass was forced to ride one-handed, her left arm roughly strapped across her body, the pain spreading now so that it felt as if her whole torso were suffused with it.

The others did not seem to know how to treat Cass. Leah grasped her hand excitedly and Sigrid gave her a brief but fierce hug, but the others' eyes flickered in Lily's direction and their congratulations were dampened.

'I did not mean to,' Cass struggled to explain when she left the field and returned to the bedraggled group, the rain still pouring down around them. 'It was not my choice. It just happened.' She spread her hands helplessly, wishing she could explain, knowing how ridiculous she sounded.

'You were victorious,' Sigrid barked tersely, giving the others a defensive glare. 'We told you to fight, and you proved yourself.'

'Nobody is disputing that she proved herself, Sigrid,' Angharad snapped, but her eyes were on Lily's downcast face. 'Though the visibility was so poor that the final bout was concealed from us.' And she looked piercingly at Cass, who blinked and lowered her visor.

They stopped only briefly at their lodgings to change into dry clothes and wait for a gap in the rain before they rode for home, a sombre procession that belied Cass's victory. And all thought of a knighthood seemed to have been left on the muddy field.

There were scouts with grave faces waiting for Angharad upon their return. Their conversations were urgent and whispered, but Cass could hear mention of Saxon bands, of war hosts encroaching, and Angharad's face creased with concern as she swept the messengers away to her chambers.

Lily was taken directly to her room, with a herbal concoction from Alys and strict instructions to rest. She did not meet Cass's beseeching gaze, and there was no opportunity to speak to her then, or in the days that followed. Her chamber door was firmly closed, guarded by pages tasked with ensuring complete rest and privacy. Nor did Cass know what she would have said even if she had been admitted. For the first time since her arrival at the manor she felt the loss of Lily's warm, vibrant presence.

As she came downstairs for breakfast a few days later, she overheard a heated discussion further along the corridor.

'—should be knighted, she has earned it!'

'And what of Lily? It was dishonourable to earn victory by obliterating one of her own! She will have to wait until next year . . .'

'And what if I . . .'

'Yes? If you retaliate? Do you think that I am not aware every day that you could ruin us with what you know is sunk within that pool?'

Cass gasped, and Angharad and Sigrid looked up, their faces guilty and surprised.

'I understand,' Cass muttered, and she abandoned the manor, suddenly not feeling hungry at all, and, taking a basket from the kitchen, slipped out into the woods instead.

She felt hot with shame and frustration as she stomped into the trees, trying to focus on foraging for the mushrooms she knew they had almost run out of in the larder, but too distracted by her own thoughts to concentrate on the task.

It was not just the way the battle had unfolded, the fear

that she had disgraced herself by attacking Lily so ruthlessly, the sickening panic that she might have lost her best friend or the awareness that she had not been able to control the power that welled up inside her. There was also another, deeper fear that throbbed beneath the rest, like a deep bruise that she felt every time she moved.

One of Mordaunt's knights knew her secret. And yes, every part of her body remembered the kiss, as if it had been some alchemy that had altered her cells, changed her skin. Yes, she felt instinctively that he would not betray her. But how could she be sure? She had exposed the entire order, and to a member of the household of their most dangerous enemy. How could she keep that concealed? But telling them would surely mean expulsion from the place she had come to call home.

And even that home seemed tainted now, and unreliable. Could Sigrid be trusted not to betray Angharad's crime? Were they even right to cover up what she had done?

Cass stumbled blindly on through the trees.

The storm had cleared, leaving behind a blustery spring breeze, and the first bluebells were beginning to nod their heads in velvet patches that carpeted the forest floor.

Cass sighed and sat down at the base of an oak tree, leaning her back against the trunk as she gently rotated her stiff shoulder.

'The motion seems better already.'

She jumped and turned to see Alys, swathed in a woollen shawl, carrying a basket full of wild garlic.

Cass nodded. 'The pain is fading. Thank you for the poultice.'

Alys set down her basket and lowered herself onto the mossy ground next to Cass.

'It cannot be easy, to return home both a hero and a villain.'

Cass nodded briefly.

'This will not be the end of the journey, Cass,' Alys said gently.

When Cass did not answer or raise her eyes, Alys continued. 'Cass, there is something I need to tell you about. Something I have been thinking about since I saw your tea leaves that day.'

Cass shrugged wearily. 'What do a bunch of leaves at the bottom of a cup matter?'

Alys smiled. 'That is a fair question.' She paused, looking thoughtfully up at the clouds.

'There are people who ask what the contents of a baby's dream matter, but I have seen how a child stricken with fever often recovers the morning after a night of terrors, and know that a dreamless sleep often foreshadows a tragic morning when there is no awakening.

'As a child, I grew up in an unusual home. It was a

community, where groups of people who were not welcome in other settlements tried to raise their families together, supporting each other. I learned from each of them. Women who knew about the plants that would help other women to make decisions about their own bodies. Who were at risk of death if the knowledge was shared more widely. People from the old communities, who shared the old ways, the things others fear and so speak of as if they are evil.'

She sighed heavily. 'They are gone now. We were not safe, in the end. And the community was scattered. So I ended up here. But I have remembered the different things they taught me. And yes, some believe it is foolish to think we can learn anything about a person from the formation of the leaves left at the bottom of their cup. But it is just another tool of interpretation, of fallible human attempts to know ourselves, and the world around us. Who are you, or I, to decide what is science and what is myth? Are not our astrologers frequently wrong? Are there not patients our doctors of physic cannot save? Are there not, now, methods and ideas seen as brilliant and ground-breaking that would have been considered lunacy just a few short years ago?'

Her voice was sad and tired. 'Cass, there is a prophecy. A promise that was whispered amongst the people who still remembered the old ways. A story that had been handed down by those who lived in these forests for a long time.

About a person who would come, who would be a light in the face of the gathering dark.'

'I am tired, Alys.' Cass rose to her feet. She could not hear any more. Already she felt as if the bright, shining future that had seemed to hover just beyond her fingertips had been snatched away. She didn't want to hear that she was special, that the thing she felt inside her was real. What good was it, if she had lost Lily? If she could not even achieve knighthood? What did it matter, now she had single-handedly threatened the survival of the whole fellowship? It was nonsense. None of it was real.

She struggled to her feet, her muscles still aching in protest.

'Thank you for trying to cheer me up.'

Alys did not attempt to stop her as she turned and trudged back the way she had come.

There was a gathering in the hall when Cass returned, the senior women of the fellowship all sitting around with Angharad and the scouts, their faces drawn and worried. There was a map unrolled before them on the table, and Vivian was pointing to different areas, muttering about incursions and risk.

Angharad banged her fist on the table in frustration. 'We should be united as a region in the face of this threat,' she said angrily. 'Not fractured and harried by Mordaunt and his men. If we cannot raise a fyrd of fighters to defend our territory because the people have been so impoverished and malnourished by his greed then we will not stand against the invaders . . .' She broke off as a young girl scampered into the hall, holding up her skirts as she raced towards the group.

'Mordaunt . . .' she panted. 'At the gates, with several men.'

'Quick!' Vivian ordered, sweeping the map and other papers from the table and thrusting them into the arms of a nearby page. Most of the women were already dressed in their daytime clothes, but a few who had been clad in armour, having come directly from training, quickly exited the hall.

They had barely composed themselves when the door opened again and Sir Mordaunt swept regally into the room, flanked by four knights in full armour. He wore a rich, full-length tunic of peacock blue, and a fine, gold-trimmed cloak fastened at the shoulder with an ornate metal brooch in the shape of an oak leaf. His thick, shaggy black hair had been partially tamed with oily pomade and swept back, which seemed to make his thin, pale lips and pointed yellow teeth all the more prominent.

Angharad rose, and stepped forward. 'Sir Mordaunt, this is an unexpected honour.'

'Let us abandon the pretence of civility, shall we, lady?' Mordaunt sneered, and Angharad stiffened.

'Forgive me, I do not understand . . .'

'Where are they?'

'My husband and his men ride on business, lord.'

'Not your husband, witch, the men you are protecting.'

'The men, lord?'

'Did you think I would not discern the truth?' Little flecks of spittle flew from his tongue and gathered at the edges of his mouth. 'Did you think me so stupid that I would not realize what was going on?'

'My lord,' Angharad's voice was controlled, humble, feminine. 'Truly, I am entirely ignorant of your meaning.'

Mordaunt scoffed with rage, his skin beginning to turn a slightly mottled purple colour. He held up his fingers and began to tick them off one by one. 'My knights being repeatedly attacked and undermined in their own territory. Attempts to steal game from my lands. An ambush on a group of my men shortly after you had berated them most discourteously for their actions in a nearby village. Do you take me for a fool?'

Angharad murmured something soft and placatory, and Cass saw how she was shrinking into the role of submission that Mordaunt expected, presenting the picture of feminine supplication and confusion that she needed him to believe.

'I am sorry to hear of this, my lord.'

Mordaunt snorted. 'You are hiding them.' He almost spat

the words out. 'These so-called "nameless knights". Sheltering them. Perhaps even working with them. Outlaw knights who have no land rights here, no authority to undermine my rule.'

For just the briefest moment Angharad tried to hide a small smile, and Mordaunt, seeing it, seemed to fly into even more of a rage.

'*Do you take me for a fool?*'

'My lord,' Angharad moved closer, her hands held out in supplication, 'I am merely struck by the absurdity of this suggestion. My ladies and I live quiet and secluded lives here in my husband's frequent absence, as well you know. The very idea of any involvement in such matters is far beyond our wildest imaginings.'

Mordaunt scowled and his voice dropped lower, dripping with threat.

'I might have believed that once. But now there is the matter of Beolin.'

Cass saw Vivian's chest rise with a sharp intake of breath, saw the colour drain from her cheeks. But Angharad stood still as stone, her expression revealing nothing.

'Yes, Sir Beolin,' Mordaunt bellowed. 'Do not pretend you have not heard of him. We know about his stays here, when you were unchaperoned, lady, so do not act the innocent with me.'

Angharad's cheeks flushed angrily, and a muscle was

twitching in Vivian's cheek, but still the women did not speak.

'And now,' Mordaunt snarled, 'Beolin, who had begged us to throw in our lot with him, who had made a pact to raise a joint war host and taken a great sum of gold from my coffers to begin to recruit men, has failed to reappear at the agreed time.'

Angharad opened and closed her mouth. 'My lord?'

'Reneged on our agreement. Disappeared with my wealth. After spending time with you. And whoever else you are sheltering in this place.' He wiped sweat from his upper lip and slammed his fist down on the table with a crash that made Cass flinch. 'And now we are left without the funds or the men to defend our lands, while the Saxon war host masses to the west.'

'No, lord, I assure you,' Angharad whispered weakly, 'we hide nothing.' But Mordaunt turned to his knights.

'Search the place,' he ordered, and they stepped forward. 'Find what they are hiding.'

Cass saw the panic ripple across the faces in the hall, saw Angharad's face convulse with fear.

'NO.' Vivian stepped forward, and Mordaunt raised his hands, staying his knights. 'No. A search will not be necessary.'

Angharad whipped round to face Vivian. Her voice was strangled. 'Vivian, do not.'

'We must tell him, my lady,' Vivian said firmly, inclining

her head towards Mordaunt. 'For Sir Beolin's decisions are his own, and we must not be blamed for them. We should not protect him.'

'Vivian.' There was a warning in Angharad's voice, but Vivian ignored it, taking another step forward.

'You are right, sir,' she addressed Mordaunt directly, her tone deliberately submissive. 'Sir Beolin did visit here, both before his meeting with you and, briefly, afterwards. He spoke of your folly, sir, I am sorry to say, in providing payment up front before the men had been raised. He spoke of taking the riches and returning home, and asked my lady to accompany him, which, of course, she immediately declined to do. We should have come to you, my lord, and revealed this, but we were afraid that you might punish us if we disclosed what we knew.'

Mordaunt's chest heaved. Angharad was staring at Vivian in disbelief.

'It was not the first time I think, lord, that he had made you look a fool,' Vivian continued, grimacing a little as if she were pained at having to reveal such delicate information. 'I believe on his first visit he hinted at the actions of some of his men in the area, who he had tasked with busying and thwarting your men to help persuade you of the threat, so that you would be more likely to join him and throw your wealth behind the endeavour.'

'If this is true,' Mordaunt wheezed, his face now a dark shade of puce, 'then Beolin will pay.' He turned to Angharad with a nasty gleam in his eyes. 'He was enamoured with you, lady, that much was plain. So we will test his loyalty to you, shall we?'

'Please, sir,' Angharad objected. 'I do not know where Sir Beolin is and have no special bond with him.'

Mordaunt gave a nasty grin. 'I would be more inclined to believe that, lady, had we not passed your stables on our way through the courtyard. There is a very fine new charger in your stalls, is there not?' He sneered at her unpleasantly. 'It bears a *striking* similarity to Beolin's steed.' He turned to his knights and snapped out his orders. 'Send scouts and messengers throughout the region. Beolin cannot have travelled more than a few days on foot and he would not have left his horse if he did not intend to return. Send word that I will meet him in single combat three days hence, at the tournament field at Gefrin. Let him face me and save his honour, or forfeit his life and the gold if I am the victor.' He stopped, and strode right up to Angharad, his wolfish teeth bared a hair's breadth from her face. 'Your household will be expected to attend, of course, *my lady.*' There was silence and the crackling of the fire.

'And if Beolin fails to take up my challenge, let it be known that I will raze this place to the ground.'

Chapter 34

The hours that followed were fraught with tension and fear. Everyone from the oldest knight to the youngest page haunted the halls of the manor in a fevered daze. Urgent, whispered conversations took place among huddled knots of women. Cass overheard some of the younger squires worrying about whether Sir Beolin would return to defend their mistress, anxiously wondering whether word would reach him in time. Cold slithered round her stomach. They didn't know that there was no possibility of his return. A few, those lucky enough to have homes to return to, or distant relatives, rolled their possessions into bundles and departed.

On the second afternoon, Cass passed the bottom of the

staircase leading to Angharad's chambers and heard her shouting, 'You cannot fix this! You have done enough!' before there was the loud slam of a door and Vivian descended the stairs, her face stained with tears.

All Cass wanted was to talk it over with Lily, their legs tucked under a sheepskin together, with a reassuring fire crackling in the background. But Lily still did not leave her room, and though her strength was said to be returning, she would not allow Cass to be admitted, no matter how many times she knocked.

The morning of the third day dawned cold and muted, the sky slate grey. Angharad sat like stone in the hall, eating nothing, drinking only a small amount of ale, Vivian grey-faced beside her.

'We could . . .'

Angharad silenced her with a small, tight shake of her head.

'We have no options left. When Beolin does not appear, I will admit the truth about my lord and offer myself to Mordaunt. It will not protect our way of life here, but it will protect our lives.'

There were gasps around the hall and a young page burst into tears.

'I am sorry.' Angharad's voice was flat and expressionless. 'I thought it was possible to create a world for ourselves within another world that does not allow us to choose our own paths. I was wrong. But I will not allow any of you to suffer for my mistake.'

'You cannot sacrifice yourself,' Vivian cried. But Angharad raised a hand to silence her and stood to lead them from the hall.

It was a stricken procession that walked the mile and a half from the manor gates to the great tournament field, traipsing disconsolately up the slopes that led towards Mordaunt's grand mansion. Angharad had ordered everyone in the sisterhood to attend, but Cass saw that their numbers were few, so many having fled. Lily was still confined to her room and both Vivian and Sigrid had flatly refused to witness the destruction of everything they had worked for.

The field sat to the west of the fortifications that made up the outer wall, a long, pleasant terrace cut into the hillside with one end open to the slopes and the other bordered by a copse of birch and hazel trees where the woods crept up the side of the hill.

Mordaunt and his court were already present, the knights and attendants surrounding their lord who sat mounted on a pure black warhorse, its muscles rippling beneath a gleaming coat. He wore a full coat of chainmail beneath the black armour, the silver antlers on his shield matching the blinding shine of his helmet.

The women filed into a small wooden stand, the sun shining warm on their faces. Cass sat mutely, staring straight ahead, her hands clutched numb in her lap. Around her, she was aware of the whispering, the craning necks, as the appointed time drew near and the younger squires strained to glimpse the knight they hoped would arrive to avenge their mistress. Of those present, only Cass and Angharad knew for certain that Sir Beolin would not arrive.

Mordaunt's face was like a granite slab behind his raised visor as the time crept agonizingly by. As the minutes stretched out into an hour, Mordaunt turned his head, slowly, deliberately, to look Angharad in the eyes. Cass turned and saw the defeat on her face and felt her own heart breaking within her as Angharad rose, preparing to approach the knight.

But before she could move, there came a low, insistent thrumming in the distance, a heartbeat that grew and swelled into the unmistakable sound of galloping hooves.

Sir Beolin burst from the copse at the far end of the field, his distinctive armour gleaming, his stallion thundering across the field, the eagle feather fluttering jauntily atop his helmet, lance already drawn and ready. Angharad faltered, her mouth falling open, and there was an excited surge of chattering and cheers from the assembled women.

Sir Mordaunt snapped his visor down and wheeled his

horse to meet the oncoming rider, couching his great, black lance with its thin silver stripe beneath his arm as he rode.

They came together with a deafening impact, splinters of wood flying in all directions as both fell from their horses and immediately leaped to their feet, drawing their swords. Cass recognized the ornate gold sheath at Beolin's hip, and the richly jewelled hilt of his sword.

The battle was fierce and fast. They hacked and hewed at one another's armour until the ground around them was stained pink with blood that dripped from superficial wounds. The women in the stands strained forward as one, their silk dresses catching the sunlight, as the two knights struggled, locked in deadly combat.

Time crept by and both knights began to tire, their blows becoming wilder and more desperate, their movements more laboured, but both clung doggedly on in the fight, grimly determined. For a moment, it looked like Mordaunt was at a disadvantage, as the other knight hacked desperately at him, forcing him gradually backwards.

Then Mordaunt seemed to gather the very last of his strength and with a roaring battle cry he threw himself forward, attacking his opponent's left flank with a mighty backhanded blow. And both Cass and Angharad saw, at the same moment, the way that the other knight's left ankle buckled, how he stumbled backwards, and knew the truth.

And Angharad cried out, a long, tortured wail that cut through Cass's bones and would live forever in her memory, as the knight fell slowly backwards and Mordaunt leaped up with a curdling victory cry. He brought his sword-point mercilessly down to pierce the leather armour straight through to the heart.

The spectators fell silent as Angharad ran onto the field, her red hair flying behind her, burnished by the sun, and Mordaunt turned to bare his wolf snarl in victory to his men, who bayed his name until it rang from the walls of the manor.

But when Mordaunt turned to approach the body of his slain opponent, seeming to bend as if he would pull off the eagle-feather helmet, Angharad threw herself forward, shielding the body with her own.

'No,' she sobbed brokenly. 'We will bury him.' And Mordaunt shrugged and moved away, seeing nothing more in it than the grief of a woman whose paramour had been slain.

'Then let this be a lesson to you, lady,' his departing words rang out, 'about the company you keep.'

She made no retort, but simply eased the helmeted head onto her silk-covered lap and wept as if she would never stop.

Chapter 35

They buried Vivian in the meadow at dawn the following morning. Angharad's sobs had subsided into the agony of silence and so the only sound was the morning song of the blackbirds and the thrushes, the warblers and the wrens, and the soft swish of silk as the squires lowered their burden into the freshly dug grave.

They had wrapped her body in white cotton, after they had prised Angharad's arms from her neck, after gently removing Beolin's armour, and they buried her with her sword clasped between her hands.

Angharad threw a single white rose into the open grave and then her whole body seemed to crumple and Rowan and Lily supported her away, leaving the rest of them to fill the grave with closely packed earth, then cover it with heavy rocks to protect it from scavengers.

Nobody knew what to do after that. Cass returned to her chamber and lay silently on her bed. Sitting in the hall without Vivian did not feel right. How would they train again knowing that pile of awful rocks was weighting her body down in the meadow? Perhaps it would not matter: nobody seemed sure whether Angharad would even be willing to continue training knights at all now that Vivian was gone. Perhaps the sisterhood would simply disband, as quietly and secretly as it had formed.

There was a soft knock at the door and Lily stood there in tunic and hose, her face wan and tired beneath a square-sided cap. 'I thought we could join Rowan for a ride,' she said, as if agonizing days had not passed since they had last spoken to each other. 'Vivian was hers, almost as much as Angharad's. She shouldn't be alone today.' Cass nodded eagerly and pulled on her riding clothes, finding that her heart could still feel a tremor of hope, in spite of everything. As they walked out to the stables, she slipped her hand into Lily's, and though she did not speak or look at her, Cass thought she felt her give the slightest squeeze.

Blyth's eyes were full of sympathy for Rowan as they saddled their horses. Pebble seemed nervous, stamping her feet and tossing her head as Cass slipped the bridle over her head.

'They have not been themselves today,' Blyth said with a concerned frown, stroking Pebble gently on the nose.

The whole stable felt restless. Horses were whinnying and pacing in their stalls, and one colt was rearing up, pounding his hooves against the sturdy, iron-studded door of his stall again and again until sparks flew from the metal rivets.

Blyth grimaced and turned to the others. 'Perhaps you should not ride today. Something doesn't seem right.' Cass felt her skin crawl as Pebble seemed to shiver beneath her. For a moment, she considered returning inside. But then she thought of the ghoulish mood within, and looked at Rowan's red, swollen eyes and she shook her head. 'Perhaps they have picked up on the atmosphere, that's all,' she said reassuringly. And before Blyth could protest any further they urged the horses out of the stables, across the courtyard and into the woods.

Somewhere, somebody was burning a bonfire: a farmer clearing a patch of woodland, perhaps. The rich, savoury smell crept into Cass's nostrils and she felt exhilarated almost in spite of herself, the experience of being surrounded by trees and plants soothing and calming her troubled mind.

They did not speak as they picked their way through the woodland paths, allowing Rowan to lead the way. Buds were swelling promisingly on hawthorn and wild cherry trees. A few early flesh-coloured petals were pushing from their cramped winter confines to stretch gleefully into bloom. The trees seemed bedecked for a wedding, not a funeral, and their exuberance jarred at first, but as they rode on, Cass began to find it soothing. Hopeful.

At last they came to open country and unleashed the full energy of their mounts. Rowan streaked ahead, her handsome chestnut mare tossing her head, her mane and tail streaming in the wind. Lily and Cass were close behind, bent low to urge their ponies forward as they scythed across the spring-softened earth.

A bump appeared on the horizon, a little smudge of brown and grey that grew quickly larger as they galloped towards it. The smell of smoke was sharper now, and more acrid, catching bitterly in the back of Cass's throat. Her eyes began to stream as the smudge expanded into a billowing column of smoke stretching upwards from the horizon until it was swept sideways by the wind. Rowan looked back at them, alarm in her eyes, and reined in her mare. They approached more cautiously, trotting alongside each other.

It was not a bonfire. It was the village they had visited the previous year, or what was left of it.

Buildings crumbling, thatch ablaze.

The unforgettable stench of burning flesh.

A little body, spreadeagled, a cowlick still sticking up in the straw-blonde hair.

A woman keening, distraught, her voice more animal than human.

A smouldering crust of men in black tunics surrounding the injured and grieving, their impassive faces mocking the brutality of what they had done.

An elderly man stumbling away from a building, pursued by a man on horseback who threw a cruelly pointed spear and felled him like a sapling being snapped off at the root.

A father, bent over the body of his child, looking up, horror and incomprehension in his eyes. 'We could not pay,' he stammered in disbelief. 'They said it was too late.'

Rowan's cry of fury as she spurred her horse forward, the whistling of her blade as it swished through the air and then sang out as it met the sword of one of the men in the black tunics embellished with silver antlers.

Without thinking, without fear, Cass drew her sword too, and charged into the fray alongside Rowan, a bright, burning fury filling her with a heat so great it seemed to radiate out of her. She dismounted and set about herself, left and right, fighting more desperately than she ever had before. She felled one man, then another, dimly aware of the clashes of other swords around her, of screams and shouts and the sickening noise of snapping bones and blades hacking into flesh.

Everything poured out of her, through her hands and into

her blade. Her grief for Vivian, the injustice of Mordaunt's abuse of his people, the fear that she was about to lose her home and her purpose. Her power took over her, completely. Ruthlessly.

Gradually, quietness fell.

There were bodies around her, on the ground, some writhing and gasping, or making awful, wet, gurgling noises, some still and silent. In the distance, some villagers were still running. In the opposite direction, a few of Mordaunt's men were riding swiftly away, retreating to his stronghold.

It was then that Rowan put her hand on Cass's shoulder, and Cass looked up and knew from her face, without her ever having to say a word.

Lily lay on her side, blood trickling from the corner of her mouth. Her eyes stared blankly, her pink lips slightly open as if to express surprise.

Cass did not stop. She did not cry or bend down to touch the body or let herself feel the impact of the grief like a great hammer to her belly. She took up her sword and mounted Pebble and rode back to the manor as if a thousand wolves were chasing her.

She clattered across the courtyard and threw the reins to Blyth, who saw her face, her bloodied sword and clothes and cried out in alarm, but she did not stop. She ran through the hall, ignoring the shocked gasps of the squires and knights

349

inside. She leaped up the stone stairs three at a time and pounded furiously at the door of Angharad's chamber.

Angharad's face was pale; her hair hung greasy. There were dark yellow circles like bruises beneath her eyes. Her eyelids were rimmed red, her lips swollen.

Cass did not have time for any of that. She could not contemplate grief or let it in because it would swallow her whole.

'Mordaunt has massacred innocent villagers. Lily is dead. We must take action.'

There was no space for emotion or unnecessary explanations. These were the facts. They were all that mattered.

Cass continued, 'We cannot stand by any longer. This is not just tyranny. It is murder. It is diabolical. It cannot be allowed to stand.'

'I agree.' Angharad's voice trembled with anger. 'We will take it to the witan.'

So before the sun had set they had gathered in the hall, every one of them, knights and squires, pages and stable hands. And before the stars had fully emerged in the black velvet sky above the meadow, they had held a witan of their own, and voted, every one of them, to act.

Chapter 36

For three long weeks they watched and waited, while the early summer sun burnished the sky with silver sunrises and spectacular rose-gold sunsets.

In the pasture at the end of the meadow three new foals joyfully tested their spindly legs and buttercups studded the grass with gold. Dogrose and stitchwort burst into flower in the hedgerows and the woods were heady with the scent of honeysuckle.

The apple trees in the village were obscene with creamy blossom when they went to bury the dead and offer succour to the survivors. Everywhere they looked, spring was ripening into summer, as if nature ridiculed the dead.

There was a day when Alys led them out into the meadow,

her white cotton dress billowing in the summer breeze, and stood over the graves and carried out funeral rites. She scattered the stones with flowers, and laid their armour beside the headstones where Iona had chiselled their names. She sang and cried and remembered them. Elaine was there, and Blyth and the others, and they stood in a circle, hands clasped, as if they could not stand alone.

Cass refused to go out, her heart too raw to bear it, and watched instead from the window of Lily's tower room. But the scent of lavender broke her open and she lay on the mattress where Lily had first slipped her arm round her and wept.

Cass barely ate or slept. She did not let herself keep still or allow her mind to rest long enough to think of Lily. She would not visit the meadow, where they had buried Lily's body next to Vivian's, a second terrible pile of pale rocks. So she practised in the woods, or alone in her chamber, building her muscles and stamina with an intensity so relentless that even Sigrid expressed her concern.

'I know what it is to be consumed with grief,' she said abruptly one evening, when she returned to their chambers to find Cass lifting heavy rocks, sweat pouring down her back, her fingernails bloody and broken. 'Your anger is like a flame. You must feed it enough to keep it alive. But if you allow it to burn too bright it will reduce you to ash before you are able to act on it.'

But Cass did not listen. She could not.

Every moment she was not training, she was crawling on her belly in the bracken that carpeted the slopes leading up to Mordaunt's manor, or keeping watch in the branches of the copse of trees at the end of his tournament field. Her eyes followed every footstep of his knights and guards, every change of the watch on the ramparts, every delivery and messenger and excursion. By the third week they could account for all the occupants: an overwhelmingly male household due to Mordaunt's lack of a wife. They knew the patterns of the watch, the movements of the servants, the entrances and exits to the manor.

'We cannot take them in open battle,' Sigrid warned, as she and Cass, Angharad and Rowan and some of the other knights pored over plans of the manor and the surrounding woods by candlelight, long into the small, cold hours of the night. 'But they are not so many that we might not succeed by stealth.'

She paused and breathed in deeply, as if steeling herself.

Then Sigrid revealed everything, about Jonathan's squire, her long, grief-fuelled mission for revenge, her secret communication with a man inside Mordaunt's court. It was a long, tense evening, as Sigrid tried to explain herself, insisting they could rely on the inside information he provided, and Angharad railed furiously against her dishonesty and betrayal.

'Sigrid was right to keep it from us,' Rowan spoke bitterly into the silence when they had both subsided and were staring angrily into the fire. 'We have been too soft. We would not have used the information in the right way, before now. We should have acted sooner. We should have taken Mordaunt and his men long ago, whatever the price. If we had, then Vivian might still be alive. And Lily too. They should all die for what they have cost so many.'

Then Cass found herself speaking, quietly, uncertainly, the pain in her chest pressing down so hard that it was difficult to get the words out. She knew they had to act, that Lily must be avenged. But she was equally certain that Gamelin did not deserve to die, and that there might be others like him. So she told them the truth. About the battle of the squires, about how he had met her in the forest, how he had saved her at the feast and forfeited the tournament title to protect her from being unmasked. She told them everything, except the kiss.

She found herself laughing, empty and hollow when they turned on her afterwards. Because it struck her that this was the first and only time she might be glad Lily wasn't there, to be as disappointed in her as the others were. But it didn't matter if they were disappointed in her now. It didn't matter what they thought of her or what happened to her. They had to stop Mordaunt. After that it didn't matter what happened.

Without Lily, time seemed to stretch ahead in one listless, empty, unbearably colourless expanse of emptiness.

She did not care that Sigrid looked at her as if she didn't know her. Didn't care that Rowan narrowed her eyes in disgust and muttered that she had guessed Cass was concealing something, ever since that day in the forest when she had plunged into the pool. Didn't even care that Angharad rose and left without even a backward glance. None of it mattered any more.

'I should have told you sooner,' Cass said flatly. 'But it doesn't change the fact that there are good people in bad places. You needed to know.'

'You only know that because you have been fraternizing with the enemy,' Rowan spat. 'After everything Angharad and Vivian have done for you. It is not the same as Sigrid working with someone she already knew to try and bring down Mordaunt. It was selfish. And stupid.'

Cass nodded wearily. The emptiness wouldn't let her find the energy to defend herself. And anyway, maybe Rowan was right. Maybe she didn't deserve to be here. Perhaps, after what came next, they would not want her to stay. But she couldn't think that far ahead. She had to focus on the here and now, because otherwise the constant, aching loss would swallow her whole.

When Cass was not scouting or training she threw

herself into any menial task that would occupy her hands and her brain: chopping wood, sharpening flints for new arrowheads, and sweeping the muck from the stables until Blyth found her, bent double in Pebble's stall, spewing thin bile into the straw and examining the bleeding blisters on her palms as if she were surprised to see them there. But when Blyth reached out a gentle hand towards her, she fled to the silence and isolation of the woods.

There was an afternoon when she wandered barefoot, hair uncovered, paying no heed to the sharp stones at her feet or the risk of discovery. She didn't know where she was going, only that she had to move because when she stood still the pain became unbearable.

Without knowing how she had come there, she was in the clearing again, staring down at the mocking silver surface of the pool, and she didn't know how long she had knelt beside it before there was a gentle hand on her shoulder and Alys stood at her side.

'Cass,' she said, and it was a great effort to hear her, as if her words echoed from under the water, or from the end of a very long tunnel. 'Cass, I know you are struggling, but I must speak with you.' Her face was troubled, her fingers twisting. 'I must speak with you about who you are.'

Cass laughed at her, then. As if it mattered, any more.

Alys pressed on, gripping her by the shoulders, trying

to force her to listen. Asking her tedious and unimportant questions, questions that made no sense, about her identity, about whether she still possessed anything from her past.

And she thought of the locket, and for the first time since that day in the orchard a lifetime ago, her mother's words came back to her. 'It is yours . . . It was never really mine.' But tears pricked her eyes when she thought of home, of the safety of the orchard and the smell of the grass and the pain she might have avoided if she had never left the kitchen that morning. And she shook Alys's hand away, and ran into the trees before she could stop her, ignoring her name as Alys called it after her.

She sharpened her sword obsessively, sliding the whetstone along it again and again, taking strange comfort in the harshness of the sound, in the sense that she was making keen the blade that would sing Lily's name as it avenged her death. She sharpened herself like a sword too, setting up sackcloth targets in the courtyard and hurling spears at them over and over until her arms screamed in protest and the stuffing spilled out onto the cobbles. She pictured herself like the length of metal Iona had forged in the fire, her heart burned to an unbearable fury by Vivian's loss, then instantly plunged into the shock of freezing water by Lily's death, leaving her hardened and cold as stone. And she folded the soft, tender parts of her deep inside like the tin, letting only

357

the sharp, relentless steel face outwards to the light.

Grief wrapped round her like a fog and everything outside her own obsessive thoughts was distant and faded. She hardly noticed that Angharad haunted the corridors and stairways like a ghost, running her hand along the walls as if she might never return. That Sigrid was more aloof and unreachable than ever, her relationship with the other senior knights strained almost beyond repair by her confession and their obvious, naked distrust. She spent days and nights at a time riding out alone, and Cass, grateful for the quiet of the chambers, did not miss her.

One morning, lying beneath a gorse bush as she waited for Mordaunt's watchmen to change their guard, she felt her eyelids begin to droop despite herself. But even when sleep came it was not an escape but a horrible, restless, uneasy thing that scratched at the inside of her skull. She was chasing Lily through the woods, calling for her to wait, to come back, always catching a glimpse of her golden curls just disappearing round the next tree trunk, never managing to catch up with her. Lily's easy laugh echoed and taunted her, mocking, out of reach. Until she was standing again, alone in the clearing, with the terrible pool. And this time the stag was there, and Lily was suddenly there too, her face blank and expressionless, her eyes white and unseeing. And the stag butted her from behind with its antlers and she fell, hard and fast, on her knees at the edge of the water. And before she could wrench herself away she was plunged beneath the surface again, only this time it was Gamelin whose face rose towards her, Gamelin with his mouth stretched wide in a silent scream, Gamelin, whose stronghold they would storm in a few short days. He reached out his hand towards her, his eyes imploring, desperate for help. She started to reach out for him, to clasp his wrist. But Lily's lifeless, cold hand wrapped round her neck and pulled her backwards, away from him, his fingertips slipping uselessly through hers.

Then she came back to herself, cold tears on her cheeks and the gorse prickling her back, and she had missed the changing of the watch.

Chapter 37

On the twenty-second day after Lily's death, they held a witan. The last witan, perhaps.

Every member of the sisterhood was present, all of them quiet and serious, even the youngest pages. 'We leave at nightfall,' Angharad told them. 'We take Mordaunt's manor and we fight for justice, for freedom, for the innocent villagers, for Vivian and Lily.' There was no cheering, no rousing applause.

Cass saw the little boy's broken body, though she tried to close her mind, to block it out. And she thought of the woman who had been so grateful for their parcel of food.

'But what happens next, we decide together,' Angharad

continued, steadying her voice after it trembled at Vivian's name.

'Vengeance,' Rowan hissed, immediately. 'Lives for lives. A brutal reckoning.' And Cass realized, with muted surprise, that she did not recognize Rowan any more in the hatchet-faced youth whose eyes were hard and hungry.

'I did not join this sisterhood to become an indiscriminate murderer,' came a quiet voice. It was Leah, standing near the fireplace. 'I came here to escape violence, not to chase it.'

'If we eschew violence,' Cass muttered angrily, her eyes on the flagstones, 'then we might as well have joined a nunnery instead for all the good we will do.'

'I did not say we should avoid it altogether,' Leah responded coolly. 'But we must be measured. I agree, Mordaunt must pay for the pain he has inflicted. But we cannot be judge and jury for him and his entire household. It would make us no better than them.'

Standing on the other side of the fireplace Sigrid kicked out at one of the logs and it shattered into a burst of sparks.

'There will be far more violence to come if we do not eliminate them,' she insisted, her fists clenched in frustration as she tried to keep her voice civil. 'Do you think they won't come after us, if we let them live—'

'It is the violence to come that we must think of, Sigrid,' Angharad countered, and there was steel in her green eyes.

'This is bigger than us, bigger than Mordaunt or Lily, or even Vivian.'

She looked round the circle. 'I have sent out scouts these past days. Arthur's knights would not have been sent so far north without urgent cause. There is a great war host massing in the west. Saxons. The Picts trouble the northern borders again. There is going to be a reckoning, sooner than any of us would like to admit. We are going to have to fight for our land, our families, our very existence. We cannot do that alone. We need Mordaunt's men, any of them who will join us. And we will need many more besides. The only way to achieve that is to be just, to show mercy.'

Leah was nodding. 'Mordaunt should be exiled. But his men may be persuaded to stay and fight for their homes. And they are more likely to join us if we have shown him mercy.'

'Mercy?' Rowan roared, and her face was creased in pain. 'How can you both speak of mercy when Vivian lies cold in the meadow?'

Angharad seemed to break then, her body physically sagging. 'Vivian gave her life for our sisterhood to survive, Rowan.' She pulled from her pocket a crumpled piece of parchment and read it aloud in a voice that was soft and cracked. 'What we have built is worth saving. You are worth saving. The cost is not too high. I love you.'

Angharad dragged her sleeve across her eyes and seemed to pull herself back with a great effort. 'She died to preserve what we have fought for. I will not fail her now. Our greatest strength,' she continued softly, shaking her head, 'is that we allow our love and grief to drive us.'

'Then open your heart to it,' Sigrid said curtly, 'but let it make you strong, not soft and weak.'

Angharad snapped down her visor and used the pad of her thumb to test the blade of her sword, drawing a fine line of blood.

'On that point you need have no fear,' she said grimly.

Cass returned to her small chamber. She found her locket and slipped it over her head not looking at it, hardly touching it, as if it might burn her fingers, but still feeling that she needed it with her. Then she added Lily's necklace on top, fumbling with the delicate clasp. For a brief, soft second, Cass closed her eyes and felt Lily's fingers at the nape of her neck, saw her quick, dimpled smile. Then it was gone, and she dragged her cloak over her shoulders and left the room without looking back.

They left the manor under the light of a bright half-moon. Angharad went first, mounted, with half a dozen other knights, all in full armour, and a score of squires, their horses' hooves muffled with cloth. Elaine rode with them, cradling her now heavily swollen stomach, in a yellow silk dress that shone softly in the moonlight, her face set and determined.

Angharad checked her horse for a moment and looked back over her shoulder, her eyes finding Elaine's in the moonlight. 'You are sure it is not too much?' Elaine nodded grimly and kicked her heels, galloping ahead.

Sigrid was next, setting off on foot with Rowan and Cass and a small group of others, all fully armed, sharp spears clutched in their hands and swords at their sides.

Leah followed with the rest of the knights, those whose skill at archery was greatest, their backs burdened with full quivers and heavy bows.

The manor was left deserted. Everyone from Alys and Blyth to the youngest pages had a role to play in what would unfold that night. The hogs were left grunting in their pens, the last of the dinner dishes piled haphazardly in the kitchen, the fireplaces cold and still. Only the two curved mounds of stone kept watch over the darkened meadow.

The thickest part of the night drew in round them like a blanket as they rode. When they came to the place where the woods gave way to slopes bearded with gorse and bracken, the manor rising above like a crouching beast, they separated. Angharad remained at the treeline, concealed in the dark shadow of the woods, with the others on horseback beside her. Sigrid and her group set off to the west, skirting the lowest slopes, making for the rear of the fortifications. Leah and her archers continued east, ready to approach from the tournament field and position themselves in the copse where Vivian had waited that terrible day, dressed in Sir Beolin's armour. And Elaine set out alone, panting slightly, her silk skirts gathered up in her hands and her eyes fixed on the single point of light that shone from the lantern of the watchman on the ramparts.

When they reached the far side of the hill, Sigrid fell silently to her knees and the others followed, beginning the laborious process of inching their way up the incline, keeping to what little shelter was available from spiny gorse bushes and scrubby trees. Cass ignored the sharp jolts as her kneecaps met rocks, ignored the burning protest of her thighs.

And as they went, they listened. From somewhere in the woods, a barn owl gave its long, harsh scream, and Cass thought of Angharad, keeping her horse tightly reined, her eyes never leaving that single point of light. Then silence again, until at last the night was rent with a pitiful cry, the wail of a labouring mother in pain. A pause, and then another anguished scream, quickly followed by a man's shout, urgent and questioning. There came no reply, and Cass pictured Elaine, falling to her knees at the edge of the moat, her dress spilling out round her like liquid gold. There was another agonizing wait, and then an order rang out, quick and sharp, followed by the squeak and creak of the lowering drawbridge, the thud of it hitting the ground and a clang as the iron bar was dropped to the floor and the great oak door pushed open.

Next came the sound of running feet, and Cass imagined the sentry rushing to Elaine's side, bending over her to lift her chin and rub her hands. She felt the shock that must rush through his body as Elaine rose up like a serpent and drew the dagger that had been concealed in her bodice. A few moments later, low, male shouts of consternation, and more running feet. Then the unmistakable whistle of a flight of arrows scything through the night sky and heavy thuds and surprised yelps of pain as they found their targets.

Silence again.

A short time later, a star seemed to fly upwards in a slow, graceful arc over the manor, hovering for a moment before it plunged back into darkness. There was a faint tinkle of shattering glass. And they knew that the watch were taken, that Elaine had sent her signal, throwing the sentry's lantern high above the ramparts with all her strength, and that somewhere on the edges of the forest, Angharad's spurs had met the sides of her horse.

Chapter 38

They did not wait to hear any more. Quickly, quietly, Cass and the others rose to their feet and rushed across the open ground until they reached the bank of the moat. Stumbling across the spongy, reed-matted ground, they slipped one by one into the water, gasping as it enveloped them. The cold was as shocking as a blinding flash of light. It lit up Cass's body with a brightness and clarity that was like a sharpened blade, focusing every part of her brain on the task ahead. Find Mordaunt. Subdue his men. Exile him.

They half-waded, half-swam the short distance to the other side. Sigrid held out her hand and Cass clasped her gauntlet-clad wrist, straining to pull herself out of the mire.

The boggy ground sucked at her feet, trying to pull her back.

They gained the cover of the curtain wall, and spread out along it, backs to the rough stone. Led by Sigrid, they inched sideways until they reached the half-concealed postern door, a sturdy oak slab, securely bolted from inside, roughly covered with a curtain of ivy. They had only learned of its existence when the long days of scouting paid off, as Cass blinked wearily in the first rays of sun one morning and noticed three squires emerging from the side of the stronghold, emptying their chamber pots and drawing up water from a nearby well to take back into the kitchen, not bothering to protect the door behind them.

It would be the perfect back entrance, and if they executed their plan correctly, it would enable Sigrid and her band to come upon Mordaunt's household from behind just as Angharad and the cavalry rode in from the front.

Cass knew there was not long to wait. Her teeth chattered furiously, her whole body shaking with cold, yet she did not feel it: it was as if her flesh had been peeled away, as if it lay numb and unfeeling under the ground with Lily. She didn't know if she would ever feel anything ever again.

The sky was beginning to lighten. Almost imperceptible streaks of amber were creeping along the horizon, pushing through the inky dark, diluting it.

There came a chattering of voices and Cass felt Rowan

stiffen beside her. Sigrid raised a finger to her lips, warning them. *Wait. Do not move. Hold your position.*

The ivy swished aside as the door swung back and three squires ambled out, rubbing their eyes. One hawked up a glob of spittle and spat it glistening on the ground just yards from where Cass was standing, her whole body tense and poised to spring. He yawned and stretched, turning his head slightly, and she recognized the pallor of his face and the straggling moustache and knew him to be Mordaunt's squire. She remembered his taunts to Lily and a burst of eager heat rushed through her limbs. She was ready.

Still, Sigrid's hand was poised in the air, her fingers taut.

The waiting was agony. At any moment, one of the squires could turn and see them, a silent line of watchers, shadowing the curtain wall in the murky daybreak. Leave it too late and they would be discovered, losing the element of surprise. But act too quickly and they risked one of the squires escaping back into the manor to raise the alarm, bolting the door behind him.

So they waited, hardly daring to breathe. A blackbird trilled brightly, as if it were just another morning. And the squires, woolly-headed with the dregs of sleep, did not turn, but slouched away from the door towards the well, just as they had every day Cass had watched them, her stiff limbs aching from their frozen position in the bushes.

When at last the three youths had moved a good distance away, one bending to empty a chamber pot onto the ground, one turning the handle to winch up the bucket, one stopping to relieve himself against the side of the well, Sigrid's hand finally dropped. Silently, the line of women moved forward, edging closer and closer.

At the very last moment, Mordaunt's squire turned, hearing some slight rustle of a leaf or a foot on a twig, and gave a little yelp of surprise, the chamber pot dropping from his hand. He reached for his sword, but it was not there, none of them having come armed from their bedchambers.

Hearing him, the others were beginning to turn, but the women were upon them before they could shout or run. Cass and Rowan lunged for Mordaunt's squire, Cass throwing herself bodily onto his back, clawing at his face like a feral cat, while Rowan took advantage of his distraction to kick him, hard, behind the knees so that he fell heavily forward. They gagged him, tying a thick piece of sackcloth tightly round his head, and bound his hands and ankles together, while the others dealt similarly with his two fellows.

Then the women trickled through the open doorway, leaving the trussed squires like helpless pigs waiting to be stuck on the roasting pole, their bodies twitching a little but the bonds holding firm.

Angharad and the others had already made their move.

As they entered the kitchen by the back stairs, Cass could hear shouts and the clash of swords. They came into a large, homely kitchen where a fire was blazing in the hearth and bacon sizzling in a pan. A small group of terrified women huddled in the corner, hands pressed to their mouths.

'Go,' Cass ordered, her voice low and brooking no argument. She drew her sword and used it to point to the narrow staircase leading to the postern wall. Then she pulled a small money bag from her belt and threw it to them. 'And consider this payment for leaving the animals you will see outside bound as you find them.'

The women took the money and fled, and Sigrid led them on, across the kitchen and through a doorway into the vaulted hall.

The scene was chaos. Across the hall, a battle seemed to be raging out in the courtyard, where the clatter of hooves and the whinnying of horses merged with the deafening clash of weapons. Through the open doorway, across the vast floor, Cass could see a blur of heaving bodies and flashing swords.

Inside the still shadowy hall, knights and squires awoken in confusion were hastening to join the melee, some pulling on armour as they went, others, as Angharad had hoped, caught in their nightclothes, racing to find swords and shields.

Sigrid gave a great war cry and leaped out of the kitchen corridor, throwing herself like a battering ram into the path

371

of a tall, burly knight, her helmeted head butting him in the stomach so that he doubled over with a grunt of pain.

Rowan followed, knocking a weasel-faced squire unconscious with her shield and racing on to pinion another against the great wooden hearth, her spear taking him through the shoulder piece of his armour and lifting him bodily into the air so that he hung there, feebly kicking his legs.

Cass and the others followed, spears flying, swords drawn, taking the men by surprise as they turned their focus from the din in the courtyard to find attackers behind them as well.

Wherever they could, they stunned their opponents, using lengths of twine they had brought with them to tie them fast as they lay reeling on the floor.

But before long they were fighting in earnest against the remaining two dozen or so men, who were better armed with swords and shields, fully awake now and spitting fury at the invasion of their stronghold.

A snarling knight with his helmet on but no other armour lunged for Cass, his sword scything down from above so fast that she only just managed to bring up her shield in time. The impact reverberated through her body, shaking her like a sapling in a storm but she held fast, waited for his momentum to bring him forward and then sprang up, throwing her shield aside.

As she rose, Cass saw Lily's body again, the blood trickling from her mouth. She saw the old man, his body faltering as the spear pierced his back. She saw the little boy with the scruffy hair. And as she sliced her sword across the man's stomach, felling him with a scream of pain and a fountain of blood, she did not feel guilt, or anguish, or horror, or any of the things she had imagined in the long nights she had lain awake and imagined this moment. She felt only peace.

The morning light was beginning to spill into the great hall, the vaulted windows glowing blood-red now, bathing the struggling knights with an eerie rose glow. Cass saw Sigrid, her helmet shining with a pinkish halo, her own sword in her right hand and another she had taken from one of Mordaunt's knights in her left. Doubly armed, Sigrid whirled through the centre of the hall with deadly speed, ruthlessly cutting down any man who dared to stand in her way, the 'J' on the pommel of her sword glinting briefly in the bloody light as she raised it above her head before it sliced down and another black tunic crumpled to the ground.

Then another man hurtled towards Sigrid, and for a moment a cry of warning jumped into Cass's throat. But then he turned, back to back with Sigrid, and drew his sword, crossing weapons with another of the black knights and letting out a tormented, curdled cry. And as she watched them standing together, battling opponents on all sides, Cass realized it was Jonathan's squire, and knew that they were locked together, in their own desperate struggle for revenge.

Rowan took another knight, the butt of her spear sending him sprawling to the ground, dazed, before he even saw her coming. Cass was knocked backwards into a table, sending pewterware clattering to the ground, by a burly knight with sideburns so bristly they resembled the tusks of a wild boar. Lying on her back on the table, she bent her knees and kicked out with all her might, catching him in the centre of his chest with both feet and sending him tumbling backwards. Rowan, standing nearby, lifted a sturdy wooden stool and brought it crashing down onto his head before he could rise again.

They were closing in on the doorway to the courtyard now, the knights remaining inside the hall almost entirely subdued. Cass burst out into the sunlight after Sigrid, leaving Rowan and a few others to finish what was left to be done inside.

Chapter 39

For a moment she stopped in her tracks at the scene outside. The twinkling candles and enchanted forest seemed like a lifetime ago. Blood ran dirty between the cobbles and the air was thick with cries of pain and the smell of sweat and open wounds.

Near the opposite side of the courtyard, where the drawbridge still lay open, she could see the scattered bodies of fallen men with arrows in their backs and necks, their limbs spreadeagled where they had dropped.

She could see that the horses had afforded their side a huge advantage: the dead were mostly Mordaunt's men. But Cass also saw Leah's body, a wound in her throat gaping open, and the bodies of a handful of squires she recognized from the manor. Joan sat gaping against the courtyard wall, her mouth slack, her hands clutched to a bleeding wound in her side.

She saw Blyth mounted on a great stallion; saw the horse rear up and trample one of the black-clad knights with lethal hooves the size of a man's head.

Up on the ramparts, Elaine was wielding a bow, sending deadly arrows flying into the chaos. Cass saw her release her bowstring and a tall knight who had been close to strangling one of the silk squires dropped like a stone.

Angharad had dismounted and was locked in combat with Mordaunt himself, his head exposed, his face contorted with fury.

In the far corner of the courtyard, Alys was struggling with a young knight, holding a shield before her with both hands, a look of pure terror on her face as he struck it again and again with his sword. Cass shook herself and leaped into action, quickly skirting the courtyard, exchanging blows with anyone who got in her way, until she was behind the knight. She dealt him a great clout with the pommel of her sword, feeling the crack of his skull at the moment of impact, and he slumped to the floor. Alys emerged, shaking, from behind the shield.

'Thank you,' she called, but Cass was already gone.

She ran past three men locked in combat and checked

herself for a moment in surprise – all wore the black livery with the silver antlers, yet one was battling the other two, their blades flashing and smashing together like lightning. The one fighting alone was Gamelin, his tunic rolled up above the elbows, no armour or chainmail, his face dripping with sweat.

'I was not at the village,' he gasped out, seeing her, as the sword sparks flew round them. 'But after the men returned that night I thought this day might come. I hoped for it.'

Cass nodded and moved on.

In a pen under the shelter of the courtyard wall, a flock of chickens were running frantically to and fro, their feathers puffed out in alarm, making little panicked screeching noises. As she ran past them, Cass came face to face with the knight Angharad had humiliated in the woods after he had robbed the villagers of their pigs, knowing him by the black feather in his helmet. She pulled out a spear that was strapped to her back and threw it, but it glanced off the chainmail that covered his torso and arms.

Turning, he drew his sword and bore down on her, pounding her with relentless, hacking blows that her light sword could not return. He was faster than any other man she had fought, preventing her from using her speed and agility to her advantage, and she felt herself giving ground as he gradually hammered her backwards until the fence

377

of the chicken pen dug into her calves, preventing her from retreating any further. Sweat streamed down her neck inside her helmet, and her arms began to shake uncontrollably with the effort of repelling his sword.

Their swords met once more and this time he did not withdraw his, but pressed it closer and closer, the blade inching towards her throat, while she struggled in vain to push it away.

Sweat dripped into her eyes, obscuring her vision as she leaned back further still. She could feel the blade on her skin now, the metal cold and deadly against her neck. She looked up into the man's face. His eyes were wild and his nostrils already flared in victory. Then an arrow buried itself in his temple and he fell forward, his sword dropping harmlessly to the floor as his body collapsed over the side of the pen and sent the chickens scattering.

Elaine stood where the man had been, her bow still raised, the sleeves of her yellow silk dress billowing round her, leaning back a little to offset the protrusion of her stomach.

The sun rose higher, bathing the scene in a soft golden light. The seething swarm of activity seemed to be calming as more and more knights fell, stunned, exhausted or hurt. The tide was turning clear in their favour: though they outnumbered Angharad's force, Mordaunt's men were simply unable to overcome the disadvantage of having been caught off guard, with so many unarmed.

They were closing in round him now, Angharad panting and grunting but still fighting on, Sigrid dealing with one of the last of Mordaunt's knights just outside the doorway to the hall, Rowan scuffling with a squire on the cobblestones, rolling over and over, swords abandoned, trading punches instead.

Another squire approached and Cass drew her sword to meet him. She surged forward, but another of Mordaunt's men, collapsed and wounded but still alive, stuck out a malicious foot and she tripped and crashed to the floor, her sword flying out of her hand and skidding away.

Before she could recover herself, there was a sudden scream and a flash of light, as Mordaunt took advantage of Angharad's exhaustion in a moment of distraction and slipped behind her, twisting one arm behind her back and sweeping his sword round to hold it pressed against her throat.

'Everybody stop!' he commanded, his voice heaving with exertion. 'Nobody move or he dies.'

They froze. Sigrid paused, sword poised in mid-air. Mordaunt's squire and Rowan rolled over and rose to their knees. Cass lay prone on the flagstones, only a shield's length behind where Mordaunt was gripping Angharad, close enough to see each individual strand of his greasy black hair.

The courtyard rang with the sudden silence.

Mordaunt panted, his hand gripping Angharad's neck roughly, his sword forced hard against her chin. He cast wildly around, his eyes swivelling, making sure that nobody was moving. Cass could hear Angharad's breath coming in short, desperate gasps.

Mordaunt bared his yellow wolf teeth, enjoying being back in control. He swaggered a little on the spot, spitting at Angharad and letting the sputum slide down the side of her closed helmet.

'Perhaps I will gut you slowly like a pig and let your men watch you die,' he mused, letting his fingers travel down her breastplate and across her groin. 'Or perhaps I will let you watch them die first, one by one, so that you can see what happens to those who are stupid enough to challenge me.'

'You!' He pointed at Sigrid. 'Drop your sword, or he dies.'

Sigrid hesitated, panting, her sword still hovering in mid-air. Cass could see her eyes flicking back and forth behind her visor, knew she was making fast calculations, trying to work out what to do.

'NOW!' Mordaunt screamed, and he dragged the blade across Angharad's neck a little, so that she cried out and Cass saw a few drops of blood drop onto the cobbles.

Sigrid's sword clanged to the ground.

'Over to the wall. Now.' Sigrid reluctantly stood

against the wall, where one of Mordaunt's remaining men immediately sprang forward to guard her, sword in hand.

'You too,' Mordaunt snapped at Rowan, and she disentangled herself from the squire, picked herself up, clutching her stomach as she gasped for breath, and began to move towards Sigrid.

The other squires moved to line up too, their weapons clattering to the floor, and Cass knew it was almost over. Once they were all disarmed and rounded up like cattle they would truly be at Mordaunt's mercy.

She was so close to Mordaunt she could almost touch him. He had not noticed her yet, lying down and out of his line of sight. This was the very last moment she could act.

Unbidden, she felt it begin. The light creeping inside her, starting to grow. She felt the warmth surge through her body and burst into her fingertips and for the first time since Lily's death, she allowed herself to feel the sheer joy and exhilaration of that sense of certainty. Of knowing. She leaped, silently, into a crouching position, ready to make a desperate dash for her sword. But Mordaunt was too quick for her. He turned, sweeping the courtyard, and saw her as she sprang to her feet. A cruel grin played across his lips as he kicked her sword further out of her reach and moved to stand in front of her.

Cass stayed perfectly still, still crouching, poised on the

balls of her feet. One wrong move could cost Angharad her life.

'This fool thought he could play the hero,' he mocked, in a high, singsong voice, and his remaining knights sniggered appreciatively.

'Shall we show him what his heroics have done?' He asked, making a theatrical show of pulling the sword hilt up to Angharad's throat, as if preparing to slit it open.

Mordaunt's knights began chanting, baying for blood. *'Kill him! Kill him! Kill him!'*

Cass could see how the frenzy was elating Mordaunt, how he responded to the chants, his mottled face flushing with pleasure, his grin widening.

'Well, youth,' he spat, clearly enjoying himself. 'Say goodbye to your master.' And he turned to face his knights as he began to draw the sword across Angharad's neck.

But the light was not done. As the awful moment seemed to slow and stretch, gaping wide in front of her, her eyes never leaving the blade of Mordaunt's sword, Cass grasped out wildly, blindly, thinking to find some rock or object she could throw, and her fingers found the handle of a sword one of the fallen knights must have dropped. She drew it up so fast it seemed to create an arc of light as it passed through the air and for a moment she thought there was a gasp but there was no time to listen, no time to stop, no time to think.

In a flash of memory, she saw Sigrid in the clearing that first day she had spent at the manor, and immediately she knew exactly what to do.

With a single, fluid motion, she threw herself forward and slashed the point of the sword across the back of Mordaunt's ankles, feeling it cut cleanly through leather and skin and tendon as effortlessly as a hot knife through butter.

The blood sprayed out as Mordaunt shrieked in rage and pain, falling forward onto his knees, and Angharad had twisted her body and relieved him of his sword before he had even stopped screaming. She stood over him, her chest heaving, blood trickling from a shallow wound in her neck.

Very slowly, keeping the sword's sharp point at the base of Mordaunt's throat, Angharad reached up and pulled off her helmet, allowing her long red hair to fall like a curtain round her shoulders.

'We have lived in fear long enough,' she said quietly, and as Mordaunt gaped and paled so fast that Cass thought he might faint or vomit, every other female knight and squire in the courtyard pulled off their own helmets too.

For what felt like a very long moment, they all stood there, in the bright morning light, their heads held high. Knights, openly, proudly, for the first time. And the shock and confusion on the faces of the men around them was sweet.

Things moved very quickly after that, though Cass, sitting

dazed on the cobblestones, Mordaunt's blood spattered across her hands, still holding the dead knight's sword, was hardly aware of what happened next.

'You will flee these lands and never return,' Angharad told Mordaunt, her voice crisp and clear, while he watched her, ashen-faced, his hands clamped to his ankle wounds.

'Or you will die now, quickly and painlessly.' She looked down at him, coldly. 'The choice is yours, but you must choose now.'

She looked round the courtyard and addressed the remaining knights and squires who cowered in their black tunics, many of them staring at the armoured women in open shock.

'All who surrender will be spared. You may follow your lord or join us without censure. The Saxons approach from the west with a great war host. The Picts harry our borders to the north and the sea wolves threaten to crawl out of the bays and estuaries. Never has it been more important for us to stand together. Our lands will not survive unless we unite. But it will not be behind this man, who has sown more discord and division than he has ever created unity.'

She looked at Mordaunt with loathing and naked hatred.

'You killed the woman I loved. But still, in her name, I show you mercy. Because she would have wanted you spared, to flee like a cur with your tail between your legs, rather than receive a hero's death on the battlefield.'

Her voice rang out round the courtyard as she addressed Mordaunt's men again. 'I do this too so that you can see I am just and will treat you fairly. There will be no needless bloodshed. Your wounds will be tended to. Join us, and together we will stand against the Saxons and restore our lands to peace and prosperity. I call on those of you who swore fealty to the nameless knights to join us now and prevent more deaths.' And Cass saw the eyes of some of the knights widen and their faces redden in shame and shock as they realized who had bested them in the forest that day. They looked uncertainly from Angharad to their master.

Angharad, with her back to Sigrid, did not see the black-armoured figure start forward until she was almost upon her. Did not see Rowan hold out her sword, her face closed and cold and her eyes deadly. But Cass did. She saw Sigrid grasp the sword and stride forward, saw the love and anguish and hatred in her eyes and knew what was about to happen. There was no time to speak, to step forward, to do anything. In front of Angharad's horrified eyes, Sigrid's sword dropped like a bolt of lightning and Mordaunt fell forward, his head cleaved in two.

Chapter 40

There was movement and talking around her.

She knew that Mordaunt's body had been dragged away, and they were starting to clear the other corpses too, wrapping them in sheets and carrying them out to the tournament field for burial.

She had sat, still half stunned, as Mordaunt's sullen followers had fled on horseback.

In her peripheral vision, Rowan and Blyth were busying themselves with the wounded, conversing with those few of Mordaunt's people who had remained.

And the noonday sun was shining hot on her uncovered head. A gentle breeze blew, lifting her matted hair a little. She had not washed it since Lily had died. But after the battle, something in her had become unstopped, somehow. There had been a release, and she knew that there was something very pressing, a destiny hanging over her, looming large in her mind.

But she just wanted to sleep. For the first time in twenty-three days, she was ready to rest. Her hands were numb and bleeding. There was a shallow wound stinging on her shoulder where a sword-point had found a gap in her armour. She knew there was much to be done, and yet she could not stand up. They had achieved a victory beyond her wildest dreams, and Lily was not here to share it with her. She laid her head down on a flagstone without removing her armour or releasing her sword and closed her eyes.

But a shadow fell across her eyelids, blocking out the glare of the sun, and she opened them again.

It was Alys, one side of her face blossoming in a purplish bruise, nursing a swollen wrist, her lip split and glistening with blood. Gently, she crouched next to Cass.

'I tried to speak to you of this, Cass, but you were not ready to listen. Perhaps you could not hear it until the thing had been done.'

'What do you mean? It is finished. Leave me alone. Let me sleep.'

'I cannot, Cass. You must hear me. There is a prophecy.

Made when I was a child, before the last of the old people had been forced from the forests. A prophecy about a great leader, a light to unite the Britons, a leader who would hold back the darkness. And we would know this leader by the drawing of a sword.'

'Yes, yes, I know all this. Everybody knows all this,' she snapped irritably. 'Arthur pulled the sword from the stone and became the High King and all Britons must swear fealty to him.'

'No, Cass.' Alys's voice trembled with urgency. 'This prophecy was made many years before Arthur's allies chose him as ruler and placed that sword in the churchyard to give their choice the stamp of divine authority. Fate played no hand in what happened that day.'

Cass groaned. Her head was ringing and her eyelids were heavy as lead.

'This prophecy concerned Northumbria, our own territories. It referred to Mordaunt's land.'

Cass shook her head bitterly. It felt heavy and painful, stuffed with wool and too full of memories and thoughts of Lily that bruised and jarred with her every movement. Vaguely, she knew that Sigrid was gone, that Angharad had banished her in a fury, telling her never to return on pain of death.

She wanted to sleep, needed to surrender to the sweet

release of unconsciousness. But Alys would not let her: she plucked at her arm insistently, pinching her skin, forcing her to look up.

'Alys!' she shouted, resentment and frustration and fury bursting out of her. 'This does not *matter* to me. None of it matters.'

'It matters a great deal,' Alys whispered, glancing around to see they were not overheard. 'For the prophecy did not speak of a king. It spoke only of a leader. A leader who would pull a sword from a stone in Gefrin in Northumbria, and become the light to drive out the gathering dark. And we would know them by the sword, with a ruby at its hilt.'

Then Cass looked down at the sword she had forgotten she was holding, the sword that she had picked up from the ground, assuming it had been discarded by another knight. The sword she had thought was simply lying there for the taking.

The ruby shimmered in the light, as it had the night she had first seen it, set in the stone, when she walked through Mordaunt's courtyard to the feast. And she realized that she had drawn it out, without even knowing it, without even meaning to. She saw it glint red as a ripple of power surged up through her, and at last she understood.

Dear Reader,

Thank you for picking up my book!

I grew up devouring Arthurian fantasy, but there was always something missing. There were only a small handful of female characters, often one-dimensional and cast in the old tropes of virgin or witch, while their male counterparts were complex, heroic and brave.

I wanted to take the richness of a setting that so many of us grew up with and adored, and to remake it with an inclusive, feminist lens. So that another generation of girls wouldn't have to grow up loving Arthur's world but feeling unrepresented there. Making room, taking up space, breaking and remaking the boundaries of what it means to be a girl: all things I want young women to feel inspired and empowered to do themselves.

We are living in unprecedented times, when somebody who tells young boys that the way to be a man is to throw a woman against the wall by her throat can reach 11.4 billion TikTok views. When a rape is reported to the police by a UK school every day of the term. Teenage girls have never faced so much vitriol and silencing, yet the popular narrative tells us girls have never had it so good.

Through my work as a feminist activist with the Everyday Sexism Project, I visit schools across the UK each week and work with tens of thousands of young people each year, listening to their experiences of sexism and sexual violence, their hopes and fears for themselves and the world around them. There is a time for rage and for action, but the girls I work with every day are also exhausted and sad. Alongside protest there is also an urgent need for feminist joy and that is what this book represents for me. Sheer delight in finding space for girls' and women's lives, stories and strength, flaws and love and friendship in a world that has historically excluded them.

Cass is a heroine I hope will resonate with the young people I work with – finding her inner power in a world that wants to force her into a footnote. She rejects the minor, submissive, supporting role that has been written for her, and exchanges it instead for an exhilarating life of adventure, power and sisterhood. Above all, she finds the strength to write her own story. This is everything I wish for my readers.

With warmest wishes,

Laura x

Acknowledgements

I've held the idea for this book close to my heart for a very long time, and I have my kind and brilliant editor Lucy Pearse to thank for helping me to bring this passion project to fruition at last. I'm so grateful to the whole brilliant team at Simon and Schuster, including Rachel Denwood, Laura Hough, Sarah Macmillan, Jess Dean, Arub Ahmed, Eve Wersocki-Morris, Olivia Horrox and all the marketing and publicity teams who work so hard to help my books find their readers! Thank you to Anna Bowles for her meticulous copyediting and to Micaela Alcaino and Sean Williams for creating the cover of my dreams. You are all ridiculously talented and I am very grateful that I get to work with you!

My agent Abigail Bergstrom is the greatest support, friend, mentor and cheerleader throughout each project we navigate together, and I am so glad to have her on my team. She is truly the best agent an author could wish for. And a huge thank you to Megan and everyone at Bergstrom Studios for all that you do.

A very special thanks to Joe, Jon, Chelsea and everyone at the Knights of Middle England and Warwick International School of Riding for teaching me to ride, joust, shoot arrows and sword fight: without a doubt the most exhilarating research I have ever done for a book. The bruises were well worth it, and I'll be back to learn some more for book two!

Finally, I am so grateful to Aileen, Lucy and Hayley, my earliest readers and generous sounding boards, and to the whole group of women who make up my own sisterhood. I wouldn't make it a week without you.

About the Author

Laura Bates is a feminist activist and bestselling author. She writes regularly for the *Guardian*, *New York Times* and others. Her Everyday Sexism Project has collected over 250,000 testimonies of gender inequality and has helped to put sexual consent on the school curriculum, change Facebook's policies on sexual violence and transform the British Transport Police's approach to sexual offences. Laura works closely with bodies like the United Nations, the Council of Europe, MPs, police forces, schools and businesses to tackle misogyny. She is a Fellow of the Royal Society of Literature, an Honorary Fellow of St John's College, Cambridge and recipient of a British Empire Medal for services to gender equality.

Pledge your allegiance

Sisters of Sword and Shadow